KARMA

A NOVEL

JUDITH BLEVINS

Cover, interior book design, and eBook design
by Blue Harvest Creative
www.blueharvestcreative.com

KARMA

Published by
Shahrazad Publishing

ISBN-13: 978-0692544716
ISBN-10: 0692544712

Visit the author at:
www.bhcauthors.com
Goodreads: Judith Blevins

Visit the author by
scanning the QR code.

ALSO BY JUDITH BLEVINS

The Legacy
Double Jeopardy
Swan Song

To Carroll Multz,
whose careers as a trial attorney, district attorney,
judge and author inspired me to write this novel.
May justice always prevail…

PROLOGUE

Wilber "Willy" McCrombie had just been released from Rikers Island Prison. Foremost in his mind and the driving force in his life was his determination to even the score with the judge and the cop that had put him away. Now that he's out, revenge was for the taking.

Willy arrived in Manhattan by bus the very day he was released from prison. He knew where the judge lived; information that was readily available on the second page of all of His Honor's novels—novels that Willy read from cover to cover. Now, Willy stands in the alcove at the rear entrance of *The Blackstone,* an upscale apartment building located in downtown Manhattan where the judge made his home. Willy smiled thinking of how easily he had burglarized the judge's eleventh floor apartment earlier that afternoon.

Willy's stint in prison wasn't all for naught. He developed some very useful skills taught to him by other inmates with unique talents. Danny "The Pick" Buchanan taught Willy how to crack any lock without leaving a trace of the intrusion. Breaching locks was the one new tool in Willy's arsenal of evil that he treasured most. He knew it would come in handy multiple times upon his release from prison.

Willy was a short stocky man with patches of gray hair on his balding head. Dull gray eyes with hooded lids were positioned close together under a large red birthmark that underscored his ruddy complexion. Willy had served twenty years of a twenty to life sentence. The five-woman seven-man jury found him guilty of first degree murder of his girlfriend, Alice Dayton, a news anchor for one of the local TV affiliates. When Judge Antonio Facinni imposed the sentence twenty years ago, Willy abruptly rose, shouted, swore and vowed revenge on both Judge Facinni and Detective Leonard Wycowski. Willy became so violent that it took three security guards to restrain him. He fought back with superhuman strength as he was being dragged from the courtroom in handcuffs and ankle chains. Now, after twenty years behind bars, Willy was out.

PART ONE

THE
FRAME

CHAPTER

1

A broad smile graces my face as I meander past the Crandall Bookstore on 42nd Street and observe an array of my novels on display there. My current novel, *End Game*, is featured and dominates the Crandall's large display window. *End Game*, my fourth novel, has been on the best-seller list for the last three weeks. The other three novels, *Fair Game*, *Fool's Game* and *Skin Game* hadn't done too well until *End Game* topped the charts. Now, all of my novels are in demand.

Fellow pedestrians channel around me as I stop to examine the life-sized poster of the author which is positioned front and center. I move closer in order to read the bio on the back of the novel:

> Author of the *Game* novels, Antonio Facinni, practiced law as a criminal trial lawyer for more than a dozen years before receiving a judicial appointment from the Supreme Court. After serving twenty-four years on the bench, Facinni retired from his position as Chief Judge for the 3rd Judicial District for the State of New

York and turned his talents to writing suspense thrillers.

In addition to his four works of fiction, *Fair Game, Fool's Game, Skin Game* and *End Game*, Facinni has written articles for *The Lawyer's Digest* as well as numerous legal opinions and technical manuals. His real life experiences, which he weaves into spell-binding murder mysteries, contribute to the realism reflected in his novels; novels that hold the reader in suspense until all is revealed in the final pages.

Facinni, a native New Yorker, lives in Manhattan with his feline friend, *Karma*. He admits that, since childhood, all of his pets have been named Karma and laughingly adds, "some good, some bad."

◆◆◆◆◆

I TURN AWAY from the display and look up the boulevard. There is a slight breeze and the autumn chill heralds the advance of the dreaded winter looming on the horizon. Red and gold leaves flutter from the trees that line the avenue and swirl about the sidewalk seeking refuge in corners and doorways where they pile up with their predecessors. Autumn is my favorite time of year and New York is my favorite city.

Finished with my shopping, and past the Crandall, I hold tightly onto my purchases as I quicken my pace. The little spring in my step reflects my buoyant mood that nothing is going to rain on my parade this day. I'm on top of the charts—and the world, for that matter.

I turn the corner and hurry down the concrete steps that lead to the subway that will take me to Mulberry Street and home. Once aboard, I grab a window seat and watch the city whiz by. Fifteen minutes later I arrive at my destination, and when I exit the station, I notice the wind has kicked up. I protectively cradle my cargo closer as I lean into the wind and cover the three-block walk from the train to my brownstone apartment building in record time.

Standing in the lobby waiting for the elevator, I juggle the grocery bags and fumble for the keys that are lodged in the corner of my jacket pocket. Soon several of the building's other occupants join me and we exchange greetings as we step into the elevator. My apartment is one of two that encompass the entire eleventh floor and I lose my companions one-by-one as we journey upward. Finally arriving home, I unlock my apartment door, and as I step inside, I find Karma waiting in the foyer eager to inspect my purchases. She agilely winds herself around my calves, purring all the while.

"Hey girl," I greet her. "You hungry?" *Dumb question, she's always hungry.* She follows me into the kitchen and jumps up on a bar stool. I've trained her from kitten-hood to stay off the counter tops. Not sure she complies with the rules when I'm absent but I've seen no sign that she transgresses.

Under the watchful eye of Karma, I unload the groceries and store my purchases. She doesn't miss a beat and when I turn toward the laundry room she jumps down from her perch. Black and sleek, Karma moves with slinky panther-like feline grace to her private dining area. I follow close behind. Purring loudly, she intertwines between my legs as I retrieve her cat food from the cabinet over the washer. After I fill her dish, she briefly looks up at me with large green cat eyes, meows once and then attacks her lunch.

"Atta girl," I say. "I respect a woman with a healthy appetite." She, of course, doesn't even flinch.

Returning to the kitchen, I put the deli-sub I had purchased for myself onto a plate and take it along with a can of cold beer into the den and flip on the television. The Jets are hosting the Colts and the game has just begun. Flopping down in my favorite recliner, I sigh as I appreciate the coolness of the leather against the back of my neck. I'm home and full of hope and expectation that the Jets will reverse the curse that has plagued them all season.

My hopes are dampened when the Colts add a touchdown to their field goal making the score ten to zip at the end of the first. I don't much relish the way the game is going so I punch the mute button on the remote and go to my desk where I'm working on my fifth novel. Lately I've been experiencing writer's block. With my time on the bench, you'd think I'd be full of ideas. Not so! *I'm beginning to think I'm full of something but it isn't plots.* Tapping the eraser end of the pencil against the glass top on my desk, I try to jar something loose in my head. No luck. I swivel around and embrace the view from the picture window overlooking Mulberry which is now lined with trees donned in fall regalia. The panorama is breathtaking from the eleventh floor any time of year — winter, summer, spring and especially fall. I have no competition in this older section of the city as there are not many tall buildings around to obstruct the view. However, I do pay dearly for the view and the solitude, but it's worth the price.

I turn back. The Jets are still losing. My eye lids have grown heavy and I'm thinking of taking a nap when the phone jars me from my reverie.

"Hello." I look at the clock on my desk. It's 4:30.

"Hey, Tony. How ya doin'?" Len asks in his patented jovial way.

Leonard Wycowski is one of my oldest and closest friends. We grew up in the same neighborhood and were classmates for twelve years. After graduating high school, I went on to college and then law school; Len pursued a career in law enforcement, retiring as head of the NYPD detective division about the same time I retired from the bench.

"Len! Ya crazy Pollack, where ya been? Thought you may have dropped off the face of the earth."

"Un-huh. You're not getting rid of me that easily." Then he pauses for a brief moment, "Guess you heard McCrombie was released yesterday."

"Yeah. FBI called to let me know. They act like I should be worried. McCrombie has had twenty years to cool his jets. I don't see him as a viable threat anymore."

"Just the same, you watch your six. Don't ever take a threat from malcontents like McCrombie lightly," Len scolds.

"Thank you, *Daddy*. Remember, he also threatened you."

"Yep. Haven't forgotten. He's a scary son-of-a-bitch. I'm taking extra precautions and suggest you do the same."

"H-m-m-m, probably good advice that I should follow as well." After a pause, I add, "I'm watching the Jets get their collective butts' beat. Wanna come over and cry in a beer with me?"

"Hell, yes! Thought you'd never ask. I'm on my way, twenty minutes give or take."

That was the last conversation I'd ever have with Len.

◆◆◆◆◆

WILLY HAD PLENTY of time on his hands while in the joint, twenty years in fact. He fueled his hatred by reading Facinni's murder mysteries. Halfway through the third novel, Willy began to hatch a plan for his revenge. *When I get outta here, I'm gonna even the score. Facinni's pretend murders may just become real ones and the high and mighty could find himself facing murder charges. Yeah, outright killing the bastard would be too easy. He needs to go through what I've just been through, and as a bonus, the inmates will surely find unique ways to keep the judge entertained.* Willy almost howled with glee just thinking about it.

It's now late afternoon and the murky October sun fades as the advancing twilight nudges it over the horizon. Shadows gradually envelop the surrounding area and soon it will be completely dark. As Willy watches, his attention is directed toward a middle-aged man who approaches the building from The Blackstone's parking garage. *Something about that guy seems familiar.* Willy scratches his head trying to remember; after all, it has been twenty years. Willy watches as the man strolls in his direction, and as he gets closer, it suddenly dawns on Willy. *I do not believe my luck—Leonard Wycowski, of all people! Finding the judge's gun when I tossed his place this afternoon was truly fortunate.* Willy's hand goes immediately to the pistol tucked into the waistband of his slacks. Reassured the gun is still there, Willy pulls his arm back and winces as he does so. He pushes up his sweater sleeve and examines the nasty scratch on his arm. *Wonder if that damn cat's been served the special treat I left in her bag of cat food. I hate cats, especially that one!* Willy readjusts his sleeve and steps back a few paces. He flips the handgun open, and satisfied it is fully loaded, he moves deeper into the shadows and waits, patiently waits.

◆◆◆◆◆

IT WAS A dismal display and I renew my vow to never watch another Jets game. Not only did the Jets loose, but Len never showed up as promised. After the passage of time, my agitation with Len now turns into concern. At half past seven, I pick up the phone. I dial Len's number and leave a message when Len doesn't answer. *Not like Len.* Now I'm full-out worried. I call several of our mutual friends and the pubs I know he frequents. Nothing! He has no family. He's been divorced for ten years and I don't know where his ex lives. I run out of places to search. I know the police won't act on a missing person call until after forty-eight hours, but I try anyway. After all, Len had been one of them.

I pick up the phone and punch in the numbers.

"911, what's the nature of your emergency?"

"I want to report a missing person. My name is Antonio Facinni. My friend, Leonard Wycowski is missing."

"How long has Mr. Wycowski been missing?"

"Just a few hours but this situation is unique."

"Our policy is to wait forty-eig…"

"I know, I know. I'm a retired judge, I know the rules. However, Len, that is Mr. Wycowski, was threatened twenty years ago by a convicted murderer. Said felon was released yesterday and Mr. Wycowski is missing today. Now, does that sound like coincidence to you?"

"Sir, I have my instruct..."

"DAMN YOUR INSTRUCTIONS! Let me talk to your supervisor."

"Hold on..."

After what seems like an eternity, another voice comes on the line. "This is Ginny Williams. I'm the night supervisor. Would you please identify yourself?"

"Yes! I'm Retired Judge Antonio Facinni..."

There is a brief pause. Ginny says, "Judge Facinni. I remember you. You were on the bench when I was a rookie. What can I do for you?"

I sigh. "Ginny, since you were on the force twenty years ago, perhaps you remember the murder of Alice Dayton."

"I vaguely remember that trial."

"The trial lasted eight weeks at the end of which Wilber McCrombie was convicted and given a twenty-to-life sentence. Because of the way things are being run now, twenty-to-life boils down to just twenty, well for McCrombie anyway. He was released yesterday."

"That so? H-m-m-m." A slight pause then Ginny says, "Now I remember. Alice Dayton was a local celebrity. Pretty gruesome stuff..."

"Yes, it was. Leonard Wycowski was the lead detective on the case. McCrombie threw a fit and threatened to kill Wycowski and me as he was being ushered from the court-room after I imposed sentence. McCrombie was released yesterday and Len is missing today—not a coincidence in my book. Can you forget the forty-eight hour rule and get someone on this right away?"

I wait. Ginny is apparently thinking over my request. After a few moments, she says, "I'll forward your request to the duty officer. I have your number and as soon as I have an answer, I'll call you back."

"Thank you, Ginny. Every second counts."

"You're welcome, Judge. Hang in there."

Now, despite all my bravado, I begin to feel uncertain, and yes, I admit it, afraid. McCrombie is not only a scary son-of-a-bitch; he's a crazy, scary son-of-a-bitch.

I pace my office waiting for Ginny to call. Finally, the phone rings and I grab it up.

"Yes?"

"Is this Judge Facinni?"

"Ginny?"

"Yes. I've convinced Sgt. Rudderd to initiate an investigation. Rudderd knew Wycowski. He told me Wycowski took him under his wing way back when and nurtured him through rookie-hood. He said 'he owes that Pollack one.'"

"Thanks, Ginny. Now, I owe *you* one."

"Just doing my job. I'm off duty now. I'll pray your friend turns up safe and sound."

"Me, too."

◆◆◆◆◆

LAURA STEIN, A resident of The Blackstone, was just returning home from having dinner with a few of her girl-friends. As she approached the entrance of her building, she saw what appeared to be the body of a man lying in the alcove. As she got closer she saw a rivulet of blood cascading over the walkway. She later told officers that her first thought was that he had fallen and hit his head, causing the blood flow. That was until she got closer and saw the massive amount of blood on the front of the man's jacket. Laura stated she then sudden-ly realized this was not an accident and dialed 911. She said her hands were shaking and she kept looking around fearing the perpetrator was still in the vicinity.

Officers David Copeland and Robbie Peterson answered the call. Laura was visibly unnerved, and by the time the cruis-er arrived on the scene, she appeared to be on the verge of hys-teria. Officer Peterson led her aside and took her statement. She was then allowed to leave the scene. Before she left, Laura was advised by Officer Peterson that she would be interviewed later by homicide detectives.

◆◆◆◆◆

"LOOKS MORE LIKE revenge than a gang hit to me," Detective Robbie Peterson says as he kneels and carefully lifts the victim's left hand with his pen and peers under it. It was then that he noticed the victim's expensive watch. "He still has his personal belongings, so I'm ruling robbery out as a motive."

Officer Copeland, journaling in a log book, doesn't look up as he responds, "That was my initial take. He was shot multiple times with what appears to be a small caliber weapon, probably a .22. You'd have to be pretty damn mad at someone to empty your gun into 'em."

"Amen to that. Any ID yet?" Peterson asks rising to his feet.

Copeland flips a page back, and after examining it, answers, "Driver's license says Leonard Wycowski. If my math is correct, he's fifty-eight."

Peterson rubs his chin, "Leonard Wycowski? Sounds familiar. I think I know him." Peterson stoops and takes another look at the victim's face. "I just picked up an APB. Seems a friend got worried when Wycowski hadn't shown up for beer and football. Yeah, now I remember. He used to be a cop—detective division. He just retired a few years ago. Well, I'll be damned. Looks like someone finally got to 'em."

◆◆◆◆◆

THE WAIT DRAGS on. I glance at the phone every so often willing it to ring bearing news of Len. After a couple of hours, I finally give up, go to bed, and fall into a restless sleep. My slumber is fraught with nightmares and Len's face keeps popping up. The storm that assaults upper Manhattan this night adds eeriness to my anxiety. I finally give it up around six and stumble into the kitchen where I put on a pot of coffee.

Once brewed, I pour myself a cup, and with mug in hand, head for my office where I flip on the television hoping to catch the scores. The local news is just beginning:

"…the bullet-riddled body has been identified as Leonard Wycowski, former…"

"OH, NO! OH, NO! Not Len," I cry into the emptiness. Before I have time to absorb the situation, the phone begins ringing.

"Yes?" I bark into the receiver.

"Judge Facinni?"

"Yes!" I'm obviously in no mood for Q and A.

"This is Sgt. Slater."

"Oh. Sorry, I apologize for my abruptness. I just turned on the news and heard about Len." I pause, "Len Wycowski was a close friend. Are you at liberty to share details of his death at this point?" I naturally assume the call is a follow up on the 911 call I placed last night.

"No, sir. It's an ongoing investigation so everything is still confidential. However, I can tell you the ME's preliminary examination puts the time of death between four and five yesterday afternoon."

I'm stunned. "But I talked to Len around four-thirty — invited him over to watch the game with me." Then I ask, "I didn't catch the entire newscast. Can you tell me where the body was discovered?"

"Yes, in the breezeway adjacent to your apartment building."

I almost drop the phone. "What?" I feel light-headed and find I'm unable to say more.

After a few moments, Sgt. Slater asks, "You there, Judge?"

I manage an answer, "Yes, I'm here…Len was that close…"

"Yes, he was that close. We'll want you to make a statement since apparently you're the last person to have had contact with him — except for the murderer, of course."

I swallow hard. The way he says that makes me wonder if I'm a suspect. I reply, "Of course, I'll be happy to oblige. When and where do you want to do this?" *Damn, I'm beginning to sound like someone that's all too anxious to prove his innocence.*

"Why don't you come down to the 42nd stationhouse after lunch, say around two-thirty. Ask for me; I'll be expecting you."

"Okay. I'll be there." Then I notice I'm talking to a dead phone. Slater had already hung up.

◆◆◆◆◆

I ARRIVE FOR the interview right on time but I'm kept waiting forty minutes. *Police tactic?* When Slater finally ushers me into an interview room, my stomach lurches and I suppress the urge to gag. The small enclosed room smells of unwashed bodies, stale liquor and vomit. The green paint is chipped and faded and the only furnishings are an institutional steel table and two straight back chairs positioned on either side. The obligatory two-way mirror is embedded in one wall and stands sentinel.

"Take a seat, *Judge.*"

I could be paranoid but I don't like the way he says "Judge." Looking around I spot the camera placed in a corner of the ceiling. I assume it's videotaping the interview. I begin to feel more-and-more like "one of the usual suspects."

Slater takes the chair opposite me, leans forward on his crossed arms and begins. "I'm recording our conversation from this point forward. That's for your information, Judge." He punches the "on" button on the recording device, and looking at me, states, "For the record, I'm going to introduce us as well as indicate the date and time of this interview."

I watch Slater shuffle papers around on the table and I catch a glimpse of a photograph of Len's dead body lying on a slab in the morgue before Slater can cover it. *Did he expose the photograph on purpose?* **Was he hoping to nudge me into something—confessing perhaps.** Clearing his throat, Slater speaks into the machine.

"My name is Sgt. Gary Slater. It is three thirty p.m., October 14, 2014. With me is retired judge Antonio Facinni." Slater looks at me and says, "Judge Facinni, please state your full name, address and date of birth for the record."

I comply: "My name is Antonio Marcello Facinni, born August 16, 1956, and my address is 2485 Mulberry, number 1137, Manhattan."

Slater clears his throat and continues, "Judge, you told me earlier you talked to the deceased, Leonard Wycowsky, at approximately four-thirty on the afternoon of October 13th."

"Yes, that's correct."

Slater scoots his chair back and crosses his legs before continuing, "What did the two of you talk about?"

Hoping not to sound too anxious, I take a few seconds, collect my thoughts, and answer:

"I was watching the game, Jets and Colts, when Len called. We joshed about not seeing each other for a time and then Len asked me if I knew McCrombie had been released."

"Hold on! Who's McCrombie?"

"Wilber McCrombie. He was convicted of murdering his girlfriend, a news anchor for one of the local TV stations, twenty years ago. Len was lead on that case and I presided over the trial and imposed sentence. McCrombie threatened both of us as he left the courtroom."

"Un-huh, I see. Go on," Slater prompts.

"I told Len the FBI had contacted me, and yes, I did know. We reminded each other that McCrombie, that is Wilber McCrombie, had threatened to kill us both."

Talking about the trial brought back memories and suddenly I'm overcome with sadness at Len's loss. Len had been a good friend for many years.

"Come to think of it, I remember that trial. Go on," Slater says.

I take deep breaths as I try to suppress my grief, then I continue. "I asked Len if he would like to come over and watch the game. He seemed very enthusiastic and readily accepted my invitation." I pause; my mouth is suddenly dry. "May I have some water?" I ask.

Slater nods and leaves the room. He soon returns with two plastic bottles of water. He hands one to me and sits down again. "Okay, Judge, please go on," he urges.

I take a long pull from the bottle before I continue. "I waited about four hours and when he didn't show, I got worried. That's when I called 911. After our talk about McCrombie being released, I was more anxious than I probably would have been otherwise."

"Un-huh. How long had you and the deceased been acquainted?" Slater asks as he absently strips the paper label from his water bottle.

I reflect on my answer for a couple of seconds then say, "H-m-m-m, probably over forty-five years. We went to the same schools, K through 12. Len was Chief of Detectives when I took the bench. I heard a lot of cases in which he was involved as assisting officer, arresting officer, or advisory witness. Before his divorce, his ex would take pity on this bachelor and invite me for dinner from time-to-time. Len and I shared our passion for football, so we would occasionally watch the Sunday afternoon game together either at his place or mine." A sob erupts from my throat and I grab my handkerchief from my hip pocket. "Sorry..."

"That's all right, Judge. Take your time." Then, after a minute, Slater asks, "What happened to the ex?"

"Roxy? I don't know." I lean forward and stuff the handkerchief into my back pocket. "After the divorce, Len never mentioned her again. They didn't have children. The last I heard, she had moved to California."

"I see. Do you think McCrombie offed Len?"

I take a few moments to think before I answer. "I'm sure Len had a plethora of enemies having been in law enforcement for so long. It just seems more than a coincidence that Len gets murdered the day after McCrombie's release. And McCrombie did threaten to kill Len and probably had the means, motive and opportunity to do so."

"Un-huh," slight pause, "ah, you own a gun?"

"Yes…I have a .22 caliber Ruger." Suddenly, the hair on the back of my neck begins to raise — I'm becoming more-and-more suspicious that I'm a suspect. I regain control and continue, "Dad and I used to go out and target practice. In fact, the gun was a Christmas gift from my Dad years-and-years ago." I pause and think about it. Then I ask, "Why? What are you suggesting?"

"H-m-m-m, as you know, we are obligated to follow all leads and investigate where the evidence takes us. I'm not suggesting anything, I'm investigating."

"Right." Now I'm really getting concerned that I'm *the number one suspect.*

"Would you willingly let us examine your weapon?"

"You mean without a search warrant?" I do not hesitate, "Of course. I have nothing to hide." *How many times have I heard that over the past decades? Even to me, I'm sounding like I'm guilty.* "I'll bring my weapon in sometime this week."

"That won't be necessary. I'm going to send Charlie home with you. She can pick up the gun."

"Sounds like you don't trust me."

"Whoa! It's not a matter of trust. Let's call it chain of custody — it's for your protection as well as ours."

Slater picks up the phone. "Send Charlie in," he demands.

After a few minutes, the door to the interview room opens and there before me stands the most intriguing creature I've ever laid eyes on. Charlie, tall and slender, scans the entire room in an instant with intelligent, inquisitive blue eyes. She obviously didn't have time to prepare and she self-consciously fusses with a few tendrils of silky black hair that have escaped from a clip positioned at the back of her neck. Although my legs have turned to jelly, I somehow manage to stand.

"Charlie," Slater says interrupting my trance. "Come in." He points to me, "This is Judge Antonio Facinni."

"Good afternoon, Judge Facinni." Her voice is music. I notice her furrow her brow. She appears to be trying to remember something. Then she asks, "Say, are you the same Facinni that writes the *Game* novels?"

With some difficulty, I find my voice and reply, "Why, yes, I am. One-and-the-same."

Feeling awkward, I continue, "It's a pleasure to meet you, *Charlie*. Have you read my novels? "

"Yes. All four of them, and the pleasure is mine. I've also followed your career. My colleagues and I have a great deal of respect..."

Charlie doesn't get to finish her sentence. Slater shows signs of impatience and he's back to business. "Charlie, I want you to accompany Judge Facinni home and pick up his .22 caliber Ruger. Preserve it as you would any chain of custody evidence."

Charlie whips around and glares at me. I feel my face flush with embarrassment.

"Yes, sir!" She responds and quickly steps back from the door to allow me to exit before her. I'm humiliated in the presence of this lovely woman.

"This way," Charlie says and takes me through a back entrance into a private parking lot where police cruisers are lined up like solders standing at attention. Charlie points to the right directing me toward the first cruiser in line.

"What about my car?" I ask.

"It'll be safe enough here at the station. I'll bring you back after we pick up the weapon."

Right. Where does this chick get her information? It's been my experience that thieves and vandals aren't particular where they commit their crimes and to whom they prey upon.

◆◆◆◆◆

I OPEN THE passenger door and cringe when I detect that the cruiser doesn't smell much better than the interview room. Once we're buckled in, Charlie puts the car in gear and backs out of the parking space. We don't talk during the trip to my neighborhood other than me giving her directions.

Once inside my apartment, I say, "This way," and point in the direction of the bedroom. I notice that Karma didn't meet us at the door and I wonder why she's hiding. It's out of character for her not to greet me when I come in. *Maybe she doesn't like cops or...did I shut her up in the office again when I left? Could have, I was pretty distraught.*

"Karma, where are you girl?" I call. No answer.

Charlie is right behind me as I make my way through the apartment. *Guess she thinks I'm going to tamper with the evidence.* Entering the master suite, I open my walk-in closet and reach up to the top shelf. No gun! I fumble around feeling for it but to no avail. Finally, I retrieve the ottoman I keep in the bedroom and climb up for a closer examination of the top shelf. Charlie stands watching. Everything seems to be in order except for the gun. It has disappeared. I shake my head in disbelief.

"It isn't here," I finally have to admit. "The box of shells I had with it is also missing," I add.

"So it seems. Mind if I take a look?"

"No, of course not, go right ahead," I step down, take her hand and help her up, then step aside allowing Charlie room to manipulate in the cramped space.

"When did you last see the gun?" she asks as she runs her hands under the folded linen I keep on the top shelf.

I take a moment to reflect on my answer before I say, "I don't know...several years at least. Dad went into assisted living a few years ago, ten—twelve, I don't remember. Since he's the only one I shoot with, I haven't had the gun out since. No reason to."

"Un-huh." Charlie steps down, puts her hands on her hips and takes a quick look around before saying, "Okay, Judge, come on. I'll take you back downtown to get your car."

Suddenly my mouth is once again as dry as cotton. "Mind if I get a drink before we leave?"

"No, go right ahead."

I head for the kitchen with Charlie still on my heels. I take a glass from the overhead cabinet and fill it with cold water from the water dispenser on the refrigerator door. As I take a sip, I glance toward the laundry room. In the wedge of light that pierces the gloom through the partially open laundry room door, I see Karma lying motionless on the tile floor in front of the washer.

"KARMA!" I cry. Setting my glass down I rush to her. However, I know instinctively that she's dead. Rigor Mortis has set in and Karma is cold to the touch indicating she has been dead for a few hours. I kneel and try to pick her up but she is too rigid and that's when I detect the odor of almonds. *Cyanide smells like almonds.* I know this from the research of types of poison I engaged in for my first novel. Then it hits me full in the face. *The burglar who broke in and stole my gun also poisoned Karma.* The hair on the back of my neck again begins to rise at the prospect and I look quickly around, *Maybe that someone is still here.*

More frightened than I ever remember being, I say, "Detective, my cat's been poisoned." Charlie is instantly at my side. I'm still on my knees so I slide over to give her room to examine the cat.

Charlie kneels beside me and carefully leans toward Karma. "I think you're right, she smells like almonds. Probably cyanide." She stands, puts her hand on her weapon and looks around. "How long were you at the station?"

I rise to my feet, lean forward and brace myself against the washer with my hands. "Don't know. Counting the time it took me to get there and the wait, probably two hours or more. Come to think of it, I don't remember seeing Karma after I fed her. Guess I assumed she was napping."

Charlie nods and places a comforting hand on my shoulder, "So you didn't see her before you left for your meeting with Slater?"

I take a moment to consider, "No, I didn't. But, that wasn't unusual as she doesn't usually escort me to the door when I leave. However, I thought it was odd she didn't greet me when we arrived a few minutes ago... now I know why."

"Un-huh," Charlie says as she pinches the bridge of her nose with her thumb and forefinger. I observe a thoughtful expression cross her face. She then says, "I'm not sure how long it takes a cat to cool after death, especially wearing a fur coat."

Good God! Does she think I killed Karma before going to the police station?

"I'll call the captain and have him dispatch our CSI team. I don't think it's a coincidence that your gun is missing and your cat has been poisoned simultaneously. At the very least, we may be able to get some prints. You should get your locks changed as soon as possible."

Stunned silence engulfs me as I try to fathom what is happening. I manage to murmur a weak response, "Okay..." Charlie's already on the phone and I don't think she heard me. She has her back to me and glances around just as I start to pick Karma up again.

"NO! Leave her until after the team has done their job," she instructs me. Then she directs her attention back to the phone, "What, no not you, I'm talking to Judge Facinni. Yes, I'll wait and preserve the scene until the team arrives."

I sit down on a bar stool. *Hope I'm not tampering with evidence by sitting down.* Charlie takes a position opposite me and stands with her crossed arms resting on the countertop.

"Take it easy, Judge. We need to collect evidence while it's still fresh...I don't believe in coincidences."

"Nor do I. Someone broke into my home, stole my gun and poisoned my cat. How sick is that? And I don't mind saying, I'm scared. If the intruder could crack my old lock, what's to keep him from doing the same to a new lock?"

"Good point. Chains?"

I just stare at her. *And when I go out who's going to attach the chain?* "How soon will the CSI team be here?" I ask.

Charlie appears to be preoccupied but finally answers, "Twenty, thirty minutes."

I'm overcome with grief at the loss of Len and now Karma so I stand and head for the office where I can avoid looking at Karma's dead body. Charlie follows me and we sit waiting. The tension is overwhelming and I can't control myself any longer.

"I didn't do it!" I blurt.

"Do what?"

"I didn't kill Len or Karma. I'm beginning to feel like a bug under a microscope."

"No one said you did. You need to calm down."

Before I can answer, the doorbell rings and Charlie hurries to answer it. She keeps her hand on her weapon as she peers through the peephole. When she opens the door, three officers carrying investigation equipment converge upon my abode.

Charlie says, "Judge Facinni, this is Sgt. Jackson Callahan. He's lead on this particular team. Over there," Charlie points toward the center of the room, "are Officers Chad Watkins and Tyson Bailey."

Callahan extends his hand, "How ya doin'?"

I shake his hand, "Okay, I guess." The other two officers wave in my direction before they resume the task of unloading their equipment. I cringe at the thought of black fingerprint dust being scattered about my place but I hold my tongue. After all, I, too, want answers.

Charlie takes charge and sends the team into the master suite to begin the destruction. I want to remove my linen from the shelf in the closet before they ruin it with the fingerprint powder, but I keep silent. My fear is that they will think I have something to hide. I go back into my office, flop down in my recliner, and lay my head back against the headrest. *Dear God, let me wake up and discover this is all a bad dream.* I sit there reflecting on the events leading up to this point and I began to be haunted by memories of those that appeared before me, when I was on the bench, with what I determined to be flimsy excuses. *How many innocent people could I have sentenced?*

I'm jerked back into reality when Charlie says, "Judge, we've finished here. However, we have to take Karma in for a *post mortem* to determine exactly what killed her." I notice the team is already at the door with their equipment and I see they also have Karma's carcass in a clear plastic evidence bag sealed with red tape.

"Of course," I say.

As soon as the team leaves, Charlie says, "Come on, I'll take you back to the station to get your car. I've called for patrol to watch the building until you can get the locks taken care of."

Sure. Lotta good that'll do – I'm on the eleventh floor and this is a pretty busy building. A patrol car circling the block every half-hour or so is really going to scare the hell out of a ruthless killer. I reply, "Thanks. I'm ready whenever you are."

◆◆◆◆◆

BLACK STORM CLOUDS hang low and lightning flashes in the east followed by loud claps of thunder. Although it's only seven, it's already dark. On the ride back to the station, we don't talk much. I am too conflicted to engage in conversation. *How can this be happening – one day I'm on top of the world and the next I'm living in hell.*

"Okay, Judge. Here we are, where did you park?" Charlie asks as she slows the cruiser down.

"The white Mercedes up ahead is mine." I point to my vehicle and am relieved to see all four wheels are still intact.

As Charlie eases up next to my car, I say, "I prefer you call me Tony. Judge is my past life."

"Sure. Tony it is. Say, that's some ride ya got there, partner."

"Well, yes, you're right. It is *some ride,*" I answer. Sensing sarcasm in her voice, I try to match it. "Look, Charlie, I don't know what's going on any more than you do. I just lost one of my best friends and a pet I've had for twelve years. I didn't kill either one of them. And I don't know what happened to my Ruger. The fact that I can afford a luxury vehicle doesn't give you the right to ridicule me with that tone of voice. I'm beginning to feel like what you would call a 'person of interest.'"

Charlie stops the cruiser and I open the door, but before I can step out, she tugs at my sleeve.

"I apologize if you thought me rude. I wasn't trying to be—I was trying to be…well, funny. Bad timing, huh? If you'll wait and let me make it up to you, I'll buy dinner. I know you from your time on the bench and your reputation is impeccable. And for what it's worth, I don't believe you'd flip out and go rogue and kill your friend and your pet. There's obviously more to this than meets the eye."

I soften and turn toward her and gaze into her big beautiful blue eyes, "Thank you for that, Charlie. I need someone to have faith in me."

"You're welcome and it would be my privilege to have dinner with one of my favorite authors."

Well, when you put it like that…"

She smiles. "I have to take the cruiser around to the parking lot and check it in. It'll take a few minutes."

"Okay. I'll be here." I close the car door and Charlie burns a U. The first drops of rain begin to fall, but suddenly things are looking up. The fact that someone believes me, especially a police officer, encourages me beyond belief. I don't feel so all alone now.

◆◆◆◆◆

WHEN CHARLIE REAPPEARS about twenty minutes later, she looks lovely. She's wearing black slacks with a matching jacket and frilly pink ruffles from a silk blouse softly frame her face. *Straight outta Vogue*. She closes her umbrella and gracefully slips onto the passenger seat.

"WOW! The Black Swan." I greet her.

"The Black Swan?"

I laugh. "I was referring to your grace and beauty."

"Un-huh. The Black Swan is one of my favorite ballets."

"Really, and why is that?" I've fallen under *her* spell which gives more credence to the black swan reference. However, I don't tell her that.

"I don't know, maybe because it mirrors so much of real life." Charlie pauses, then she continues, "If you remember, the White Swan must find love so she can be released from a curse. She falls in love with Leroy, but alas, she has competition — the dark and reckless Black Swan. As in real life, Black and White volley for Leroy's affection. However, Leroy, jerk that he is, doesn't deserve either one of them. It's just an ego trip for him."

"But…" I cut in but was cut off as she continues.

"As the story progresses, the swans' rivalry turns into a twisted friendship and Black's dark and reckless side threatens to destroy her…"

Feeling pretty fragile, I throw my hands up, "OY! I surrender!"

Her laughter sounds like a melody. "Okay, truce. I usually don't take prisoners but in your case…" She softens, "You asked and I was just explaining *my* theory of how the ballet mirrors real life." After a pause, she asks, "Where would you like to go for dinner?"

"Oh, no you don't. I haven't made too many good choices today; since you're buying, you pick."

"H-m-m-m. If we go to the hotdog stand on the corner, we'd have to stand in the rain," she jokes. "How about the Horizon Room on top of the Keystone. The view is breathtaking, even in the rain."

"Okay, works for me. One of my favorites." I put the flivver in gear, and as I ease out into traffic, I just avoid being hit by an SUV that suddenly swerves into my lane.

"IDIOT!" I shout. Then, with my heart still thumping like a jungle drum, I glance at Charlie. "Reckless drivers are infuriating. Seems to me, for some reason or other, motorists forget how to drive when the weather turns bad."

"How well I know," Charlie says as she fastens her seat-belt. "Our business picks up considerably during the winter months when the weather and people's patience chill."

◆◆◆◆◆

WE ARRIVE SAFELY at the Horizon Room, and fortunately, we do not have long to wait for a table. In fact, we are escorted to a coveted table by the large windows overlooking the city from twenty stories up. As we're being seated, I say, "Maybe the storm has deterred many from venturing out and it's not as crowded as it normally would be."

"I like it. At least we can talk without having to shout," Charlie says and raises her eyebrows.

We peruse the menu, and after a few moments, we both agree on the featured selection, fresh tilapia. As we admire the view, I take a sip of water and ask, "'Charlie,' that's an unusual name for a female. Is it a nickname?"

Before Charlie can answer, the waiter is back with our salads and a bottle of white zin. He pours the wine and then retreats.

Charlie places her napkin in her lap, and with her fork, she takes a few pokes at her salad before answering, "No. But I get that a lot." She smiles at me. "My dad, Charles Sabastian Whitaker, III, desperately wanted a son to carry on the family name. The son was predestined to be Charles Sabastian Whitaker, IV. After having six daughters, Mom threatened Dad with castration if he didn't give it up."

Still toying with her salad, Charlie continues, "Since I was then declared to be the last of the brood, Mom relented, after a battle royal, and allowed Dad to name me Charlie. However, she refused to go the whole nine yards to Charles Sabastian Whitaker, IV. I simply emerged as Charlie Whitaker. This satisfied Dad, and believe it or not, they're still married; almost fifty years now. We — that is, me and my five siblings — are planning a big bash for their fiftieth."

"That's quite a story." I pause and take a drink of wine. Then I ask, "Do your sisters live in New York?"

"Oddly enough, yes, they all do. Yvonne, Annette, Cecile, Marie and Emily are scattered across the state, but close enough that we spend most holidays together. It's our family tradition. Doesn't matter which holiday it is, we first get up and go to Mass at St. Peter's before starting the festivities. Mom rules with an iron fist and insists that we all stay at the old family mansion which they have maintained all these years and which, by the way, is large enough to accommodate all of us and our extended families. My sisters and I have planned to surprise Mom and Dad by sending them on a cruise for their fiftieth anniversary. That'll blow Mom away."

Just then the waiter reappears with our dinners; he tops off the water glasses and retreats. Charlie, setting her partially eaten salad aside, says, "Looks like I'm doing all the talking. I get carried away when I talk about family. What about you? Is your family close?"

"I'm enjoying every minute of it," I say as I dissect my fish. "You're very entertaining and I love hearing about your family. My story isn't as interesting as yours. In fact, it's down-right boring in comparison." As I take my first bite, I realize that something Charlie said struck a chord with me, so I ask, "Your sisters' names sound familiar. Were they ever in show business?"

She tosses her head back and laughs. "Maybe in their dreams, but no. You may have heard of the Dionne quintuplets that were born in Canada in 1934. As a child, Mom was fascinated by them. They were born before all of the fertility drugs hit the market and Mom considered them one of God's miracles. She even clipped a picture of them from a magazine and has it pasted in her scrapbook. At that time, of course, she didn't know she was going to have six daughters."

Charlie twists her wine glass between her thumb and forefinger as she continues, "My sisters, Yvonne and Annette, were the first born. They are identical twins but we're all close together in age and we look very much alike. I'm only five years younger than the twins."

My God. There are five more out there that look like this god-dess! "Six daughters under the age of five? Sounds like Mom had her hands full."

"Yes, and for many years. Throw Dad into the mix, and what can I say; Mom's a saint!" Charlie says. then takes a sip from her wine glass.

"I'd agree to that." Remembering my mother is bitter-sweet and I pause for a moment before offering, "So was my Mom, a saint, that is. I had only one sibling, a brother that was three years my senior. He was killed in Viet Nam."

Charlie rests her fork on the side of her dinner plate and looks at me with sympathy in her eyes. "Oh, Tony, how terrible. What a waste that was! To cause so many so much pain and suffering and for what? "

The bite of salad I have on my fork is suspended in midair on the way to my mouth; I put my fork down before continuing. "My mother never really got over it. She died a few years after Martez was killed. I'm sure losing Martez contributed to her early demise." Remembering my mother and brother further erode my current state of mind and my emotions threaten to take control. I quickly take a drink of water before uttering, "I still miss them both very much."

"I'm so sorry, Tony."

I sense Charlie realizes how fragile I've become when she changes the subject. "Where does your father live?"

I'm relieved for the reprieve. I answer, "My dad's sharp as a tack but needs help with everyday functions. He lives in an assisted living facility in Rochester. I try to visit him as often as possible. He's my most ardent fan and keeps pressuring me to write faster." Mimicking Dad, I say "After all, Sonny, I don't have much time left." Then I suddenly stop and reflect on my father's fragile health. *God, I pray my fears are just that, unwarrant-ed fears. If I'm indicted for murder, that would surely kill Dad.*

After dinner, I drive Charlie back to the police station where she had left her car. She tells me that employees park in the same lot as the police vehicles so I stop in the front of the station to drop her off.

"Thank you, Charlie, for a pleasant dinner. I enjoyed it very much."

"You're welcome, Tony. So did I." Charlie opens her door and has one foot on the curb when she stops, turns to face me, and asks, "Why is it a handsome, talented man like you never married?"

I'm caught off guard at the unexpected and personal question. I don't want to reveal that I was married many years ago and that Joanna, my wife of two years, finally got fed up with my working eighty-hour weeks plus most weekends. According to her, and I suspect she was right, the only time I was home was when I was sleeping.

Our marriage gradually disintegrated. One night, after a grueling day in court, when I arrived home I found the note from Joanna telling me that she had left with another man. I still loved her and I couldn't blame her for her departure. I chastised myself but held out hope that she would return to me. After about six months with no word from her, I quietly obtained a divorce.

I blink back the memory and manage a flip answer to Charlie's question. "Guess I never found the right woman."

"I see," she smiles. Then she was gone.

◆◆◆◆◆

SLATER WAS LEAVING just as Charlie entered the rear door of the 42nd station.

"Say, you look nice. Where you goin' all dressed up?" he asks.

"Already been. Had dinner with Facinni."

"Trying to get him to confess?" Slater asks and then, after a pause, adds, "Did you get the Ruger?"

"No. It was missing along with a box of shells and…and someone had broken into his place and poisoned his cat."

"The hell you say! Is that why you had the CSI team dispatched?"

"Yes."

"Did you see signs of a break in?" he chides.

"No. The doors and windows were secure. That's still a mystery. I had CSI process the scene. We'll know more after we examine the evidence."

"There's something fishy about this whole thing. Personally, I think Facinni is our man," Slater smirks.

"And to what end?" Charlie sarcastically throws back at him.

Slater squints as he looks at Charlie, "Publicity to promote book sales comes to mind or maybe the guy's just plain nuts."

"Come on, Slater, you know that's stretching it. His novels are selling like hot cakes."

"Maybe, maybe not, but…" Slater looks over his shoulder, then back at Charlie. *Has she got the hots for Facinni?* "Anyway, it's late. Go on home. See you tomorrow."

2

D arkness approaches as the fading daylight comingles with the advancing twilight. Willy, sitting in Doreen Lancaster's living room, casually cleans his fingernails with the hunting knife he recently purchased from Rockford's Sporting Goods Store at the mall. He admires the elk head embossed on the imitation ivory handle as he runs his thumb along the polished six-inch blade. *Very nice, my lovely, very nice.* Satisfied, Willy smiles as he pulls on a pair of leather gloves. He then takes a handkerchief from his hip pocket and thoroughly wipes the knife.

Now, sitting there in the gloom, Willy occasionally glances through the bay window as he waits for his prey. Minutes tick slowly by. When Willy finally hears a key rattle in the lock on the front door, he slowly rises and stealthily moves into the shadows of the room. There, he stands very still, waiting.

♦♦♦♦♦

I FINALLY GIVE up the fight and get out of bed after a very restless night. I jam my feet into my slippers and mosey over to the bedroom window. I stand there a few minutes and watch as the sun volleys for dominance. However, the weatherman says the clouds will win today and rain is imminent. I turn and shuffle to the kitchen where I start coffee before going to the front door to retrieve the morning paper. On my way back to the kitchen, I flip the paper open, and when I read the headlines, I stop dead in my tracks.

LOCAL WOMAN FOUND MURDERED IN HER HOME

The article began:

Doreen Lancaster...

As soon as I read the name, shock rolls over me and I feel light headed. Doreen had been my clerk for twenty-five years. I barely make it to the sofa where I collapse onto the soft cushions as I read the gruesome details of her murder.

> Doreen Lancaster, 68, was discovered dead in her home at 1040 Melrose Avenue, Queens, the evening of October 18 by her daughter, Linda Overmeyer.

> Overmeyer became concerned when her mother failed to show up for a prearranged dinner with the Overmeyer family. When Lancaster didn't answer her daughter's telephone calls, Overmeyer went to her mother's home to investigate and found her body lying in the living room with a knife protruding from her chest. There were no signs of forced entry.

> The murder weapon is described as a hunting knife with an elk's head etched in the ivory handle. The homicide is being investigated by the NYPD and no further details are available at this time.

My hands shake as I set the paper aside. The murder and the murder weapon are exactly as described in my third novel. *First Karma then Len, both killed as were the victims in my first two novels, Fair Game and Fool's Game. Now Doreen, mirroring the murder in my third novel, Skin Game. What the hell's going on!* I run my hands through my hair and try to piece it together. *It has to be McCrombie – there's no other explanation. Should I go to the police? They'll find out sooner or later that Doreen was my clerk and it may look suspicious if I don't come forward. Holy crap!* Then it suddenly occurs to me: *Detective Charlie Whitaker has read all my novels. Holy crap!*

Just as I am about to make the call, the doorbell rings. I jump like I'd been shot and rush to the bedroom where I struggle into my robe and fumble with the sash as I hurry to the door. I look out the peep hole. Charlie is waiting in the corridor flanked by two uniformed officers. I open the door.

"Morning, Tony," Charlie says. "Mind if we come in?"

"Not at all. In fact, I was just getting ready to call you."

"Un-huh."

I don't like the sound of that so I just stand waiting, afraid to say anything else. If I had a lawyer present, I'm sure he would advise me to keep my trap shut. So I take my imaginary lawyer's advice and keep my trap shut. After a few awkward moments, Charlie tosses a plastic evidence bag on the table in the foyer.

"That look familiar?" she asks. "We pried it from the cold dead hands of Doreen Lancaster."

I wince as I think that sounds pretty much like an ad for the NRA. I pick up the bag and stare at the content, a tie tack with the emblem of New York State Judicial Branch engraved into the metal.

Finally, I find my voice, "Yes. Yes, it does look familiar. I have one just like it," I murmur.

"Un-huh. May I see yours?"

"Of course. It will just take a moment to get..."

"I'll come with you," she says.

"Sure." I turn toward the bedroom. She's right on my heels.

I go to the small wooden jewelry box atop my dresser and lift the hinged cover. It's empty. Everything is gone. I jerk around gulping air, "I…I,"

"Get dressed, Tony. You're coming downtown with us. Orders from headquarters."

"Sure, okay. Is this an arrest?" *Dammit! Wish I hadn't said that.*

"No. Slater just wants to talk to you."

I wait but no further explanation is forthcoming so I turn and go into my walk-in closet where I select a pair of slacks and a sweater. Then I ask, "May I dress in privacy?"

Charlie glares at me with steely eyes before shouting to an officer in the other room. "Rocky, get in here and keep an eye on the judge while he changes." Then she turns and walks away. I notice she's back to calling me *Judge* and my heart sinks at this sudden change in her demeanor.

◆◆◆◆◆

I SIT IN the backseat with Charlie, and needless to say, the ride to the station is pretty tense. She stares ahead not looking at me. Once we arrive at the 42nd, Slater is waiting in the same interview room that we used before. I'm roughly ushered in by Charlie's uniformed entourage.

"Well, we meet again," Slater smirks.

I'm no Sherlock, but I am beginning to get the impression Slater doesn't care too much for me. Or, for that matter, anyone else, including Charlie, or so it seems.

"Take a seat, Judge."

His voice drips with contempt. I nod and comply. *Keep your cool. Don't say anything. Exercise your right to have an attorney present during questioning. God, my hands are sweating – sure sign of guilt?*

Slater studies his eyes on me as he states, "For the record, I'm going to establish who we are and the date and time of this interview."

I nod. *Been here before…*

"My name is Sgt. Gary Slater, he says after pushing the "on" button on the recorder. "The interviewee is Antonio Facinni. Today is October 19, 2014, 8:38 a.m." Slater clears his throat, "Judge Facinni, please state your full name, address and date of birth for the record."

I do so.

"Did you know Doreen Lancaster?"

"Yes."

"And how is it you are acquainted with her?"

"She worked for the State of New York and was my clerk during the time I served as District Court Judge for the third judicial district. That would be approximately twenty years."

Slater scribbles something on his notepad. "When was the last time you saw Doreen?"

I take a moment to recollect when I saw Doreen last before answering. "At her retirement party approximately six, seven years ago."

"Did you get along with her during the time she worked for you?"

"Absolutely. We were not only co-workers but good friends."

"Un-huh. That makes two of your *good friends* that have been murdered this past week — plus your cat," he pauses for effect.

I don't say anything.

"Do you have any idea who would want Doreen dead?"

I hesitate. *Should I mention McCrombie. No! Not yet. I need a lawyer.* "No," I answer.

"Where were you yesterday, say from between five and seven in the evening?"

I look at Charlie who was leaning against the ugly green wall with her arms crossed. "I was home," I say.

"Can you prove that?"

Now I have to start providing alibis. This definitely does not look good — is he trying to railroad me? "I live alone — how do you expect me to prove it?" Then I look straight into Slater's eyes and say, "I want a lawyer. I believe that this *interview* is over."

Slater slaps his thighs with his palms and stands. He goes to the door and shouts, "Clancy, bring a phone in here."

When the phone is brought in and connected, Slater motions for me to make the call. He leans back in his chair and stares at me. I stare back. I'm determined not to be intimidated this time around. I pull my wallet from my hip pocket and find my attorney's business card and dial his number.

"Jeff Wilkinson," Jeff says in a cheerful voice.

"Jeff, this is Tony Facinni."

"Hey, Judge. What's up?" Jeff asks, his voice laced with concern.

"I'm down at the 42ⁿᵈ precinct. I'm in trouble and need legal advice. Are you available? Now?"

Jeff doesn't even pause before saying, "Of course, I have the morning free."

"How soon can you be here?"

◆◆◆◆◆

TWENTY-FIVE STRAINED MINUTES later, Jeffery Wilkinson is escorted into the interview room.

He takes a quick look around and then orders, "Give us some privacy!" Slater, appearing to be somewhat reluctant, stands and slowly leaves the room. Charlie had left earlier.

Jeff turns to me. "What gives, Tony?" he asks.

I bring Jeff up to speed leaving out nothing including my suspicions that Wilber McCrombie is behind the murders – the *Game* novel murders. *Oh, my God.* I suddenly remember I have another novel out there.

Jeff must have noticed the look on my face. "What is it, Tony?"

"Jeff, the killer...the killer is duplicating the murders in my novels. In *Fool's Game* the victim was a detective shot in an alley four times with a .22. My gun is a .22 Ruger. In fact, that's why I used that model; I'm familiar with it."

"H-m-m-m. Interesting but not..."

I rub my face with my hands and continue. "That's not all, Jeff. Karma and Doreen were murdered exactly as the victims in *Fair Game and Skin Game*. Don't you see? McCrombie is setting me up. I have another novel out there and there is another innocent person at risk of becoming victim number four. Oh, my God, Jeff, we gotta do something."

"Hold on, Tony. Who the hell is Karma?"

"Oh, sorry. Karma is, er...was my cat. She was poisoned with cyanide." I pause then say, "Someone broke into my place, killed my cat and stole my gun and jewelry.

"Have you told your theory to the cops?"

"NO! Not yet anyway. I wanted to talk to you before making any statements."

"You're pretty smart for a judge," he joked.

"Yeah. Well, apparently not too smart or I wouldn't be in this predicament. I didn't want to believe it but now I'm sure Doreen's murder was duplicated from my third novel. Telling you the details made me realize the events surrounding Len's murder were in my second novel and Karma, my first. However, the victim in the first was a person, not a cat."

"Tony, in the fourth novel, how is the victim killed?" Jeff asks.

"Hogie, the *End Game* victim, plunges off a hairpin curve in the Catskills. His business partner had severed the brake fluid line on Hogie's Escalade."

"I see. Well, at least that's a start but now that we suspect we know how the copycat killing is going to happen, how do we narrow down the identity of who the fourth victim will be? The only thing the first three have in common is that they were all associated with you in some fashion. Is it possible that you have a very narrow coterie of friends and acquaintances that we could canvass?"

I shrug and say to Jeff, "Unfortunately, no. However, I don't see McCrombie leaving this jurisdiction. He obviously wants me to be the goat for all of his crimes. Leaving the reservation would impede that plan so that narrows it down a bit."

"What do you call a bit?" Jeff asks.

I slump in my chair as I realize our quest is hopeless. There's no way we could narrow down potential victims — even if we had the time. "Okay, I see your point. Way too many to count. Dammit! Do you think I should bring the cops in on my theory? If they book me, I'll be out of circulation. Then what's McCrombie gonna do?" I pause. "Come to think of it, that may be a good way to save victim number four."

"Throw yourself on your sword, so to speak," Jeff quips. I notice a thoughtful look cross his face before he says, "However, my advice is for you to say nothing, at least for now. At any rate, I don't think they have enough, at this point, to hold you, and even if you did share your theory, it wouldn't change that fact. If they had solid reason to think you're their man and evidence to back it up, you'd have been read your rights and we'd be having this conversation in a cell. What they have is mostly circumstantial. If they're smart, and most cops are, they wouldn't want it to be known they have a viable suspect until they have enough to nail your ass." Jeff pauses then asks, "Have you ever been printed?"

I place my elbows on the table and rub my temples as I think back, "No, not that I recall."

"Not even when you received the appointment?"

"No. When I took the bench, background checks were minimal and prints weren't required. Things are different now. NYCIC and NCIC checks, as well as FBI fingerprint comparisons are now an absolute necessity.

"When Slater brought me in, I wasn't booked so I wasn't printed. He referred to our meeting as an *interview*. However, for all intents and purposes, it seemed to me more like an *interrogation*. He told me I wasn't being arrested and I could leave any time I wanted."

As I sat there with Jeff discussing my treatment by Slater, I become angry all over again. I suddenly stand, slap the steel table with my palms and announce, "Since I'm free to leave at any time; I want that time to be *now!*"

Jeff smiles. "Okay, Cowboy, I'm your posse. We're bustin' outta here." Jeff stood and slid his legal pad into his valise. Clutching it under his arm, he states, "We're walkin' outta here together." Before reaching the door, he turns to me and adds, "I don't think you should go home — it isn't safe. You're welcome to stay at my place until things change."

I'm touched by Jeff's kindness. "Thanks, Jeff. That's the best offer I've had all day but I don't want to run from this maniac. I had my locks changed and chains put on the doors. If I use myself as bait, we may be able to catch him sooner than later, and hopefully, before anyone else gets killed." I cringe at the thought of someone else falling victim because of me.

"Sure, Tony. I really don't like the idea, but suit yourself. The offer is open ended."

Jeff opens the door. As soon as we exit the interview room, he announces to Slater, "We're leaving now."

"What do you mean 'we'?" Slater sneers as he sharply eyes me.

Jeff bristles, "If you have something to hold my client on, book 'em!" Jeff slams his right fist into his left palm. "Right damn now! Book 'em! Otherwise, *we're* leaving."

Slater backs off and jams his hands into his pants pockets. Then looking at me, he says, "Okay, go on. But don't be leaving town, ya hear?"

"We know the drill. Don't worry. That won't happen," Jeff says as he roughly pushes past Slater and I follow close behind. *I love this guy — he's smart and tough and has the guts to back it up.*

◆◆◆◆◆

AS SOON AS we exit the police station, the crisp morning air caresses my face. I look up at a blue sky adorned with white puffy clouds. Freedom takes on a whole different meaning and in this moment, I embrace it with my whole being. *But for how long?*

"Where'd you park?" Jeff asks as we descend the cascade of cement steps leading to the walkway.

"Didn't. I was chauffeured."

"Un-huh. Come on, I'll take you home." Jeff gently takes my elbow and guides me toward his vintage luxury Lincoln Continental parked up the block. As we approach, I suddenly recall the day Jeff got the MADE N USA vanity plates. He was so excited, he made a special trip to my office at the courthouse to show them off. Jeff is American through-and-through and didn't mind flaunting it. He did a stint in Viet Nam and saw plenty of action. According to Jeff, the lyrics of the *Star Spangled Banner* should be changed to "…the land of the free *because* of the brave."

As we get closer to the Lincoln, I notice the original black paint looks like new as does the plush black interior. I open the passenger door and ease myself onto the genuine leather seat and lay my head back. *Dear God, please let me wake up from this nightmare.* Jeff goes around the car, slips in behind the steering wheel and gently closes the door. He inserts the key into the ignition and the powerful V8 springs to life. One quick look over his shoulder and we're off like a flash.

Jeff expertly maneuvers his pride and joy through NYC traffic. When we reach my place, I say, "Hey, Pilgrim, I missed breakfast. If you'd like to come up, I'll make us an omelet… served with mimosas."

"Shucks, Partner, I'd be a fool to turn that offer down," he replies as he puts the car back into gear and proceeds to drive around to the parking garage behind the building.

As I exit the vehicle, I notice a stranger walking through the parking garage looking as though he forgot where he parked his car. He looks familiar. I rack my brain and scratch my head trying to remember, but I can't place him.

"Well, come on, Tonto. Them mimosas is awaitin'," Jeff teases with a southern drawl.

I shrug off the uneasy feeling that's swarming all over me. *Guess I'm just tense, frustrated and scared.* I fall in beside Jeff as we approach the back entrance of the building.

◆◆◆◆◆

DURING BREAKFAST, JEFF and I examine the evidence against me to date. I verbally put the events into chronological order:

"First, on October 13, my cat is poisoned with cyanide mirroring the murder in my first novel. Then, later that same day, Len is shot just outside my apartment building mirroring the murder in the second novel. And coincidentally, my gun, same caliber as the murder weapon used to kill Len, went missing."

Jeff interrupts, "I don't believe in coincidences."

I nod and continue. "Next, on October 18, my long-time friend and clerk, Doreen Lancaster, is stabbed to death with the exact same kind of knife that is depicted in my third novel. A tie tack, exclusive to the New York Judicial Branch and identical to one I *had*, was clutched in her hand. I can't produce mine. Its missing along with my .22 and the rest of my jewelry." I pause, reflecting on these events leaves me drained and I'm too emotional to say more.

We sit silent for a few minutes. After examining the case against me murder-by-murder, I'm devastated. I finally manage to say, "Looks pretty bleak, doesn't it?"

Jeff, obviously, has been mentally designing a defense. That's what defense attorneys do.

He doesn't miss a beat. "That, my friend, is defeatist. Let's look at the other side." He holds up his right hand, and touching his fingers with his thumb, he begins to tick off positive points:

"What possible motive could you have for any of it? I don't see a jury buying the 'to boost book sales' theory as a motive. Your arch-enemy was released from prison the day before your cat was poisoned and Len was murdered. McCrombie is probably the burglar and poisoned your cat at the same time he burglarized your home. What's more, he had threatened you and Len. The idiotic notion that you left evidence at the crime scenes that directly points the finger at you is ludicrous on its face. The only thing that makes sense is that someone is framing you — in all likelihood — McCrombie."

I nod. Jeff makes perfect sense. My spirits are lifted and I'm feeling much better.

"Okay, Tony. Enough for now," Jeff says as he drains the last of his mimosa and looks at his watch. "I have an appointment at two, so I'd better hit the road. I know it's easy for me to say, but don't let this wear you down. We have a damn good defense if it comes to that. I'll phone you tomorrow."

I walk Jeff to the door and we shake hands. "Thanks for the grub," he says. "You run a pretty mean chuck wagon."

I laugh, "Thank you for the advice and encouragement. I was beginning to feel like I had already been tried and convicted."

"They're going to need a lot more than they have to date to initiate anything. Let's just wait and see where this takes us."

◆◆◆◆◆

AFTER JEFF LEAVES I clean up our breakfast dishes and go into my office. I cringe when I look at the mess on my desk. *Didn't I just sort through the mail a few days ago? I don't understand how the post office can be in financial trouble with all the junk mail they're delivering on a daily basis.* I spend the next few hours sorting, shredding, writing checks and answering the incoming mail. My head aches and my eyes burn when finally I reach the bottom of the stack. The paper chase was something I tried to avoid in my professional life and something I would avoid in retirement if I could.

Retreating from my desk, I head for the kitchen. Jeff and I hadn't finished the pitcher of mimosas and it would be sinful to let the residue go to waste. I'm part way to the kitchen when the phone rings so I rush back into the office to answer it.

"Hello."

"Tony, its Charlie. All right if I come over? I need to talk to you."

The vision of her standing in the interview room looking at me with accusing eyes washes over me. "I'll be here all afternoon so come whenever you like." *Wonder what this is all about. Is Slater sending in Tokyo Rose to immerse me in propaganda or to seduce me into a confession?*

"Thirty minutes."

"Sure. I'll be expecting you." I probably did a lousy job of filtering the sarcasm from my voice. Wonder if I pissed her off when, three hours later, I'm still waiting and getting pretty pissed off myself. I'm about to head out to walk off some of my pent-up anger when the phone rings again.

"Tony," she says, and I detect sadness in her voice.

"Yeah. What happened, I've been waiting for you..."

"Jeff Wilkinson is dead."

I stagger, almost fall, and began to shake all over. "How, what..."

"Traffic accident. He went off an embankment just this side of the Catskills. There were no skid marks. It was like he didn't even hit the brakes. It just doesn't look right to me, but we'll know more after the investigation."

End Game! "Oh, my God! Oh, my God!" was all I could say remembering the conversation I had with Jeff only a few hours before.

"Tony, it could have been the brakes."

I'm shocked and remain silent. Then it hits me. *The stranger I saw moseying around in the garage when Jeff and I arrived was McCrombie. That dirty rotten son-of-a-bitch. When we were having breakfast he cut Jeff's brake fluid line. The accident must've happened shortly after Jeff left here. Oh, my God!*

"Can you come over now?" I ask Charlie. "I need to talk to you." *I'm still not sure I can trust her after the cold shoulder she displayed this morning. However, there's only one way to find out if she's friend or foe.*

"As soon as I finish up here. I'm still at the scene. Two hours, give-or-take," she says.

"Okay."

I hang up the phone and sit down on the sofa cradling my head in my hands and for the first time since this horror began, I weep. No, actually, I full-out cry. I want to scream and throw things. At the end of my tirade, I'm spent—emotionally, physically and mentally. I curl up on the sofa, pull the green Jets stadium blanket over me and fall into a haunting restless slumber. I'm not sure how long I'd been lying there when the doorbell rings. I jump up and almost run to the door. Charlie, dirty and bedraggled, moves to embrace me but thinks better of it after she looks down at her soiled uniform. I motion for her to come in.

"Oh, Tony. I'm so, so sorry."

"Is this ever going to end?" I murmur and turn back toward the office.

She just stands there for a minute, what can she say?

"I'm sorry, Charlie. I didn't mean to...come on in."

"Understandable." Looking down at her clothing again, she asks, "May I use your bathroom to clean up? I don't want to soil your furniture. We have a lot to talk about. Slater is hot on your trail, but you've probably figured that out by now."

I nod. "That's pretty much what we decided, Jeff and I." I rub my eyes and push back another flood of tears that threatens to burst forth as I reflect on this morning's conversation with Jeff. "You're welcome to take a shower. There's a robe hanging on the back of the bathroom door, you can use it if you like."

"Thanks. I won't be long." She turns toward the bathroom adding, "Preliminary investigation looks like the brake line was cut. Let me clean up and I'll fill you in on the details."

"Brake line, huh?" I follow her and notice she didn't refer to *End Game*. I turn so she can't see my expression and procure a clean bath towel for her. When I hear the shower running, I go to the kitchen and start a pot of coffee, mostly because I need something to do. That *déjà vu* feeling slowly creeps up on me. *End Game!*

When Charlie reappears, her hair is hanging in wet tendrils. Her freshly washed face is clean and shiny and she smells of gardenias.

"Fresh coffee." I point to the coffee maker, "Want a cup?"

"Thanks. I could use something stronger but coffee will do for now." She eases up on a bar stood and tightly secures the white terry robe around her.

I place a steaming cup of java before her and stand waiting. Finally, growing impatient, I say, "Well..."

Looking up, she exclaims, "Oh, sorry. I've been preoccupied." She pauses, then says, "I don't believe it was an accident."

"I guessed as much," I say when I'm hit with this. My fears are confirmed.

Charlie absently stirs her coffee as she says, "Looked like he was headed for the Catskills and lost control on a hairpin curve. There were no skid marks; he just plummeted over the edge. According to the ME's initial report, he died instantly."

"Oh, my God, it's my fault, my fault..." a sob escapes, and embarrassed, I bury my head in my hands.

Charlie climbs from her bar stool, comes around and embraces me. "That's nonsense, how could it have been your fault?"

It takes me a few moments to regain control of my emotions. Finally, I say, "We came here when we left the station. I fixed breakfast and we went over some details concerning the recent events."

"How long was he here?"

"Hour, hour and a half, maybe. We came in the back way so he could park off the street in the garage. Before we entered the building, I noticed a stranger lurking around. I think it could have been McCrombie. It's been twenty years since I've seen him but...if I'd been more alert, I could have prevented this, it's my fault! My fault!"

"I'm so sorry, Tony, but it wasn't your fault. You're not responsible for the actions of another."

"I should have recognized him. I could have prevented..."

Charlie, still cradling me, says, "Don't be so hard on yourself."

"Do you believe me?" I ask with a touch of panic in my voice as I jerk away from her embrace.

She doesn't hesitate. "Yes, I believe you. I was here when you found Karma, and I don't think you could have contrived your reaction. That's not the only reason. The frame-up is much too obvious. You'd have to be really dumb to do it or really smart to pull it off."

I blanch. "What do you mean?"

"Well, if you were the perp, staging a break-in and leaving personal items at the various crime scenes would be really dumb...or, on the other hand, really smart in order to make it look like a frame up."

"Ah, I see. Motive?"

"Yet to be determined, but according to Slater, to bolster book sales. He's sure your novels are going to skyrocket as soon as word gets out about the copycat murders."

"H-m-m-m. My book sales are already skyrocketing. *End Game* has been on the best-seller list now for over three weeks, and incidentally, took the other three with it. The printer can't keep up with the demand. Guess again."

"I don't know." Charlie takes a sip of coffee then adds, "Maybe you just left the reservation and started murdering people for the fun of it. Hands on experience, so to speak."

"Try holding that theory up in court."

My agitation must have bled through.

"Calm down, Slugger. I was just being the devil's advocate and looking at it from Slater's perspective. Of course, I don't believe you did any of it." She pauses before adding, "I'm going to request an APB for Willard McCrombie but I need Slater's approval to do so. Perhaps if we bring him in, he may sing or at least trip himself up. After all, he certainly would want *you* to know he's the one that masterminded your demise, sick bastard that he is."

"He may be a sick bastard, but he's also a cunning one. Do you think Slater would approve your request?"

"Maybe, maybe not. He thinks he's got his man."

"Yeah. That's what I thought." After a pause, I add, "Even if you did question him, you'd be hard pressed to trip McCrombie up."

"Maybe, but you haven't seen *my* interrogation talents yet. I have many persuasive skills including bamboo shoots." She pauses for an instant. "Tony, I haven't eaten since, since I can't even remember when. If you have some eggs, and with your permission, I'd like to make us an omelet. Would you share one with me — I am a pretty good cook."

Yep, I'm sure of it — that among many other things. "I'm sure you are, ah, a good cook that is. I do have eggs and your suggestion sounds like an excellent one. The kitchen is yours."

I make toast and watch Charlie chop the various items she pulls from the refrigerator into tiny pieces, then add eggs and seasoning. She sculpts her creation into one of the best omelets I've ever eaten.

"You're amazing," I say through a mouthful. "What do you think of my toast?"

She picks up a slice, turns it over and back again and smirks, "And you did this all by yourself?" We share a laugh which I desperately needed. It felt good.

When we finish, since Charlie did the cooking, I do the cleanup while she watches with a thoughtful expression on her face. Afterward, we take fresh coffee into the living room to watch the news. There was a small piece concerning Jeff's accident but not much since it was still under investigation.

Stretching, Charlie remarks, "I'd better get going."

"Oh, so soon?"

"I have an early day tomorrow. Thanks for the shower and loan of the robe. I'll just get dressed..."

She stands and takes her cup to the kitchen, places it in the dishwasher, then goes to the bedroom. Minutes later she reappears in the soiled uniform. I rise and walk her to the door.

"Thanks for coming by. I don't know how I could have made it through facing another death alone." After a slight pause, I ask, "Do you think Slater is going to want to interview me again?"

"I'm sure he will but don't let him rattle you. He has a way of alienating people — even those he works with. Remember, I believe you and I'm a pretty tough nut to crack."

I open the door and she gives me a quick peck on the cheek, then she's gone. I touch the damp spot left by her lips as I turn back to the now empty apartment and prepare to face another sleepless night. As I drag myself through my nightly ritual, I detect signs of Charlie that linger in the bathroom. A hairclip on the bathroom sink, a wet washcloth that smells of gardenias, toothpaste smears on the faucet...I'm missing her already.

CHAPTER

3

The ringing of the phone jolts me from my slumber. I feel as though I had just barely dozed off. I pick up the receiver and take a quick look at the clock; it's eight-thirty.

"Lo," my mouth is dry and my voice cracks when I speak.

"Good morning, Judge Facinni. This is Sgt. Slater."

I sit up and take a quick sip of water from the carafe on my nightstand, "Yes, good morning to you as well." *Here it comes.*

"I'd like to meet with you sometime this morning here at the station. I guess you know Wilkinson's death is being investigated as a homicide."

"No, I didn't know that. Am I suspect in that as well?" *Wish I hadn't said that.*

"Not that I know of. Since you're probably the last person to have seen him alive, I thought any information you can provide may be helpful. How does ten o'clock sound to you?"

"Sure, I'll be there." We hang up and dread encompasses me again. I throw back the colorful flower garden quilt my grandmother made me many years ago. Back then it was my security blanket. It's now worn and faded but priceless. I still feel grandmother's much-needed love and comfort surround me when I curl up in it.

◆◆◆◆◆

SLATER MEETS ME as I enter the station and we go into his office. *Wonder why he's abandoned the cold sterile stinky interview room.* "Take a seat," he beckons with a wave of his hand. I sit down and cross my legs trying to look relaxed. Slater eyes me suspiciously before he turns on the recorder and memorializes our names, the date and the time. Then he pushes the recorder closer to me and asks,

"Judge Facinni, when did you last see Jeff Wilkinson?"

"Yesterday morning." I volunteer no further information.

"And why was that?"

I look at Slater and wonder if he had forgotten our confrontation yesterday morning. He looks as though he sees the confusion on my face so he adds, "Even though I know the answer, this is for the record, Judge Facinni," and he points to the recording device.

I nod, "Mr. Wilkinson is, or was, my attorney. He came here, to the police station, at my bidding when you were interrogating me concerning a homicide…"

"Correction! I was not interrogating you, I was interviewing you. Just as we are now," Slater says in a very indignant tone before he continues. "What did you do after you left here yesterday morning?"

"We went to my home. I was without transportation since your crew chauffeured me down here for the *interview*. Jeff took me home." *He's going to have to ask the questions, I'm not volunteering anything.*

"Then what?"

"I made us breakfast."

"And…" I could sense the frustration in his voice.

"And we talked."

"About what?"

"That's confidential. Attorney/client privilege. I do not have to reveal that to you."

"No, you don't. But it would be better if you did."

"Better? Better in what way? Am I a suspect? All four victims were close personal friends of mine—even Karma. What possible motive would I have to kill anyone much less my close friends. You're treating me more like a suspect than an interviewee."

Slater leans forward across his desk, "Calm down, Judge. Like I said before, we have to follow the evidence." He pauses before looking up at me. "We would like to fingerprint you. If you won't give them voluntarily, I'm afraid I'll have to book you."

"On what charge, may I ask?"

"Oh, I'll think of something."

I'll just bet you will, you bastard. "I have nothing to hide. Go ahead, print me."

Slater looks surprised then says, "Okay, hold on a minute." He picks up the phone and directs someone on the other end of the line to come get me in order to collect my prints. A minute later a uniformed officer appears. His name tag identifies him as Trace Younger. Younger escorts me to a fingerprint alcove, and upon completing the process, points to a sink and instructs me to wash. I wash as much of the black ink from my fingertips as possible, then I'm escorted back to Slater's office.

"That was quick," Slater says when I reenter.

"Yeah, not much business out there this time of day. I know from my experience on the bench that most crimes are committed in the late afternoon, evening or night."

"So it seems." Slater frowns as he fiddles with some paperwork on his desk. Finally he asks, "Is there anything you wish to tell me before leaving?"

"Nope." *Does the dope think I'm going to confess to something I didn't do?*

It appears to me that Slater is expecting something and is detaining me purposefully. Moments pass and I sit waiting. Slater finally slaps his desktop with his palms and pushes his chair back. "Okay then, thanks for coming in. You're free to leave."

I stand and turn toward the door. "There is one more thing…" Slater stops me and scratches his temple. *He's missing the cigar and trench coat if he's trying to use Columbo tactics on me.*

"What's that?"

"It's not wise to withhold information from the authorities."

"So it seems," I say. Then I was out the door.

♦♦♦♦♦

AS SOON AS Judge Facinni leaves, Slater picks up the phone. "Taylor, have you had time to compare Facinni's prints to the ones we found on the undercarriage of Wilkinson's car?"

"No, sir. We just barely have it up on the rack. I'll let you know as soon as I get some results."

"Speed it up, will ya?"

Taylor suppresses the desire to tell Slater to shove it, but answers, "We're moving as fast as we can."

Slater spent an anxious few minutes pacing his office waiting for the call. When the phone finally rang, he barked into the receiver, "Yes!"

"They match."

"They match?"

"They match."

"Son-of-a-bitch. He's our man. I want to arrest him myself."

♦♦♦♦♦

SLATER KEPT A log of the events surrounding the recent murders, stored on his computer. When he was informed the fingerprints matched Judge Facinni's, he knew he had probable cause to get an arrest warrant. He immediately opened his computer file and added the language required to obtain an arrest warrant. Slater, satisfied with his affidavit establishing probable cause, printed the document. Once he had the printed document in hand, he found Officers Taylor and Gardner in the locker room just reporting for their shift. He instructed the officers to accompany him to the police parking lot where they obtained a cruiser and the three of them drove to the courthouse. Slater was on a quest to find a judge to review and issue his affidavit and arrest warrant. Once signed by a sitting judge, the document would officially give the officers permission to take Tony Facinni into custody and charge him with murder.

Slater whipped into a reserved parking slot in front of the courthouse. "You guys wait here, I won't be long," he said as he jumped from the cruiser and rushed into the courthouse. Judge Lombardi had just finished his docket and was secluded in his chambers looking over his next day's calendar when Slater entered the judge's outer office and approached the judge's clerk.

"Hi Joyce," Slater said. "Is Judge Lombardi in? I have an emergency arrest warrant I'd like for him to take a look at."

"Hello, Gary. Judge just left the bench. Let me ask him," Joyce replied as she picked up the phone. After a brief conversation, Joyce pointed to the Judge's chamber door and indicated it was okay for Slater to go in.

"Hey, Gary," Judge Lombardi greeted Slater. "What's up?"

"Good afternoon, Your Honor. I have an urgent situation concerning the copycat murders. It looks like Tony Facinni may be the perp," Slater said.

"WHAT! I don't believe it. Let me see that," the Judge said as he reached for the warrant with one hand and pointed to a chair with the other.

Slater passed the warrant to the judge and sat on the edge of the proffered chair waiting impatiently. Once Judge Lombardi finished reading the affidavit, he shook his head, apparently in disbelief. He reluctantly picked up his pen and signed the paperwork, then passed it back to Slater.

"Thank you, Your Honor." Slater was already on his feet heading for the door.

The Judge just nodded, looking as though he was still in shock.

◆◆◆◆◆

I LEAVE THE station feeling pretty depressed. Not only had I lost close friends, I was suspected of killing them, or *so it seems*. I was just getting into my car when, from behind me, a familiar voice says, "Need some company?" I turn and smile when I see Charlie walking toward me. She looks stunning, even in her blues.

"You bettcha." Standing there, I awkwardly flip my car keys in my hand as I wait for her to catch up to me. "You had breakfast yet?" I ask, and immediately sense something has gone terribly wrong—and probably not to my advantage. "Let's go to my place and try that omelet again."

"Not a good idea." Charlie fidgets and looks around before saying, "Apparently fingerprints taken from the undercarriage of Wilkinson's vehicle match yours."

"WHAT? That's impossible."

"Prints don't lie."

"But, but, I don't understand…"

"Tony, I could get fired for this, but anyway, here goes. Slater is headed for your apartment. An arrest is imminent."

"Oh, God! Did Slater get an arrest warrant?"

"Not yet but he was all fired up and in the process of preparing one when I left. That's been a while ago. I had to check out before leaving and have been looking for you for several minutes. My guess is he has it ready by now and is in the process of getting it issued by a judge. He's going to execute it himself. She pauses and looks around again before saying, "I'm off duty, let's go to my place."

"Why would you put yourself in that position?"

"I believe in you, Tony. Everything that's happened appears to me like a setup to incriminate you. It's all too convenient, and as you pointed out, McCrombie is out and apparently seeking revenge. Besides, I'm not one of Slater's biggest fans—I know some things he's done that aren't exactly kosher."

"Really? That's no surprise if the way he *interviewed* me is any indication of his tactics."

"Yep." Then Charlie looks around again before saying, "I'll get my car from the lot, you follow me home."

"Okay." My spine tingles and I, too, glance around. *Does she think we're being watched?*

Charlie adds, turning toward the parking lot, "I have underground parking so just follow me into the garage. Once secure, we'll at least have time to decipher your situation and devise a plan before you're picked up."

"Picked up?" *Can this really be happening?*

◆◆◆◆◆

IN ROUTE TO Facinni's apartment to make the arrest, Slater mumbles, "I'd like to have searched the garage at The Blackstone for unusual amounts of brake fluid. But, dammit, since so many vehicles are in an out of that facility and not even knowing where Wilkinson had parked, is problematic. Quite obviously, the brake line wasn't completely severed to begin with. Otherwise all of the fluid would have leaked out before Wilkinson reached the Catskills. In all probability, just a trace amount would be in the garage which doesn't help our case any."

"Agreed," Taylor replied. "And at any rate, if there had been an unusual amount of fluid on the garage floor, other vehicles would have already passed through it thus making it impossible to determine how much was originally there."

Officer Gardner nods and says, "The Blackstone is an eleven-story complex. My mother-in-law lives there on the sixth floor. Often, when we go to visit her, it's difficult to find a parking spot in that garage. The residents, of course, have designated parking slots but visitors are pretty much on their own."

"Yeah. That's what I thought. Anyway, if we did find something, how would we tie it in with Wilkinson's vehicle because of the high amount of traffic in and out," Slater says pondering the possibility as he stares out the windshield.

Once the officers arrive at The Blackstone, they go straight to Facinni's apartment and ring the doorbell. There is no answer. Slater turns and looks up and down the corridor. Everything is quiet.

"Gardner, you stay here but out of sight. Get into that stairwell — you should be able to see his door from there. Taylor, go down to the lobby and take up a position but stay out of sight. I'm going to move the cruiser but I'll be around. When you see him don't move on him, just let me know right away. This is *my* collar," Slater said putting his hand on his weapon.

Both officers nod and leave to take up their assigned positions.

◆◆◆◆◆

UPON PARKING WHEN we reach Charlie's apartment, we walk up a flight of steps to the second floor. She unlocks the door and ushers me inside. Her abode is small but tastefully furnished. Two sofas, upholstered with a floral design in various shades of pink, green and cream are centered in the living room facing each other, separated by a glass top oak coffee table. Lush green potted plants stand sentinel in the corners of the room. Under other circumstances, I could imagine myself in a flower garden. The galley kitchen opens into the dining area which is just big enough for a round table, four chairs and buffet. I immediately feel comfortable in this place. It's warm and friendly.

"Grab a seat and relax while I change," she says and disappears down a hallway.

"Okay," I answer and jamb my hands into my pants pockets and head toward the living room. As I pass a bookcase, I notice Charlie has all four of my novels on display. I'm flattered and pause to examine the other titles she obviously has read. I run my finger across the spines and stop when I reach Carroll Multz' *Justice Denied*. How ironic, that's exactly what I worry will happen in my case. I leaf through the book, remembering the falsely accused came to a sad ending. Self-pity threatens to engulf me so I replace the novel next to Multz' other five works of fiction and continue my journey to the living room. As I pass the fireplace, I notice an array of photographs neatly arranged on the mantel. Charlie's sisters are indeed as lovely as she. One picture in particular catches my eye. I pick it up for a closer look. It's a picture of a young woman standing with a handsome man who is wearing an Army uniform. The woman could be Charlie, or it could be any one of her sisters.

I suddenly sense Charlie behind me. I turn; she's dressed in jeans and a green Jets sweatshirt. She gently takes the photograph from me and reverently places it back on the mantel.

"That is a picture of Thomas and me. We were engaged;" she pauses then continues, "he was killed in action shortly after he was deployed to Iraq. That was over five years ago."

"Oh, I'm so sorry." I say. I'm embarrassed and feel as though I've transgressed into her personal life.

"Thank you for your condolences." I notice sadness in her eyes as she continues, "Not only did I lose my fiancé and best friend, but the world lost a wonderful person." She looks at the photograph for a few moments then says, "Come on into the kitchen and keep me company while I fix that omelet. Or would you rather have hot oatmeal?"

I'm relieved for the distraction and answer, "You decide. If I'm incarcerated who knows when I'll get another decent meal." Standing there leaning against the counter, I feel awkward. I look around hoping to find something to do. I ask, "What can I do to help?"

"Just stand by." Charlie says as she selects a plump grapefruit from a basket of fruit on the counter and cuts it in half. She hands me the paring knife and says, "Here ya go. You can section the grapefruit and set the table."

I stand next to her, gently slicing through the grapefruit sections. Charlie asks, "If you're incarcerated, would you be able to post bond?"

"On a million dollars? Not likely. Book sales aren't that good."

She sighs and I watch her graceful movements as she busies herself cooking. *I need to focus on my situation, so don't even go there – at least not yet.*

I change the subject. "How long have you lived here?" I ask.

"H-m-m-m," she pauses looking as though she's thinking about it. "I guess almost as long as I've been on the force – that's roughly twenty years."

I glance around, "This is very nice."

Charlie looks up from her slicing and dicing. "Thank you." Then she points out of the kitchen window. "The view is spectacular, that's what sold me. I love the fountain and the lake. Sometimes my place seems too small, but the upside is that I don't have overnight company." Charlie turns toward the range, and scooping the chopped vegetables into a hot skillet, she adds, "As I previously stated, my sisters stay with my parents when they're in town. My parents love the company and my sisters feel at home."

"Did you say that was here in the city?"

"Yes. Over on the west side."

I nod. "Say, that's beginning to smell good. I think I'm hungrier than I thought."

"I've always loved the smell of onions being sautéed," she says as she stirs the mixture with a wooden spoon. "It won't be long now. Go ahead and set the table. The dishes are in that cabinet."

I can't help but notice how organized Charlie's kitchen is as I remove two plates from the cabinet.

"The silverware is in that drawer," she says, pointing with the spoon, "and, if you don't mind, you can pour us each a glass of juice. Hope you like orange?"

"Yep. My favorite," I say as I take the juice from the refrigerator.

Minutes later, Charlie announces, "Looks like brunch is served," and she places a serving dish heaped with omelet, hash browns and toast on the table.

Charlie agilely slides onto a chair and wiggles into place as she says, "This is my chair, I always sit with my back to the wall."

"H-m-m-m. Guess you know that didn't work out too well for Wild Bill. Jack McCall got 'em anyway."

Charlie smiles at my analogy. "Well, Hickok didn't keep his eye on the ball and was blindsided by McCall. I don't intend to let that happen."

"Well, neither did I but…look where I am now. I should be the one sitting with my back to the wall."

"Quit whining. I'm not trading places with you. Let's eat, the omelet is getting cold." She dishes a generous portion onto my plate and I dig in.

After we finish brunch, I help Charlie clear the dishes. "We've been ignoring the elephant in the room, Charlie. I'm a wanted man. Where do we go from here?" I ask.

"We need to talk about that, Tony. As far as anyone knows, I was not aware you were targeted for arrest when I invited you over so my job isn't jeopardized for fraternizing with you. At least not yet. I think your best bet is to give yourself up. Since you're a pillar of the community, the arraigning judge may be lenient concerning your bond."

"Not a chance. Most judges stick to the bond schedule and a million is the going rate for murder one. Slater will probably hit me with three counts of murder. That makes the situation even more aggravated. And, those of us who wear white hats are held to a higher standard." I shake my head. "Can't imagine how my prints got on the undercarriage of the Lincoln."

"I can. Haven't you heard of cases where the evidence was forged or fabricated? We had a class at the academy regarding just that, forgery and fabrication. That was where I learned that fingerprints can be lifted from a surface using tape and then transferred to another surface by pressing the tape against the receiving surface. For example, prints could have been taken from your kitchen counter and transferred to the undercarriage of the victim's car. Since your place was broken into, this theory isn't too far off the mark. McCrombie could have lifted your prints from any surface in your apartment, kept them in a safe place, and when the opportunity presented itself, transferred them to the undercarriage of Wilkinson's vehicle at the same time he cut the brake line."

"Of course. I should have remembered that. I'm not thinking clearly these days." I massage my temples with my forefingers. "Add that to the other evidence against me, I'm a dead duck."

"Not necessarily. However, you do need a good criminal lawyer. I'm sure you probably know who the best is from your experience on the bench."

I'm stunned. *I'm going to be arrested and I need a good criminal lawyer.* My mind whirls and I feel light-headed, again. *My blood pressure must be off the charts.* Finally, I respond, "Yes, yes I do know the best. That would be Theobald Raddison. He's never lost a case and he's had some pretty tough ones." I hesitate before adding, "And you're right. I should surrender." I pause for a brief moment. "But first, I need to go see Dad and tell him in person what's going on. I don't want my Dad to hear it from an outside source and suffer more anxiety than necessary over this ordeal." I had begun to trust Charlie, so I ask, "How do you suggest I proceed with the surrender?"

Charlie bites at her thumb nail and I notice the thoughtful expression on her face. She finally answers, "Don't go home. Whatever you do, Tony, do not go home. They'll be waiting for you. If they do intercept you, make sure your hands are always in plain view; any sudden move on your part would give them an excuse to shoot you."

Now I'm really scared. *Shoot me?* I zone out. My brain is unable to function.

Charlie asks, "How long will it take you to go see your father?"

I'm so preoccupied, I don't hear her question at first. She persists. "Earth to Tony! Hey, Slugger. How long will it take to go see your father," she asks again.

I blink. "Ah, just a few hours."

Charlie says, "Don't take your car. When you don't show up at home they'll put out an APB. Any alert cop that spots your vehicle can arrest you."

I'm stymied, "Dammit! I can't use public transportation either."

Charlie rubs the back of her neck. "I've nothing to do the rest of the day. I'll take you."

I glance up at her. "That's very generous of you, Charlie, but I can't let you take any more chances than you already have."

"What? Are you suggesting that a drive through the countryside on a beautiful day is against the law? Not a bit of it. Why, I have a sister who lives in Rochester."

I hold my hands up in surrender. "Okay, point made." Then I add, "You're an angel."

"And *you're* a good judge of character. Call Raddison before you do anything else and bring him up to speed. Ask him for advice on how to turn yourself in. If he agrees with our plan, have him meet you at the 42nd sometime late this afternoon."

I'm suddenly in survival mode and my brain finally kicks in. I say, "Okay. That's a start. May I use your phone?"

"I'd rather you not. I don't want any record of you being here."

"Of course. I should have thought of that. My cell phone is in my car. I'll call Theo from there. Ah, do you think it would be okay if I use your phonebook to look up his number?"

"Smartass! I'll do it for you."

I raise my eyebrows. "You are thorough, aren't you?"

"I like to call it self-preservation." Charlie thumbs through the phonebook. "Here's his number."

I write the number on the palm of my hand with a pen Charlie provides. "I'm also going to call my Dad so he'll be expecting us. I don't want to surprise him with an unexpected visit. He's pretty fragile..." I stop midsentence. Charlie puts her hand on my shoulder. I can no longer keep up the bravado and slump as I bury my face in my hands and break down and sob. Charlie wraps her arms around me and holds me close.

When I regain control, I dab at my eyes with my palms. I'm embarrassed by my breakdown. As I stand, ready to leave, I look down and notice my tears have eradicated Theo's number. I hold my hand up for Charlie to see. "I'll need that phone number again. It seems to have disappeared."

"So it seems." She opens the phonebook and looks up the number again. "You go make your calls while I change into something more presentable. I'll meet you in the garage in a few minutes."

"Okay" is all I can manage. I'm conflicted and emotional. *Is my trust in her misplaced? Will she call Slater as soon as I walk out the door? I have to trust her. I have nowhere else to turn.*

I reach my car, retrieve my cell phone and call Theo's office.

"Raddison, Vincent and Martinson. How may I direct your call?" a pleasant voice on the other end responds.

"This is Judge Facinni. If Mr. Raddison is available, I need to speak to him immediately." After a slight pause, I'm connected.

"Why, hello Judge. To what do I owe this honor, Your Honor?" He laughs at his little play on words.

"That's good, Theo" I manage a slight chuckle. "I'm in a jam." I proceed to explain the circumstances surrounding the recent events and my plan to surrender.

"Hell's fire and damnation, Judge!" He pauses. *Is he going to turn me down?* Then, "Of course I'll help you. What time do you think you'll be back from Rochester?"

"Probably around four, four-thirty."

"That works and I agree with your plan of surrender. It'll add credibility to your innocence. I'll meet you at the 42nd and I'll get there early enough to ensure I'm present when you arrive. Good luck with your father and give him my regards."

Relief washes over me and I reply, "Thanks, Theo. See you later."

Before I can call Dad, Charlie appears. She's wearing black slacks and white sweater and looking pretty darn sweet. *There you go again. Get a grip!*

"Just hung up from talking to Theo. He's on board." I watch her expression relax.

"That's wonderful!"

"Hold on while I call Dad."

●●●●●

CHARLIE IS QUIET during the trip to Rochester. *Wonder if she's having second thoughts about helping me?*

I finally ask, "Are you all right?"

"Yes. Why do you ask?"

"It's just that you're so quiet. I wonder if you're having second thoughts?"

"No, not at all. I've been mentally sorting through the evidence trying to find a flaw. McCrombie certainly buttoned you up, but it's been my experience that criminals always make a mistake. We just have to ferret it out."

"Yeah, the proverbial needle in the haystack."

"You got it. Difficult, but not impossible."

I like Charlie and her attitude. She keeps me buoyed, focused and hopeful.

When we arrive at the Rochester Assisted Living Center, we find Dad waiting in the lobby. The facility is upscale and cheerful. Dad seems to be pretty satisfied living here.

"Hello, Sonny." Sonny is Dad's pet name for me. Hearing him say it opens the gates and memories of my childhood come pouring in. I feel myself getting emotional again and bite my lip to stave off the tears. *I've got to hold it together. Can't breakdown in front of Dad. He has enough to cope with.*

Dad continues, "It's good to see you, but...I sense something is wrong." Then he looks past me at Charlie and asks, "Who's the eye-candy?"

Charlie smiles, steps forward and extends her hand. "Hello, Mr. Facinni. I'm Charlie Whitaker, a friend of your son's."

"Happy to meet you. Charlie is it?"

"Yes, it's Charlie, and it's a long story."

Dad laughs and turns to me. "Come on, let's go out to the courtyard and enjoy the fresh autumn weather."

I push Dad's wheelchair out the sliding glass doors into the courtyard. Charlie follows. We position ourselves on a concrete bench under a large oak tree in the courtyard. It is indeed pleasant. The afternoon is cool, the air is fresh and I'm with my Dad. When we're all situated, Dad folds his hands in his lap and looks expectantly at me.

"So, what's going on, Son?"

I tell Dad the story from beginning to end leaving out nothing. He doesn't interrupt, just sits and listens. At the end of my dissertation, he reaches out and squeezes my hand.

"Thank you for the head's up, Sonny. What happens now?"

I look away, then back at my father. "I'm going to surrender and face whatever comes. I have an excellent lawyer..."

Dad squeezes my hand again. "That's good." He pauses. "How are you fixed financially?"

"Well, I anticipate a million dollar bond, if not higher. I don't have enough to pay a bondsman the ten percent to bail me out and give my lawyer a retainer so I may have to sit in jail until the trial."

"That's not going to happen," Dad says indignantly, "you need to be actively involved in your defense and doing it from a jail cell...well," Dad reaches into his pants pocket and produces a small key. "Here, take this."

Puzzled, I say, "Okay...but what is it?"

"It's a key to a safety deposit box at the Rochester branch of World Bank. Remember about fifteen, twenty years ago I had you take me to get a safety deposit box and had you sign the signature card as well. That signature gives you access to it. I have approximately three hundred thousand stashed..."

"WHAT?"

"Yep, I invested in dot.com stocks back in the eighties. My investment ballooned into three hundred thousand, and it's yours. It was always meant for you. I didn't want to take a chance on losing it in the vacillating market, so I just tucked it away. Probably not the most lucrative thing to do, but at least I had the peace of mind knowing it was safe. Use it for whatever it takes to clear the family name. I'm well taken care of and won't need it—ever."

I sit in stunned silence hardly able to fathom what is happening. Finally, Charlie clears her throat bringing me back into the moment.

My voice cracks. I say, "Dad, are you sure?"

"Are you kidding me, Sonny? Of course I'm sure! You're all I have left."

I kneel before him, put my arms around his waist and lay my head in his lap. He strokes my head and my back as we both shed tears. I notice Charlie turn away and dab at her eyes with a tissue.

CHAPTER

4

Charlie takes me back to her place to pick up my car. I had put the cash from Dad's safety deposit box in a shoebox Charlie had in her car. When we arrive at Charlie's, I open the car door and prepare to exit. "Thanks, Charlie, for everything." I look at my watch and pat the shoebox. "I still have time to get to the bank before they close."

"You're welcome, Tony, and" she put her hand on my arm, "good luck."

I smile and squeeze her hand. At that moment something shifts inside me. *I'm falling in love. Wouldn't you just know it–as soon as my life lands in the toilet, I meet the perfect woman.*

Charlie parks in her designated slot; I back out of the visitor's space. I glance in her direction as I drive past. A warm fuzzy feeling envelops me. I like it!

♦♦♦♦♦

WHEN I ARRIVE at the bank, I ask to see a personal banker. A perky teller shows me into a private office and leaves.

Soon afterward Ashley Dexter comes in and closes the door behind her.

"Tony, how nice to see you."

"And you as well, Ashley."

She takes a seat behind the desk and asks as she points me toward a chair opposite, "How can I help you?"

I slide onto the leather chair and say, "I have a sizable amount of cash to deposit."

"Okay?" I hear the question in her voice. "But you could have done that at a window..."

I open the shoebox. She gasps.

"Well, Tony, I know your novels are good, but..."

I laugh and say, "In my dreams." Then I add, "I have approximately three hundred thou here. It's wrapped in ten-thousand-dollar bundles."

"This is highly unusual...I mean that much actual cash."

Once again, I'm feeling like a criminal. "I don't have time to explain but trust me, it is honest money. Will you deposit this into my checking account?"

Ashley adjusts her glasses before saying, "Yes, of course, but I have to count it first. And Tony, I never doubted that it was honest." She takes the shoebox and carefully lines the bundles up across her desk quickly counting them as she does.

"You have three hundred thousand, seven hundred and fifty dollars. You want this all in your checking account?"

"Yes."

Ashley looks up and flips an errant strand of hair back. She starts to say something but abandons the thought. She places the bundles back in the shoebox and leaves the office. A few minutes later she returns with my deposit slip.

"Here you go," she smiles.

I take my deposit slip and look at the total: $300,750.00. Satisfied, I thank Ashley and hurry out. I have ten minutes to get to the police station.

◆◆◆◆◆

WHEN I ARRIVE at the station, Theo is waiting in the lobby. He stands when I enter.

"Hey, Tony, you made it." Theo extends his hand in greeting.

"Yep, and it looks like just under the wire," I shake his hand.

Theo looks around apparently making sure we're not being overheard, then says, "I talked to Sgt. Slater. He looked disappointed when I told him you were on your way in to surrender. He's waiting in his office to take you into custody. You will have to spend the night in jail since it's too late in the day to get you before a judge. I have you on the docket at eight tomorrow morning."

I also take a look around. I want to flee, but know I can't. I jam my hands in my pockets and say, "Thanks, Theo. Who am I appearing before?"

I watch as Theo studies the floor for a moment before replying, "We got lucky—Judge Marcus Ochoa."

"Marcus? Good! I've always had a good repport with Marcus."

Theo smiles. "I know. That's why we're lucky it's his week to do arraignments. With your reputation and connections to the community, I don't see any problem with getting a bond set."

Slater must have seen me enter. I look up as he approaches, jangling a set of handcuffs.

Theo apparently notices the cuffs as well and says, "There's no need to cuff my client. He's voluntarily surrendering."

Slater bristles. "Don't tell me how to do my job, Raddison! I'm following protocol and you have no say in the matter."

"Theo," I say, "its okay. He's just doing his job."

Theo starts to say something, but apparently thinks better of it. He just stands with his arms folded across his chest.

"You wait here in the lobby while I book the suspect." Slater sneers at Theo and forcefully grabs my arm.

"Theo, no need to wait," I say. "I know how this works. You go on home. I'll see you tomorrow morning."

Theo fidgets for a minute, then replies, "I'll be here." Then he looks at Slater. "And there better not be any sign of mistreatment or violation of my client's rights." Theo takes his cell phone from his pocket and begins snapping pictures of me from all angles.

"Hey, what do you think you're doing?" Slater demands. "Give me that…"

"Step away," Theo puts a restraining hand on Slater's chest, backing him down. "I'm memorializing my client's physical condition as he appears before I turn him over to you."

"You can't do that." Slater stammers.

"And why not? You have no right to take my phone—we're in the lobby where use of cell phones is permitted. You do not have my client in custody. You haven't even read him his rights so I can do whatever I like."

Slater turns red and runs his hands through his hair. Then he pulls a small card from his shirt pocket and half-assed reads me my *Miranda* rights. "Do you understand your rights as read to you?"

"Yes, I understand my rights." I watch Theo closely. He has also recorded the reading of my rights on his phone. Preparing to leave, he pockets his phone. Turning to Slater he says, "I'll be here before eight tomorrow morning. Make sure my client is ready to go. His court appearance is at eight sharp." Then he nods to me and walks toward the exit.

I watch him go and my heart sinks. I feel totally alone for the first time in my life that I can remember.

Slater jerks my arm and roughly walks me toward the adjacent detention facility. He leaves me with the duty officer. After my career on the bench, this is almost more than I can bear. *Be strong. Don't let them see your anxiety.* I comply with every command. They take my clothes and personal items and bag them with an identifying tag. Then, after a thorough and humiliating body search, I'm given a set of orange jail garb. I'm photographed, fingerprinted, for the second time, booked and locked in a holding cell.

The cell is cold and stark, fitted only with a stainless steel sink, toilet and bunk. The bunk is unmade. *Wonder if they moved someone out so I could have the penthouse suite.* I'm so exhausted I can't think. I sit down on the bunk and before long I'm curled up in a ball with the foul smelling olive-colored wool blanket pulled up around my neck. I fall into a dreamless sleep.

The night passes without incident and I'm awakened at six o'clock.

"Time to rise and shine," a much-too-cheerful deputy says as he drags a metal cup across the bars of my cell. I open my eyes and rub them. It feels like I used sandpaper. My arms itch and I remember I'm allergic to wool. The bunk is too small for my six-foot-two, hundred-and eighty-pound frame, and as I uncurl, I struggle to stand. My cramped legs resist movement but I manage to ease my way over to the toilet. I'm too miserable to care if anyone watches me pee. I splash cold water on my face. Now I'm really wide awake and the reality of my situation begins to worm its way into my consciousness. *Oh, my God! This isn't a bad dream. What if I'm convicted? This would be it for the rest of my life – the death penalty may be preferable.*

"Hey, you! Put your hands on your head and stand back against the wall. I'm bringing your breakfast in," another deputy orders.

I move to the far wall and press myself against it with my hands on my head. This guy appears to be a loose cannon and I don't want to give him an excuse to execute me on his own. When the deputy leaves, I examine breakfast. Gooey oatmeal, warm milk and burnt toast. I eat it anyway. I'm smart enough to know I need to keep my body nourished for the upcoming ordeal. As soon as I finish breakfast, I look up when I hear a familiar, friendly voice.

"Tony." Theo is standing with a deputy outside my cell. "Open it and let me in," he instructs the deputy. Once inside, Theo asks, "How'd the night go?"

"Slept like a baby, you know, sleep a couple of hours, wake up and cry, sleep a couple of hours, wake up and cry…"

Theo grins at my little joke. "I get the picture, Tony, and it shows. You don't look too good. Let's see what we can do to get you presentable before we go to court." Theo takes me to the sink and wets my hair smoothing it back. He takes a clean handkerchief from his pants pocket, wets it, and swipes it across my face a few times.

"That'll have to do," he announces, looking me over, searching for other repairs that can be implemented before we leave.

"Okay, Tony, when we get to court, let me do the talking."

I sigh audibly and answer, "I have no problem with that."

I pick up on Theo's hem-hawing. After a few moments, he finally asks, "Are you financially able to post bond?"

"If it isn't more than a million, yes, I am."

Theo's eyebrows raise. "Swell. This shouldn't take long at all. You'll be out by noon."

Just then, we hear loud voices coming into the pod and two guards approach my cell.

"Time to go, *Judge.*"

Theo puts a restraining hand on my arm and stands, turning toward the guard that spoke.

"You knock off the attitude right now!" he states in a loud voice. "Understand?"

The guard looks sheepish and nods.

"I need an answer!" Theo demands.

"Yes, sir, I understand."

"Good. Let's go."

We make our way through the tunnel that connects the detention facility with the justice center and take a private elevator to the fifth floor. I'm ushered into the inmate waiting area and Theo enters the courtroom. My case is third on the docket, and when it's called, I'm pulled out of the herd by one of the guards.

This is one of the older courtrooms. The cream-colored walls are graced with wide mahogany woodwork with etched borders. The wooden baseboards are at least six inches wide and ornately carved. The chandeliers are vintage and nostalgic. There are two tables facing the bench just inside the railing that separates the spectators from the spectacles. One is designated for the prosecution, the other for the defense. The bench is positioned on a raised platform so the judge can preside over his domain with ease. A semicircle balcony is positioned above the defense/prosecution tables. It is adorned with an elaborate wooden railing matching the décor of rest of the courtroom.

I see Theo seated at the defense table and he looks around as I'm ushered in. He stands and pulls out the second chair for me. When we're all in position, Judge Ochoa adjusts his glasses, picks up my court file and carefully looks it over. Then he looks at me for a few seconds. *I know what he's thinking. He's wondering how a law-abiding citizen and officer of the court got himself into such a mess.*

"I believe counsel has a copy of the affidavit and arrest warrant. Is that correct?"

"Yes, Your Honor." Theo answers.

"Have you had time to study it?"

"Yes, Your Honor." Theo pauses, "May I address the Court?"

"Yes, go ahead."

Theo stands. "As you know, my client has lived in New York his entire life. He maintains a home here. His roots are here. He served the People of the State of New York for over twenty-five years and has a distinguished place in the judicial archives." Theo turns and puts his hand on my shoulder. "Judge Facinni is not a flight risk. We are requesting the court to set bond at this hearing." Theo takes his seat and waits.

The judge looks at the prosecutor, a mousey little man by the name of Chester Kendall who is a deputy district attorney and appearing for the arraignment hearing only. Apparently the district attorney didn't think a bond would be authorized, and if so, that I would be unable to post it in the anticipated amount.

"Mr. Kendall, do the People object?"

"Yes, Your Honor, we do. Judge Facinni is expected to be charged with three counts of murder one — and animal cruelty, which indicates the vicious propensity of the defendant. The People emphatically object to any bond whatsoever."

Judge Ochoa looks as though he has heard it all before. He looks at Theo, "Do you want to rebut, Mr. Raddison?"

"Thank you, Your Honor, I do." Theo stands and addresses the court, "Judge Facinni is an accomplished author of four best-selling novels. His face is on his books in every city in America. If he were to flee the jurisdiction, he'd be tagged and picked up within hours. Judge Facinni is also wise enough to know the consequences for bond jumping. Plus, it is not in his nature to flee to avoid prosecution."

Before Kendall can object, Ochoa states, "The Court agrees with defense counsel and sets bond at a million dollars, cash or surety."

"Thank you, Your Honor." Theo sits down and I breathe a sigh of relief. *I can do this. I can make bail.*

Judge Ochoa signals the hearing is over as he closes the file and sets it aside. Looking at his clerk, says, "Call the next case!"

Theo and I rise. Kendall just shrugs his shoulders as we leave the courtroom. He did his job and the court setting bond is no skin off his nose.

I'm officially still in custody and have to go back into the holding cell to wait for the other inmates to conclude their hearings at which time we all will be escorted back to the detention facility.

As we walk toward the double oak doors that lead into the corridor outside the courtroom, Theo asks, "How long will it take you to get the hundred K for the bondsman?"

"I have it, cash — well, in my checking account."

"WHAT! You have that much money in your checking account? I didn't see a bank robbery charge in the affidavit. Either that or your novels must all be selling like hot cakes."

"Dad," was all I offered.

"I see. Do you have a preference or shall I pick a bondsman?"

"You're more up-to-date since I've been out of touch for a few years. You pick."

"Will do. I'll have you out before lunch."

"I'm really counting on that especially if breakfast was any indication of what lunch will be like."

Theo laughs and slaps me on the back, then a deputy leads me back into the holding cell. My fellow inmates move aside and give me space.

♦♦♦♦♦

AT THE CONCLUSION of all the arraignments, we're herded back to our pods and individual cells. It's eleven o'clock when a deputy approaches my cell. "Your ticket out of here just arrived."

He opens my cell and escorts me to the property room where my clothing and personal items are returned to me.

"Go ahead and change. I'll wait out here," the deputy says.

When I'm ready, the deputy takes me to the front desk. Theo and Sully, of Sullivan's Bail Bonds, are waiting for me at the front counter.

"Tony!" Sully offers his hand and I shake it. He looks up at the clerk at the counter who nods. Sully says, "We're done here; let's go."

As we approach the parking lot, Theo offers to buy lunch.

"Since we each have a vehicle here," he says, "I can drive or we can meet at the restaurant. How does the Del Rio sound?"

"Perfect. I'll take my car and meet you there," Sully says, "no need to come back here, at least not today. If I beat you, I'll get us a table and…a pitcher of margaritas."

"Works for me," I chime in. "I'll take my car as well. The longer I can stay away from this place, the better I like it."

♦♦♦♦♦

WHEN WE'RE ALL seated comfortably in a booth at the Del Rio, I clear my throat. "I'd like to get business out of the way before we order." I pull my checkbook from my breast pocket. First, I write a check for one hundred thousand dollars and hand it to Sully. He takes it and makes a display of kissing it.

"I like the way you do business, Tony...so will my ex."

"Anything to keep peace in the family." Then I write a check for another hundred thousand and hand it to Theo. He raises his eyebrows when he sees the amount of the check.

"This is quite a retainer, Tony."

"You'll earn it if I read Slater correctly. He's determined to burn me." I pause for a moment. "Is Ray Schaffer still in the investigation racket?"

"Yes. I use him frequently and he's still the best there is. These young punks don't know their ass from a hole in the ground."

The margaritas arrive. Sully pours all around and raises his glass.

"Here's to you, Tony," he says. "And a positive outcome at the end of trial."

"I'll drink to that," Theo and I say at the same time. The three of us raise our glasses in a salute before taking a drink.

PART TWO

THE
BLAME

CHAPTER

5

Willy, sitting on the cheap sofa in the combination living/ dining/kitchen area of a dingy apartment in the Bronx, tosses the newspaper aside. He rubs his eyes, stretches his legs and leans his head back against the dirty worn upholstery. He just finished the article regarding Judge Antonio Facinni's arrest. The headlines read:

SUSPECT ARRESTED IN COPYCAT MURDERS

Retired Judge Antonio Facinni voluntarily entered the 42nd Precinct Police Stationhouse late yesterday afternoon and surrendered when he learned that there was a warrant for his arrest and that he was a suspect in the copycat murders that have been terrorizing the citizens of New York.

District Attorney Edison Hammond has charged the former judge with three counts of first degree murder and one count of animal cruelty. Facinni appeared at the early morning arraign-ment unshaven and in jail garb. Criminal Court

Judge Marcus Ochoa set bond set at $1,000,000. Facinni's attorney, Theo Raddison, told report- ers that Facinni had made arrangements to post bond and that it was anticipated he would be released from custody by mid-morning.

Antonio Facinni was appointed to the bench and served as Criminal Court Judge for the State of New York for over twenty years. Upon retire- ment from the bench, Facinni began writing novels. He has authored four mystery thrillers: *Fair Game, Fool's Game, Skin Game* and *End Game.* An unnamed source at the district attor- ney's office said the recent murders appear to mirror the crimes depicted in Facinni's works of fiction. No motive for the crimes was cited. A bond return hearing is scheduled for October 31 at 9:00 a.m.

◆◆◆◆◆

WILLY WAS FULL of himself for being so artful in fram- ing his adversary. *So the judge was able to bond out was he? Judge- ships must pay a pretty penny. He can buy his way out of jail but not a conviction.* Willy was very pleased with himself having snuffed the detective who engineered his arrest and provided the key testimony that sealed his conviction. Now, he would turn the table on the judge who sentenced him.

Willy rises and walks to the cheap beat-up dresser. There, lying on top in plain sight, are the remnants of his raid on Facinni's apartment. He toys with the items: a pair of New York Judicial Branch cufflinks, a monogramed handkerchief, and a ring with the words New York School of Law encircling an insignia of the Statue of Liberty. The words, Antonio Facin- ni—1974 are etched on the inside of the gold band. Willy picks up the cufflinks and ring and roll them around like dice in his hand. *Picking the lock on the judge's place was like taking candy*

from a baby. Except for that damn cat. Bitch scratched the hell out-
ta me when I picked her up. Should have wrung her neck but that
wouldn't fit in with my scheme. Wish the bastard had written more
novels so I'd have a couple of more victims to blame on him. It's a
shame to waste this evidence but I can't deviate from my plan. I'll
just save these as souvenirs of my victory. Then Willy howled. The
maniacal laugh resounded off the walls.

◆◆◆◆◆

IT WAS HER day off and Detective Charlie Whitaker
sat at her dining room table absent-mindedly stirring her coffee. *Wonder if I can get a search warrant for McCrombie's place.*
There must be some incriminating evidence left from the burglary.
He wouldn't go to all this trouble to frame Tony and not keep tro-
phies. Eh! Slater would never approve a search warrant. He's got his
man *and I don't dare go over his head.* Charlie suddenly snapped
her fingers. *That's it! I'll talk to Emory and suggest McCrombie*
has been using drugs. Emory has zero tolerance for druggies, as do
most parole officers, and he's allowed to search without a warrant. I'll
accompany Em for his protection.

Emory Nelson had been a parole officer for the better part of
twenty years. Having seen so many parolees violate their parole,
he had become jaded. He doggedly pursued any hint of violation
and slammed the violator back into the penal system.

Charlie immediately telephoned Emory.

"Hey, Charlie! How do I rate?" Emory greeted her.

"Hello, Emory. I…er, I have an urgent matter I need to discuss with you. Are you free for lunch?"

Emory didn't hesitate. "You bet. I like being seen with the
most beautiful woman in the world."

"Haven't changed much, have you?" Charlie teased.

"Nope. And I hope you haven't either. Where do you want
to have this rendezvous?"

"Rendezvous? That's a stretch, but if you insist. I was
thinking about Louie's just up the street from your office."

"Sure. Maybe some of my protégés will see me with you and turn green with envy."

"Of course they will...how about eleven so we can beat the noon crowd?" Charlie suggested.

"That works for me since my next appointment isn't until one. I'm looking forward to seeing you," Emory said.

"Thanks, Em. I, too, am looking forward to seeing you."

◆◆◆◆◆

EMORY WAS SEATED at a table where he could watch the entrance, and when Charlie arrived, waved as she entered. Charlie smiled and waved back then she snaked her way through the tables to where Emory was seated.

"Thank you so much!" was the first thing Emory said to her.

Charlie looked around to see who he was addressing. Then realizing it was her, she asked,. "For what?"

"For not changing. You're still stunning."

"And you're still full of it," Charlie replied as she smiled.

They embrace briefly, and when Charlie was situated, Emory handed her a menu.

Pursuing the bill-o-fare, Charlie asked, "Umm, what appeals to you, Em?"

"You really want to know?"

Charlie blushed. "Ah, let me rephrase that. How does the chicken salad sound?"

"Heavenly."

The waitress approached with a pad in hand.

Emory looked at Charlie and she nodded. "We'll both have the chicken salad," he said.

"Very good, sir. What would you like to drink?" Emory pointed in Charlie's direction.

"Water for me," Charlie replied.

"Same for me, with a lemon wedge," Emory said without looking away from Charlie.

When the waitress retreated to place their orders, Emory looked into Charlie's eyes.

"What's troubling you, Beautiful?"

"Well," Charlie began, "I have reason to believe one of your parolees is using, selling, or both." She then looked down, ashamed of her pretext.

Emory stiffened, "What? Who?"

"Willy McCrombie."

"That slimy pig. I knew I couldn't trust him. However," Emory furrows his brow, "he hasn't had a hot UA."

"Well, then he's probably just selling or smart enough to stay clean until after being tested."

"Probably both. I'm going to pay Wee Willy Weirdo a surprise visit."

"But…but don't you want to get a search warrant first?"

"That's a good idea. However, I don't need one. One of the conditions of parole is that the parolee prospectively allows searches by his parole officer any time, day or night."

"But if you find something, won't you need a warrant?"

"Never received a definitive answer from the DA, but as a matter of protocol, we usually do. However, I'll have Willy's ass immediately thrown in jail then I'll get the warrant."

Charlie sat toying with her lunch.

"Not hungry?"

"What? Oh, no. I was just thinking. I'd like to accompany you when you do the surprise visit."

"Why? McCrombie is a weasel, a no-good, dyed-in-the-wool killer."

"Exactly. My interest is personal and I can't go into it now. Besides, I may be useful when you get his ass thrown in jail."

"Okay. Don't you think I can handle it myself?"

"Just trust me, Em. Like you said, he's a born killer."

Emory held up two fingers forming a V, the universal sign of peace. "How can I resist you under any circumstances? I'll keep you in the loop."

"Thanks, you're a love."

"Yeah, I get that a lot from my parolees."

Charlie laughed at his sarcasm.

◆◆◆◆◆

THE NEXT DAY when Charlie arrived at the stationhouse, she had a voice mail message from Emory. "Hey, Beautiful, I took your advice and had one of the DDAs review a warrant I prepared. He agreed with me that my having received a hot tip regarding Willy's using and/or selling was enough for probable cause to get a search warrant. He gave me the go ahead. I'm on my way to see a judge as we speak. I'll let you know when the warrant's issued. I'm free to execute it any time before three; let me know your schedule."

Charlie carelessly tossed her jacket onto the coatrack in the corner and immediately dialed Emory's office phone.

The answering machine picked up. "Emory Nelson is not available to take your call. Please leave a message."

"Em, this is Charlie. Got your message and I can go any time. Call me on my cell, 241-9032, and let me know as soon as the warrant is issued. I don't think we need a team. You and I can probably handle the little creep."

Charlie hung up the phone. Then the wait began. She took her cell phone from her pocket and placed it on her desk. She tried to concentrate on the pile of files overflowing in her in-basket, but her mind kept taking her in another direction. Every so often she would glance at her cell phone to make sure it was still charged and that she hadn't missed the call. Charlie looked at the clock on the wall. It was now eleven twenty-five. "Come on, Emory!" she coaxed as she tapped her nails against her desktop.

As if saying it made it happen, Charlie's cell phone rang. She grabbed it up. "Em?"

"Yep, got the warrant. Meet me at the weasel's as soon as you can get there."

"Will do, fifteen minutes. I'll be in my personal vehicle. I don't want to alert McCrombie by taking a cruiser," Charlie said.

"Okay. I'm just leaving the courthouse and it'll probably take fifteen minutes for me to get there as well.

Charlie jumped up knocking her chair against the wall. She grabbed her jacket from the coatrack, and as she rushed from the building, she encountered Sgt. Slater who was just arriving.

"Hey, where ya goin' in such a rush? You get a hot tip?"

"What? Ah, no, err, I just remembered I have a luncheon date with Margo and I'm running late," Charlie said, racing past Slater toward the exit.

Slater just shook his head as he watched her fly out the double glass doors and down the concrete steps to the spot where she had parked her car.

◆◆◆◆◆

CHARLIE AND EMORY arrive at the rundown apartment building at approximately the same time. "It's such a cheap sleazy joint, it doesn't even have a name," Charlie commented to Emory. The faded sign hanging over the door announced "ROOMS FOR RENT." The dilapidated structure was located in the more seedy part of town, and gang-bangers wandered up and down the street eying Charlie's car as they passed. *I just dare them to vandalize my car…*

Emory looked around in disgust. Then he asked, "How do you wanna play this?"

"Just like any other surprise visit. Knock on the door and you announce who you are. He'll know you're paying an unscheduled visit to check up on him. If he doesn't answer, we bust in."

"Oh boy, and I'm just two years from retirement."

"Hey, cowboy up. It'll be just fine. He thinks he's pretty clever. He'll be delighted to see you."

Emory plunged his hands into his pockets and looked around again, "Yeah. I get that a lot, too."

Charlie playfully punched Emory's arm. They stood in the lobby of the ratty establishment looking up the steep, rickety staircase. Finally Charlie took a step toward the stairs but Emory pulled her back."Me first," he said. Charlie stepped back and Emory took the lead as they started up the stairs to the fourth floor.

Charlie had been fumbling around in one pocket and then the next. About halfway up the stairs she stopped. "Dammit anyway! Wait, Em. I can't find my badge…must have left it in the car in my haste to get here. You hold on; I'll run back and get it."

"Okay. I'll meet you at the top."

"NO! You wait right here. That's an order."

"Yes, ma'am." Emory salutes.

"I mean it, Em! Right here," Charlie said as she turned and ran down the two flights of stairs and out onto the street in the direction of her car. Once there, it took her awhile to locate her badge. She finally found it under the driver's seat. When she had it in her hand, she rushed back into the building, arriving in time to hear Emory scream just before he landed in a crumpled heap at her feet.

◆◆◆◆◆

CHARLIE STOOD IN the lobby of the hotel with the medical examiner as the EMTs gently placed Emory's body on a gurney. Only one patrol car answered the call since it was reported as an accident, and there was no need for the CSIs to investigate. When the ME confirmed it appeared to be an accident, the NYPD officers left the scene to the EMTs to clean up.

"His neck was broken on impact," Dr. Dillard told Charlie. "He died instantly."

Charlie, apparently still in a state of shock, just nodded.

Dillard put his hands on his hips and looked around at the interior of the structure. "What in hell's name were you two doing here in the first place?"

"Em, er, Emory was checking on one of his parolees."

"U-m-m-m. I see." Looking up the steep climb, Dillard added, "I can see how easy it would be to fall down these stairs, but to go over the railing..."

Charlie stood in silence. *That rotten son-of-a-bitch Willy pushed him. If I hadn't left him or even tricked him into coming... Oh, God! I'll get him. Em; I'll get him!* Charlie roughly swiped at the tears running down her cheeks and looked up as one of the EMTs approached.

"Well, Doc, we're done here," he said.

Looking around again, Dillard replied, "Okay, you go on ahead and I'll meet you at the morgue." He then looked at Charlie. "You need a ride?"

"No, thank you anyway. I'm okay. I've got my wheels out front."

As soon as the medical personnel left the scene, Charlie slowly made her way back up the stairs. When she reached the fourth-floor landing, she carefully looked around for any sign of a scuffle. There was none. She eyed Willy's door across from where she was standing. *Willy could have seen or heard someone outside his door,* and *peering out, spotted Em, who no doubt was leaning over the railing trying to keep a lookout for me.* Charlie slumped, awash with guilt. She turned and descended the stairs.

Once Charlie was in her car, she dialed Tony's number.

Tony answered on the first ring. "Hello?" His greeting sounded like a question.

"Tony, I'm glad I caught you. Are you going to be home for a while? I need to see you."

"Yes. I intend to be here the rest of the day and all night. What's up?"

"It's a long story. I'm on my way."

◆◆◆◆◆

WHILE I WAIT for Charlie, I light a fire in the fireplace to ward off the damp chill that permeates the air. I turn the television down and go to the kitchen to make a fresh pot of brew. *What the hell now? I don't like the way this sounds. Maybe I'm just paranoid, but anymore, everything sounds like disaster.*

Because I'm expecting her, I open the door as soon as Charlie rings the bell. She looks cold and frazzled.

"Come on in," I say and hold the door wide. Recently, I've developed the habit of sticking my head out and looking up and down the corridor — just in case someone is lurking around out there. Charlie enters and gravitates toward the fire rubbing her hands together. I'm not sure if she's trying to warm them or if it's a nervous reaction to something. In my current state, I, of course, select the latter option.

"May I sit down, Tony?"

This is feeling more-and-more like bad news.

"By all means. Here, take this chair by the fire." I hold the chair for her. Once she is comfortable, I go to the kitchen and return with two steaming mugs of java. "Okay, tell me what's going on."

"Did you know Emory Nelson, the parole officer?" she asks.

"Yes I do." *Why did she say 'did'.*

"He was killed this afternoon."

"Oh, no. Traffic accident?"

"No. McCrombie."

I drop my cup on the floor and sway as I try to stave off a fainting spell. Charlie jumps up and helps me into the chair she had just vacated. She pats my hand and calls my name. I respond and when she's sure I'm okay, she runs to the kitchen and returns with a roll of paper towels and cleans up the coffee mess. When she's finished, she pulls another chair up beside me. She takes my hand and proceeds to tell me details of the events that led up to Emory's death.

"I'm the reason he's dead, so add another notch to my belt," I say at the conclusion of her narration.

Charlie, in a fit of frustration, throws her hands up into the air. "Nonsense! If anyone is to blame, it's me, so get off it will ya?" Then she adds, "However, neither of us are to blame.

McCrombie is the reason Emory is dead. McCrombie killed him in cold blood just as he did the others."

I drop my head into my hands and try to absorb this revelation. The past two weeks have left me mentally drained and emotionally numb. Finally, I ask, "What happened to the warrant?"

"I have it. I took it off of Em's body before the medical personnel arrived."

I nod. "What do you intend to do with it?"

"Wait a few days and execute it myself."

"Don't think so, Charlie. There's no way I'd agree to let you do such a thing."

"You don't have to agree. It's not your decision. Anyway, do you have a better idea?"

I sit for a moment thinking. "No. Can't say that I do. But there's no way I can allow you to risk your life to save mine."

"Well, let me worry about the consequences. If I do execute it, I'll be accompanied by several of NYC's finest. However, I don't have much hope we'll find anything since McCrombie has now been alerted. He, no doubt, has already disposed of anything and everything of an incriminatory nature."

I nod. Then it strikes me: "Did he see you?"

"Don't think so." Charlie rubs the back of her neck. "Can't say for sure. I was pretty stunned when Emory landed at my feet. I didn't look up. Wish I had though."

"Double-edged sword. If you didn't see him, chances are he didn't see you either, at least not your face."

Charlie rises and looks into my eyes. "That's probably true. I should go now. I'm beyond exhausted."

Now I'm fearful that she's in danger. "Charlie, call me when you're safe at home. If he did see you and recognized you…"

"Gottcha! I'll call as soon as I'm inside my place." Then she smiles at me and runs her hand up my arm. "Don't get jealous, but I'm going to sleep with Roscoe from now on."

This remark takes me by surprise. *Probably a dog.* I say, "I'm not the jealous type, but who the hell is Roscoe?"

"He's my .45 caliber equalizer, and I'd love to introduce Roscoe to our friend."

"Yep, me too. Keeping Roscoe within reach is a very good idea." *I want to say, "You could stay here," but I don't. Dammit, the timing is off. If we cohabitate, her job and my trial will both be jeopardized.*

I rise to walk her to the door. She slips her arm into mine and leans on my shoulder. "I promise you, we'll get the bastard — one way or another."

Wonder what she means by that? I open the door and we stand there for a moment. She reaches up, kisses my cheek, and leaves. *This is getting to be a habit...one that I certainly could get used to – the kissing that is, not the leaving.*

Thirty minutes later I get the call from Charlie.

"I'm safe and sound...well safe anyway. Nothing out of the ordinary happened, so I'm confident he either didn't see me, or didn't recognize me if he did."

"That's a more likely supposition. However, let's not be too confident. He's sneaky and strikes when you least expect it. You get some rest and I'll talk to you tomorrow. How about dinner?"

"Absolutely. Until tomorrow then."

◆◆◆◆◆

AFTER PUSHING HIS parole officer over the railing, Willy retreated into his room. He sat quietly listening to the commotion taking place four floors below him. *What an idiot! Did Nelson think I'd just let him in? That pest, Charlie Whitaker, is also asking for it.*

Willy rubbed his hands together. *I've got to get rid of the loot.* He looked around for a hiding place. *There's no place here that the cops wouldn't find it.*

Willy pondered what to do with the stolen jewelry and decided to get rid of it. Having made the decision, Willy wiped the items to erase fingerprints and tied the ring and cufflinks into the handkerchief that bore the judge's initials, then put them into his pants pocket. He opened his door a crack and looked up and down the dingy, dirty hallway. When he was sure the hall was empty, he slipped out and went up the stairs to the roof. There, he gingerly crossed a catwalk to the next building. The door on the roof of the next building was open and Willy creeped in. He stood and listened for a while before he descended the stairs to the ground level. He was stealthy and carefully surveyed his surroundings. Everything looked normal, so Willy exited the front entrance and proceeded down the street in the opposite direction from his hotel. He walked downtown, stopping once in a while to look around making sure he wasn't being tailed. His destination loomed before him: a children's playground. Willy crossed the boulevard and continued up a path that led through the playground to a more deserted area.

Park benches were scattered throughout the venue and Willy chose one that was positioned close to a sewer drain. He picked up the newspaper that someone had left on the bench and pretended to read it, all the while observing the activity around him with his shifty eyes. When he was certain he was not being watched, he removed the handkerchief and its contents from his pocket and bent over pretending to tie his shoelace. He turned his head left, then right, looking around again just to be sure he was not being observed. Satisfied he was safe, he slipped the handkerchief into the sewer drain. It was almost weightless, and though he didn't hear it hit the water, he was sure it had. Willy breathed a sigh of relief at having rid himself of incriminating evidence and made his way back home. *Let 'em come now. They won't find a damn thing.* He had to control himself to keep from howling.

✦✦✦✦✦

CHARLIE ATTENDED EMORY'S funeral. The church was packed with mourners. Some Charlie knew and many she didn't. She took special interest in an older woman who seemed somewhat masculine. Her makeup looked like it had been applied with a spatula. Charlie was reminded of female impersonators she had seen although this one was grotesque. Using her cell phone, Charlie surreptitiously took pictures of the woman. *Wonder who that is?* She continued snapping. *Maybe one of Em's parolees – a cross dresser?* For a moment, she thought it might be Willy but immediately put the thought out of her mind knowing Willy was dumb but not stupid.

CHAPTER

6

I didn't attend Emory's funeral as I was just a casual acquaintance, and since my arrest, I've made myself scarce and am seldom seen in public. Theo advised me to keep a low profile. We agree we don't want a change of venue for the trial, so keeping my name out of the newspapers is paramount when it comes to selecting a jury that isn't prejudiced. Theo also doesn't want to expose me to McCrombie's possible change in strategy—not waiting to let the criminal justice system determine my fate. I advised Theo that that was unlikely, as McCrombie was enjoying watching me squirm.

◆◆◆◆◆

WHEN CHARLIE RETURNED home after the funeral, she was angry and conflicted, still wrestling with the pros and cons of executing the search warrant. She sat on a sofa in her living room with her feet propped up on the coffee table. The search warrant lay on the sofa beside her. After a few thoughtful minutes, she grabbed it, wadded it up in a ball, and tossed it into the kitchen trash. *I don't need a warrant to nail your ugly*

*ass, you sick, sad, sorry, son-of-a-bitch. When you least expect it, I'll
be there…*

♦♦♦♦♦

WHEN IT COMES to Charlie, I feel like a school boy. I'm
impatient, and instead of waiting for her to call me, I call her.

"Hey, you. I'm glad you called," she says in a saucy voice.

"So am I." *Good grief! Now what do I say? I can write three,
four, even five hundred page novels but can't think of a thing to say
to this woman.* After a moment, I recover and continue, "How'd
it go today? The funeral, I mean?" *Dumb ass, how'd ya think it
went?* I chastise myself for being so insensitive.

"Actually, the service was beautiful and uplifting," Charlie responds. "Wish you could have been there."

"I'd like to hear about it. Have you had dinner yet?"

"Just getting there. How about you?"

"Not yet. Would you join me? I'd like to see you."

"Of course. I have something I want to run by you anyway. I'll come over as soon as I change."

"No! I mean, I have cabin fever and thought we could go
out — perhaps we can try the Horizon Room again."

Without hesitation she answers, "I'd love to."

"Wonderful! I'll swing by and pick you up, say twenty
minutes?"

"I'll be ready. I'll wait for you downstairs so you won't
have to come up."

"No! I don't want you exposed with that maniac running
loose. We don't know if he knows who you are but don't take
any chances," I caution her.

"Remember my little friend, Roscoe?"

"Yep. Just the same, I'll come up and get you. No arguments."

"Okay, Tony. I'll be ready."

♦♦♦♦♦

WHEN WE ARRIVE at The Horizon Room, we find that there's a fifteen minute wait for a table so we go into the lounge and order a glass of wine. After we're served our drinks, I say, "What is it you wanted to tell me?"

Charlie looks around and in a hushed tone says, "Well, it's more of a show-and-tell type answer. I don't think this is a good environment to bring it up."

More anxious than ever, my voice trembles as I say, "Okay…" *Now what?* My nerves are frayed, and overall, I'm a complete mess. Suddenly, I just want to go home. I take some deep calming breaths, put on my game face and convince myself I can tough it out. Fifteen minutes into our wait, we're escorted to a table. When the waiter hands each of us a menu, my eyes go directly to the prime rib dinner selection. My eating and sleeping habits have been severely compromised by the recent siege of events, and suddenly, I realize I'm famished. I look at Charlie and say, "Prime rib?"

She nods and we both order the prime rib, agreeing on a side of fresh ground-horse radish.

The waiter brings us our dinners in record time, and when I take the first bite, I must admit the rib is cooked to perfection and is delicious. It was well worth the wait.

Because the restaurant is pretty noisy, we don't converse much as we eat. Just being in Charlie's presence makes me happier than I've been in a long, long time. It suddenly occurs to me, we don't need to talk; just being together is a form of communication in-and-of itself.

After dinner, on the way to the parking garage, I again ask, "What is it you want to run by me?"

"Patience, my dear. Like I said, its show-and-tell.' When you take me home, we'll have a nightcap and I'll explain."

In my current state, I'm more anxious than eager to know what she's talking about, but I temper my impatience. "Guess I can wait a few more minutes," I say, all the while wondering what Charlie has on her mind.

◆◆◆◆◆

AS SOON AS we enter Charlie's condo, she kicks off her stilettos. "Torture chambers probably contrived by some woman-hater," she says as she slips out of her navy blue jacket and tosses it onto a chair. She points. "Over there in the glass hutch I have an assortment of liquor. You decide what we want to drink and I'll be right back."

"My pleasure," I reply, even though I'm at the end of my rope with the cloak-and-dagger routine. I watch her retreat before sauntering toward the liquor cabinet. After perusing the choices, I select a bottle of bourbon and take it to the kitchen. I look in the frig for soda to mix with our drinks and discover a bottle of white zin. That being my favorite alcoholic beverage, I put the bourbon back where I found it and pour two glasses of wine. Just as I enter the living room, Charlie reappears. She is swathed in a sexy black gossamer negligée. I blink twice and whistle.

"Does that mean you like?"

"Well, yes. You've just won the Good Housekeeping seal of approval." The wine glasses suddenly become very heavy; I set them down on the coffee table. I shut everything out of my mind except Charlie. I can't keep my eyes off this perfect specimen of womanhood.

Charlie cocks her head to one side and swirls around, letting her arm gently glide around my waist as she does so with the ethereal garment flowing out behind her. I feel as though I'm hypnotized. *Is this really happening or is it anther cruel joke?*

After her version of the dance of the seven vails, Charlie gracefully sits down on the sofa, crosses her lovely legs, and pats the cushion beside her beckoning me to sit. I obey. I'm suddenly a school boy on my first date. Charlie, however, is not so shy. After all, this is *her* party. She scoots over ever so close and hands me my drink. The scent of gardenias permeates my senses and my brain ceases to function — again. My heart races; my head spins; my eyes glaze over and I'm on another planet.

I hold the glass as if I don't know what to do with it. I'm afraid if I move or even breathe this moment will disappear.

Charlie takes her glass and clinks it against mine as she says, "Here's to living, loving and laughing and may your life be filled with an abundance of each."

She raises her glass to her lips and takes a sip. My eyes follow her every move as I, obedient little robot that I've become, do the same. She then takes the glass from my hand and sets it down on the coffee table along with hers. I don't remember how she got on my lap, but there she is all the same, and I eagerly embrace her. She returns the embrace. Once again, I'm dreaming, but this time it isn't a nightmare.

◆◆◆◆◆

NIGHT FADES INTO morning and the cruel sun snaps me back from Xanadu. I lay there next to Charlie, half awake, all naked. She is still asleep and cuddled up next to me. Strands of her black hair are entangled in the chain which secures a small gold cross around her neck. I examine her beautiful face as she slumbers. Her skin is silk and she still smells of gardenias. *Oh, my God. I'm in love with this woman. How is it You bring someone so wonderful into my life when my life could be coming to an end. Is this a taste of the hell that awaits me on the other side?*

Charlie stirs and awakens.

"Hey, Snow White, thought you were going to sleep forever."

She stretches and says, "Morning, Slugger." She stifles a yawn. "Wine has that effect on me. How'd you sleep?"

I'm still star-struck, but I manage to reply, "Very well; very well indeed. I like your brand of sleeping aides."

Once again, her laugh is music. "Don't go away. I'll take a quick shower and make breakfast. And remember, I still have something to run by you."

I had almost forgotten about that. Any wonder? I reply, "If it's anything like last night, bring it on!"

"I have no idea what you're talking about, Your Honor," she teases as she wiggles from my embrace. She grabs her pillow and gently presses it into my face as she throws the sheet back and makes a wild dash for the bathroom.

For the first time in months, I realize I'm happy. I'm not just happy, I'm ecstatic—at least for this moment in time. *Please, God, please let this last...*

◆◆◆◆◆

AS WE LINGER over our breakfast of hot oatmeal, toast and coffee, I remind her, "Well, Shahrazad, I believe you have a story to tell. You've kept me in suspense long enough."

"Oh, right. I seem to get sidetracked a lot here lately, especially when I'm with you." Charlie graces me with an innocent smile as she takes her cell phone from her back jeans' pocket and begins flipping through screens.

"Ah, here it is." She holds the phone up for me to see the image.

"Okay, so it's some old woman—very ugly, I might add." *Is this what she's been so protective about showing me?* I feel myself getting aggravated. I was led to believe she had something important to share with me concerning my recent dilemma.

"Look closer."

I do as I'm told and I know in my heart, from this day forward, I will do whatever Charlie directs me to do. I'm no longer in control—I'm head-over-heels, and she's driving this bus. I lean forward and take a closer look at the picture on the cell phone.

"My Holy God! Its Willy McCrombie."

"That's what I thought! Showing up at Em's funeral after killing him! Why that...that...that...I can't think of a word bad enough to describe him."

"I can but I don't talk like that in the presence of a lady." I study the photo, "You took this at the funeral?"

"Yes. Something spoke to me when I saw her, er him, or whatever." Charlie pauses, then adds, "Guess now he knows who I am. He was behind me when I signed the guest register."

This revelation hits me like a punch in the gut. *If Willy knows who Charlie is, where she lives, and what she means to me, Charlie is in grave danger. I need to take care of him before he kills anyone else...but how?*

I squirm in my chair and ask, "What time do you go in today?"

"Oh, I'm off today. Thought I'd get some shopping done; why?"

"Frankly, Charlie, I'm concerned for your safety. Willy's pretty shrewd and resourceful. He'll find you if he wants to... and apparently locks don't faze him."

"Come on, Tony. I'm a trained police officer. I've had instruction in jujitsu, karate and even Taebo. I can chop with the best of them." Charlie raises her arm across her chest karate style and fakes a chop in my direction. "Also, I'm an excellent shot, and if need be, I can run like hell."

"Not funny. This is not a joking matter. I'm seriously worried he'll try to get you, especially if he knows we, well, I mean..."

"Gottcha," she replies, saving me from trying to describe our relationship.

Grateful for the reprieve, I continue, "I'm going on the hunt myself. Maybe I can get him first."

"Oh no you don't. You'll do nothing of the sort. You're out on bond and you know the consequences of violation of same. Let me handle this creep."

Now I'm really worried for Charlie, so I say, "I'll make a pact with you. We'll do it together. I won't do anything without involving you if you'll promise to do likewise. DEAL?"

I watch Charlie raise her eyebrows. She's still for a few moments but finally says, "Deal! But you've got to promise me you will not, under any circumstances, go it alone."

"Okay, I promise," I say, then add, "Anyway, you're the only one with a gun."

"Bingo…and I know how to use it." Charlie points her finger at the wall and pulls an imaginary trigger.

"Well, at least we know where he lives, or used to live. Hopefully, he hasn't moved since he killed Emory. How do you suggest we proceed?" I ask.

"I believe I got a glimpse of him leaving the funeral. If that was him, he drives a beat up wreck. It's a faded-red older-model Chevy pickup. I wasn't close enough to get the license number, but at least that's another lead. If we see a vehicle matching that description dogging either one of us…"

"He won't have to dog us—he knows where we both live."

"Right. H-m-m-m, we can't watch his place either. There are too many exits to cover. We could flush him out using me as bait," Charlie offers.

I slam my hand on the table; Charlie jumps. "NO! That is not now, nor will it ever be, an option."

"Okay, okay. Settle down. I'm just trying to catch a killer."

"I know, but putting yourself at risk is not the answer."

"What is the answer?"

I sit there pondering. "I don't know. We need to get some evidence that puts him at the crime scenes. Otherwise, we have no probable cause to bring him in." We're silent for a few moments, then I say, "As much as I hate to say so, I should go home. I want to check my mail and messages. Let's table this discussion to give us time to think about it."

"You're right. We need proceed with caution and explore all avenues," she says. Then, after a slight pause adds, "I'd like to make you dinner tonight. My culinary skills go beyond omelets and oatmeal. Brave enough to test the waters?"

I pause then ask, "What's for dessert?"

With a twinkle in her eye, Charlie replies, "It's a carefully guarded family secret. Do I take your response as a yes?"

I lean over and kiss her as I pull my jacket from the back of the chair. She encircles my face with her hands and pulls me in closer. We share a passionate and lingering kiss.

When I, reluctantly I might add, pull back, I say, "If that's the appetizer, I'm all in for a seven-course dinner."

"You may be pleasantly surprised."

"I'm already pleasantly surprised!" I force myself to start for the door; she falls in beside me linking her arm through mine. We share another quick kiss at the door, and before I know it, I'm out in the corridor. The door closes behind me and I look back with a feeling of longing. If I could, I'd jump up and click my heels together. I'm on an emotional roller coaster. One minute I'm way, way up and the next, I'm way, way down. *God knows what will become of me!*

◆◆◆◆◆

WHEN I ARRIVE home late that same morning, my answering machine is blinking wildly. I punch the answer button and listen to my messages. One in particular captures my interest.

"Ah, hello, Judge Facinni. My name is Helen Rothburg. I believe I have something that belongs to you. Would you please return my call as soon as possible? My number is 261-6657. Thank you."

Wonder what this is all about. I hope it isn't more bad news. Without hesitation, I dial the number.

The same voice that is on my answering machine says, "Hello."

"Yes, hello. This is Tony Facinni. I'm returning a call to Ms. Rothburg."

"YES! I'm Helen Rothburg. How are you, Judge Facinni?"

"Just fine," I lie. "And you?"

"I'm well, thank you for asking. The reason I called you is, a few days ago, I took my five-year-old-son, Phillip, to Stay and Play children's playground on 33rd. He was playing hide-'n-seek with some other children. While hiding in the bushes, he saw what he describes as a scruffy man drop something into the storm drain. Being a curious child, as all children are, he investigated after the man left. He was able to retrieve the item. It was a handkerchief with a ring and a set of cufflinks wrapped in it. The ring has your name inscribed on the inside."

I almost drop the phone. "Yes, they're probably mine. I was the victim of a burglary earlier this month. May I come by and pick up the items, Ms. Rothburg?"

"Certainly. I'm home all day."

"Wonderful. Will your son be there? I'd like to ask him a couple of questions."

"Well, I don't know. I don't want to traumatize him. He wasn't even sure he should have given me the items. He was afraid he'd be in trouble. Any further discussion may frighten him even more."

I soften my voice. "Trust me, I won't frighten the child. I just want a description of the scruffy man if he can give me one. If an arrest comes from his information, you may be entitled to a Crime Stoppers reward." This was a long shot—a very, very long shot—but money seems to open many doors.

"Well, since you put it that way, of course you can talk to him. Our address is 817 Spring Run Boulevard."

"I'll be there within the hour." Then remembering my pact with Charlie, I add, "I'm bringing a police detective with me. She is very nice, so you have nothing to fear from her either."

"Well, all right," a slight hesitation before she continues, "I'll be expecting you." The line went dead.

I immediately dial Charlie's number. She answers on the third ring. I explain the situation and can hear the excitement in her voice.

"I'll come get you. After we meet, we'll come back here—dinner, remember?"

"Sounds like a plan; a darn-good plan. And yes, I remember dinner—especially dessert," I reply.

"Damn straight. I like a man that gets excited over dessert. There for a moment, I thought I was losing my touch."

"Right! That'll be the day…"

"I'm heading out the door right now—fifteen minutes?" Charlie says.

"I'm ready…" but I was talking to a dead phone. *Does that woman ever say goodbye?*

◆◆◆◆◆

I WAIT IN the lobby of my building. When Charlie drives up, I go out to meet her. When I open the passenger door, I'm greeted with the now-familiar sweet fragrance of gardenias. She squeezes my hand and says, "Hey, Slugger."

"Hey yourself, Gorgeous."

I'm not sure she heard me. She was concentrating on pulling back out into traffic but the corner of her lip turns up in a smile. She says, "Where are we headed?"

I had written the address on a slip of paper which I pull from my pocket. "817 Spring Run Boulevard, the Rothburg's."

"Okay, that's good. I'm familiar with the Spring Run area. One of my school chums lived there for a short time. It's a pretty nice neighborhood."

"I'm impressed," I say. "I need to invest in a GPS. I can get lost in a paper bag."

"Well, I do have an advantage. My early days on patrol certainly helped me find my way around the city." She looks back, changes lanes then exits onto a less-busy avenue. After a few minutes, she says, "We're almost there."

Charlie expertly navigates through the neighborhood and pulls up in front of a red-brick three-story mansion which is graced with white pillars reminiscent of antebellum homes in the south. A large stone fountain sits in the middle of the perfectly manicured lawn. The flower beds surrounding the mansion are resplendent with an array of fall flowers, and maple and oak trees grace the premises.

Perhaps I didn't have to dangle the Crime Stopper reward after all.

"Wow!" Charlie utters as we exit the vehicle.

We gingerly walk to the door and ring the bell. The door instantly opens and a pleasant looking woman, probably in her early thirties, greets us with a warm smile.

"Welcome. I'm Helen Rothburg. Please come in."

Once inside, I turn to Charlie and introduce her. "This is Detective Charlie Whitaker who is with the NYPD."

Charlie extends her hand and the two women greet one another.

"So happy to meet you, Detective Whitaker."

"And I you, but please call me Charlie."

"Okay, I will. But, you must then call me Helen." She turns in my direction, "That means you must be Antonio Facinni," Helen says, extending her hand.

"Yes, logical deduction, Watson." We all share a laugh. "But in keeping with the mode of the day, please call me Tony."

"I'd be honored to. I've read every one of your novels. I eagerly await the fifth. Will you have it out soon?"

"I'm working on it. Well, would you just look at the two of you? I have a fan club standing right here in your foyer."

We laugh again, and I hope my put-off didn't insult Helen.

"Come in and make yourselves comfortable," Helen says as she leads us into a warm comfortable library where the fire in the fireplace is dancing merrily. Helen ushers us towards a pair of soft green sofas facing each other and positioned in front of the fireplace. Charlie and I take a seat side-by-side on one of the sofas and Helen sits on the other.

When we're settled, Helen reaches into her pocket and retrieves a handkerchief. I immediately recognize it. My initials are in plain view. She hands the handkerchief to me and I carefully open it. There, nestled inside, are my cufflinks and ring. I should not have been surprised but seeing the objects was a jolt. I take a quick breath and look at Helen.

"These are mine. They were stolen from me about a month ago. Thank you for returning them."

"Not returning them was never an option. Of course, having your name engraved in the ring made the return much easier."

"Well, thank you again. These items have sentimental value." I hesitate before asking, "Is your son, Phillip, available?"

"He is. I'll go get him. Can I make you a drink while you wait?"

"Oh, no. I'm fine." Then I look at Charlie. She shakes her head and replies, "Thank you, Helen, but I'm good."

Helen nods and disappears into the interior of the home. I finger my jewelry and we sit in silence.

Minutes pass slowly as we wait for Helen to return with Phillip. Finally, the door opens and Helen walks in with her five-year-old son by her side. He is clinging to his mother's hand. Phillip appears to be a normal five-year-old except he is wearing some pretty thick glasses. This causes me to wonder how accurate his vision could have been from what must have been a significant distance when he saw Willy deposit the handkerchief in the storm drain.

I rise and greet the boy. "Phillip, what a pleasure it is to meet you. My name is Tony and this is Charlie." When I extend my hand to Phillip, he ducks and slips behind his mother. He holds a wad of her skirt in his hand as he peeks from behind her legs.

"Phillip," Helen turns and beckons to the lad, "come on out and talk to this gentleman. The ring and links you found belong to Judge Facinni. He's here to thank you for returning them."

Phillip slowly creeps out, but puts his arms around one of Helen's legs holding on for dear life. I sit back down and hope I look less intimidating. Before I can speak again, Charlie intervenes. "Phillip, those are great shoes." The boy looks down at his feet. His tennis shoes are equipped with lights that flash when he walks. Phillip smiles.

"Mommy got them," he says, almost in a whisper.

"Well, Mommy has great taste. Maybe I should get a pair."

The boy giggles and relinquishes his hold on his mother's leg. Helen reclaims her seat on the sofa opposite ours and says, "Come sit by Mommy," and pats the cushion next to her. Phillip complies.

"You're doing great," I whisper to Charlie. "Ask him if he can identify the thief."

Charlie nods then says, "Do you go to school?"

"Kndrgartn..."

"That's good. Do you like school?"

"Yes..."

"I liked school. Recess was my favorite class." Phillip giggles again. Charlie pauses, then goes on,. "Say, Phillip, do you remember anything about the man you saw hide Judge Facinni's stuff at the playground?"

"He...he was scary. He had funny hair. It was messed up and he was dirty." Phillip scoots closer to Helen.

"Was he as tall as...say, as tall as Judge Facinni?"

Phillip shakes his head and points to his mother.

"He was as tall as your mother?"

Phillip nods.

"Did he have a Santa Claus tummy, you know, jolly and fat?"

Phillip smiles and shakes his head. "He was skinny and dirty."

"What kind of clothes did he have on?"

"Jeans and a checked shirt. They were dirty."

"Un-huh. Do you remember what color the shirt was?"

"H-m-m-m, don't remember. Maybe brown, but dirty.

I'm thinking, *This kid has a Mr. Clean fetish.*

"How far away were you from the man?"

"Not very far."

"Did the man have any marks that you could see. Like... like on his face?" Charlie asks.

Phillip thinks for a minute and points to his forehead. "Here."

"What did it look like?"

"A big red thing..."

I almost jump for joy. McCrombie has a large red birthmark on his forehead in that exact same spot—much like Mikhail Gorbachev.

I can't help myself. I ask, "Do you think you would know him if you saw him again?"

"I don't want to see him…" Phillip crawled onto his mother's lap and buried his face in her bosom.

"No," I say, "you don't have to see *him*. Would you know him if you saw a picture of him?"

"Don't know…"

Everyone is silent. *I blew it.*

Helen scowls at me.

After a few awkward moments, Charlie says, "We should probably leave, Tony."

Helen nods.

"Sure, good idea." We stand to go. Helen extracts herself from Phillip's grasp and stands with us. On the way to the door, I ask, "Would it be okay if we bring a picture and come back in a couple of days?"

Helen looks over her shoulder at the boy sitting on the sofa. "I think that would be all right," she finally answers.

"Thank you so much for your hospitality," Charlie says as we exit.

"You're welcome."

I add as we go through the open door, "And thank you for rescuing my property. I don't think these items would bring much at a hock shop, but they mean an awful lot to me."

"I understand." Helen shakes our hands and we leave.

"You did just great," I say to Charlie as we drive off.

"Yep. I have a few nieces and nephews, so I know how to talk to kids. Phillip remembering the birthmark is really a stroke of luck. Otherwise, his description could fit every bum on the street."

"Agreed—what a break! Will you come back with me when I get a mug of McCrombie?" I ask Charlie.

"Absolutely. That is, if you'll let me do the talkin'."

"Guess I almost blew it, huh?"

"Close."

"Okay, deal. You can do the talkin'."

Charlie then says, "We need to assemble a lineup for Phillip. I'll put something together. Unfortunately, the only mug we have of Willy is over twenty years old."

"It's a long shot, but worth the effort. Thank you for... well, for everything. I truly don't know what I'd do without you and your championing my cause. It means the world to me." *Good Lord, am I getting soft and mushy!*

"Wouldn't have it any other way. I kinda like you," she says, "and if you're not too tired, that dinner invitation is still on the table."

"Ha! Nice play on words." *I cannot imagine any place I'd rather be, now and forever.* I say, "I accept wholeheartedly with admiration, appreciation and affection."

"Holy smokes! I hope my dinner lives up to your flowery acceptance."

"Babe, whatever it is, it's the best I've ever had."

"I'm talking about food."

"I know."

Charlie blushes and I grin.

The spaghetti was delicious, the wine was delectable, the dessert was divine, and it was just as spectacular as the night before.

CHAPTER

7

Mid-week I telephone Helen Rothburg to make arrangements for Charlie and me to come by with a photo lineup.

Rothburg shouts into the phone, "NO! You cannot come to our house ever again."

I'm stunned. *I didn't think my behavior was that bad.* "Mrs. Rothburg, may I ask what happened to change your mind?"

"YOU…you…you charlatan. I hadn't put it together until some members of my bridge club recognized you and brought it to my attention that you're the one charged with the multiple copycat murders. How dare you come into our home! Please, do not ever bother us again."

The phone went dead. I pulled the receiver from my ear and stared at it for a few seconds before slamming my receiver down. *Willy wins again.*

I phone Charlie and tell her the bad news. I hear the disappointment in her voice as she says, "That was the only real lead we had to connect Willy to the burglary. Without an ID, we don't have anything to link him to burglarizing your home and the theft of the items left at the crime scenes."

I am well aware of that, but upon hearing Charlie say it, my heart and hope sink. I say, "I know." Then I add, "Thank you for your support. It means a lot to me."

◆◆◆◆◆

WHEN WE LEFT the Rothburg's, after our initial visit, Charlie took control of the Rothburg find knowing that she had to turn the evidence over to the PD evidence custodian when she filed her report. The next day, Charlie confirmed that when she told me that after she submitted her report of our encounter with the Rothburgs, Slater exploded.

Charlie related her conversation with Slater. She told me he stammered though a spray of spittle, "How is it you were involved in this anyway? Dammit! You...you...you're officially off the case. Do I need to suspend you to get through to you?" Charlie said she did not respond. There wasn't any excuse for her actions so she remained silent. She said Slater's anger turned into rage and that she cringed as he banged his fist on his desk. Then she told me, after his tirade, Slater calmed down and said to her, "Okay, missy, since you've already made the contact, you put together a photo lineup, take a uniformed officer and go back out there and see if you can get an ID from the kid." She said he slammed his door behind her when she left.

"I'm sorry, Charlie, for dragging you into this."

"Nonsense. You didn't drag me into anything. I volunteered: remember our deal? Besides, I kinda like yankin' Slater's chain occasionally. He turns the brightest shades of red." Then she smiled. *Probably reliving her encounter with Slater, evil woman that she is.*

◆◆◆◆◆

LATER THAT EVENING, over dinner, which was now becoming a habit, Charlie related to me the following encounter with Helen Rothburg. After leaving Slater's office, Charlie put together a photo lineup, then went to the ready room to select an officer to accompany her to the Rothburgs'. Looking around, she selected Matt Ferguson. She knew Matt had five kids of his own, and in all likelihood, knew how to communicate with youngsters.

On the ride to the Rothburg residence, Charlie filled Ferguson in on our first visit. Charlie told me Ferguson nodded from time-to-time, indicating he understood the circumstances. Mrs. Rothburg swung the door open as soon as they arrived, before they could ring the bell. She apparently had seen them through the etched glass window in the door. As soon as the door was open, Rothburg demanded, "Yes, now what do you want?"

"Good day, Helen," Charlie said and watched Rothburg's eyes travel from her to Ferguson. Upon seeing Ferguson, Rothburg instantly changed her demeanor. *Funny how a uniform can make a difference.* Charlie introduced Ferguson, then said, "We'd like to see Phillip." Rothburg stood her ground and didn't reply.

Ferguson then politely tipped his hat in greeting. "Nice to meet you, ma'am," he said.

Mrs. Rothburg nodded again but didn't reply. Charlie continued, "When I was here last, we talked about having Phillip view a photo lineup." Still no response or offer to let them enter the premises. Ferguson was intuitive so he turned and looked up and down the boulevard, then asked, "May we come in?"

Apparently Mrs. Rothburg hadn't yet realized her neighbors may be curious as to why a uniformed police officer was standing at her door. She suddenly had a horror-stricken expression on her face as she, too, quickly looked around at the neighboring homes and then stepped aside allowing them to enter the foyer.

I helped Charlie clear the dinner dishes from the dining room table while she continued relating to me the following conversation she and Ferguson had with Helen Rothburg after they entered the residence:

"Helen," Charlie began.

"That's Mrs. Rothburg to you," Helen snapped in a snarky tone.

"Yes, of course. Well, *Mrs. Rothburg,* I have a photo lineup I'd like Phillip to look at. Is he home?"

"Why…why, no. No, he isn't," Rothburg stammered.

Ferguson didn't miss a beat. He asked, "Do you have more than one son?"

"No! Why?"

Ferguson pointed to the interior of the home and said, "H-m-m-m. I saw a lad dart into the other room as we entered."

Helen Rothburg flushed, obviously embarrassed at being caught in a lie. However, she recovered in a split second, saying, "Even so, you can't see him…"

"It'd be better for both of you if you cooperated." Ferguson said, cutting her off. Charlie knew there wasn't much they could do short of getting a court order but, she played along by staying silent.

"In what way?" Helen snarled.

"Okay, if that's the way…" Ferguson let the sentence dangle in midair. He put his hat on and turned to leave.

"Oh, all right." Helen said. She jammed her hands in her apron pockets and called, "Phillip, come in here."

After a few moments, Phillip timidly entered the foyer. Helen coaxed him to her and put a protective arm around his shoulders. "The officers have some pictures they would like for you to look at," she explained.

Phillip looked up at his mother and said, "But I thought…"

"Never mind!" his mother said, "It's all right, Phillip. Just look at the pictures."

Charlie said she had a sneaky hunch that mom had coached Phillip, in the event we returned, advising him not to point out anyone in the photos. However she still had hope as she took the lineup from her valise and spread it on the cool marble table top in the foyer. Beckoning Phillip over, Charlie stepped aside so he could view the photos without her hovering.

According to Charlie, Phillip stepped up to the table, adjusted his glasses and scanned the six photos. In less than ten seconds he looked up at his mother and said, "I don't see him."

Helen gathered Phillip to her and said, "There! Are you satisfied? I'm requesting that you leave, now!" She stalked to the front door and stood holding it open.

"No, I'm not satisfied," Charlie answered as she picked up the photo lineup and stashed it back in her valise. "McCrombie is a killer. I sense you've coached Phillip, and if that's the case, you can be charged with obstruction of justice. Right now, I have no proof so I can't take you into custody. However, if I do find out that you have indeed coaxed Phillip to lie, I will be back."

"Please leave!" Helen sputtered in exasperation.

◆◆◆◆◆

CHARLIE AND I finish cleaning the kitchen and take our carrot cake into the living room where we snuggle up on one of the sofas. When Charlie concludes her rendition concerning her encounter with Helen and Phillip, I say, "I'm not surprised. In fact, I would have been surprised if it had gone the other way. It's okay, Charlie. Thank you for trying. I'm sorry Slater jumped you for going with me in the first place. I should have seen that one coming."

"No need for you to apologize. I was on my own time. He does not dictate what I do with my time off—unless, of course, it's illegal." Charlie sighs heavily and continues, "Do you think Helen is so jaded that she would deliberately withhold evidence to see you convicted?"

We're silent for a minute or two. Finally, I say, "Looks like. But unless they volunteer to assist, there's not much we can do."

Charlie squeezes my hand—I squeeze back. "I'm going to see Dad this weekend. I want to touch base with him. Don't think I'll have much time to do so until after the trial — and that's provided I'm still a free man." I hesitate, then ask hopefully, "Wanna go with me?"

She does not hesitate. "Yes. Yes, Tony, I'd love to go."

◆◆◆◆◆

DAD IS IN his usual spot when we arrive. I phoned ahead, so he was expecting us. I try not to spring any surprises on him. I'm not sure how fragile he is and I want to keep him around as long as possible.

"Sonny!" Dad throws his arms up beckoning me to hug him, which I do.

"Dad, you look good. How are you faring?"

"I'm well and better now that you're here. I see you brought Ms. Charlie back." Dad holds his hands out to Charlie, "How are you young lady?"

Charlie is emboldened and steps up to give Dad a big hug.

"Mr. Facinni, I'm well and so happy to see you again."

Dad smiles up at Charlie. "You smell like gardenias. Tony's mother loved gardenias. Her bridal bouquet was a spray of white gardenias. It's funny how smell can excite memories." Dad's eyes take on a distant look. "I can still see her walking up the aisle — she was a beauty."

I don't think I can handle a stroll down memory lane in my present state, so I suggest, "Let's go outside, Dad. It's still warm enough to enjoy the afternoon."

Dad nods. Tears are visible in his eyes. I push Dad's wheelchair out to the oak tree we sat under when we were last here and I take the spot on the bench next to Dad's chair.

"Sonny, is something wrong?"

"No, Dad. There is nothing different since our last visit. I just wanted to see you before my trial starts and thank you in person for the generous gift. I'd be in the slammer until the end of trial if it hadn't been for you."

"No thanks necessary. You're my son and I love you dearly." Dad pauses. I detect anxiety in his voice when he asks, "How is that going?"

"Too soon to predict. I have the best attorney money can buy and I've been doing some snooping around myself; that is, with Charlie's help. It never hurts to have a cop on your side,. I smile at Charlie and she winks at me.

Dad raises his eyebrows. "I kinda suspect Charlie is more than just a friendly cop." Dad could always read me like a book. I just look down and clasp my hands in my lap. Dad picks up on my embarrassment and changes the subject. "Say, have you started number five yet?"

"Not yet, but I'm taking notes. This ordeal that has been foisted on me has given me a plethora of ideas for a plot."

"Wonderful! I find that other authors bore me now that you're writing."

"I totally agree," Charlie interjects. "I'm as eager as you for number five, Mr. Facinni."

"The two of you keep my spirits buoyed at a time I most need it. Bless you both," I say. Now, I'm close to tears.

Charlie moves in closer to Dad and stoops down so they are face-to-face, "Mr. Facinni, is there anything you need — can we do anything for you?"

"Thank you, Charlie, for the offer. I'm very well cared for here. I want for nothing. Sonny keeps in touch with management to ensure I'm doing well."

"You bet. You're my number one-concern." I glance at my watch. "It'll be dark soon so we should be going."

"Keep me updated, Sonny, good or bad. I'm just a phone call away and I'll be praying for you each and every day."

"I know, as I will for you." I lean down and embrace him, plant a kiss on his forehead and turn to go. I'm anxious to leave before I breakdown. I don't want him to know how fragile I've become over this whole mess.

Charlie takes Dad's hands in hers. "I'll make sure you're in the loop, Mr. Facinni. You take care."

"It's always a pleasure to see you. Be sure to come back."

"You can count on it."

As we walk back to the car, I whisper, "Don't think I could take losing Dad any time soon."

Charlie squeezes my hand. "I don't think you'll have to."

CHAPTER

8

Autumn finally gives it up and the frigid winter takes control. The holidays have come and gone and suddenly it's
January. Temperatures plummet to record lows and the remnants of an early snowfall, desecrated with dirt and debris, linger. The bitter weather and the bleakness of the city add to my
depression.

My trial is scheduled for eight weeks commencing January
7th. Theo and his team of experts and investigators have worked
their butts off putting our case together, and in theory, it looks
pretty good. I've participated in the strategizing and endless
meetings. We know our case backwards and forwards. Theo
leaves nothing to chance. I think he must have written the book
on *By the Book*. We also know the prosecution's theory. We were
given a taste of what to expect at the preliminary hearing last
November. I hate to say it, but their case looks as good, or maybe even better, than ours. The bottom line is we've done all we
possibly can. I just hope and pray the jury will render the right
decision at the end of the eight torturous weeks.

◆◆◆◆◆

THE COURTROOM IS packed with potential jurors, members of the press, and curiosity seekers. I've been in this arena almost my entire adult life, but being the accused instead of a participant is unnerving. Judge Harold Duckworth, also known as Ducky, will preside over my case. Ducky is a moniker the bar bestowed upon His Honor. *Wonder what was pinned on me when I was judge?*

I snap back to the moment when the bailiff brings the courtroom to order. "Hear ye, hear ye. This court is now in session. Please rise." We all stand as Ducky makes his grand entrance. He is resplendent in his specially-tailored black robe. Every snow-white hair on his head is in place and one gets the impression that not a single hair would dare stray thus betraying His Honor's image. Ducky looks out at the courtroom with a stern expression on his face. Having bestowed his distain upon those of us in attendance, he takes a seat in his high-backed black leather chair positioned behind an impressive oak desk, all of which are perched on an elevated platform at the front of the courtroom. I feel embarrassed and humiliated. I want to hide. I pray I'm up to the challenge.

Ducky surveys his domain for a moment or two, then says, "Be seated." It's a command not a suggestion. He continues with authority in his voice, "Do we have any matters to address before we start jury selection?"

Both sides state they do not.

"Very well, then. Bailiff, proceed with calling the names."

The bailiff, Billy Dexter, reaches into a canister that contains the names of all those summoned for jury duty and withdraws twelve names. Those challenged with and without cause are replaced so that there are always twelve in the jury box.

Both the prosecution and the defense are allowed to question each juror in order to determine if he or she has any prejudices or other reasons why he or she cannot qualify as a fair and impartial juror. Selection continues throughout the morning, and after a lunch break, into the late afternoon. By the end of the day, we do not have a jury, nor did we expect to.

Its five o'clock when Ducky announces, "We'll adjourn for the day, but those of you summoned for jury duty that have not otherwise been excused are under strict orders to return here tomorrow at nine a.m. sharp. If you fail to appear, a warrant will be issued for your arrest." A pause for effect, then he slams his gavel down. "Court adjourned!"

Out of the corner of my eye, I notice several of the prospective jurors jump at the loud and unexpected noise. Some even cringe. *Can't blame them. This has been a grueling day and tomorrow we're looking at more of the same.* Ray Schaffer, our lead investigator and designated advisory witness is seated at the defense table with us. When Theo stands, so do Ray and I and gather our notes and other items that are scattered about the table.

The courtroom has cleared by the time we are ready to leave. Dusk is rapidly approaching when we finally make it to the parking lot adjacent to the courthouse. Theo is upbeat and discusses the jurors we have already seated. "I feel as though we have a good panel thus far," he says and looks at me. "What do you think, Tony?"

I hesitate momentarily, then answer, "It's been my experience that jurors are unpredictable, and basically, it's a crap shoot. I remember one case I presided over where a potential juror was determined to be empaneled and failed to disclose that a close family member was the victim of a brutal murder. This was also a high-profile first-degree murder case that encompassed eight weeks of judicial time and expense. A few years after the defendant was found guilty and incarcerated, the defense somehow found out about the deceit and filed a motion seeking a reversal of the conviction, and a new trial. The motion, of course, was granted."

"I remember that case," Theo says. "The defendant was found guilty at the second trial, as well. Much judicial time and resources were wasted because of one juror's deception."

"Exactly," I say "My point is there is no way to determine a juror's credibility unless you have a crystal ball. You're tethered to your gut instinct."

"H-m-m-m, perhaps but not totally. However, instinct does play a significant role in the selection," Theo says. "Our defense team has conducted background checks and thoroughly examined all two hundred potentials. I think we have a shot at seating a fair and impartial jury."

I'm encouraged. I smile at Theo and say, "With that kind of confidence and a miracle, perhaps we do have a chance."

We stop once we approach my vehicle and huddle in a small group trying to ward off the cold. Theo says, "Hey, Tony, hold that thought. Remember, it's not over 'til it's over. See you tomorrow morning." Then Theo and Ray walk away towards their respective rides.

◆◆◆◆◆

CHARLIE IS SUBPOENAED as a witness for the prosecution. Witnesses have been sequestered and are not allowed into the courtroom. We previously agreed not to be seen in public together during trial. However, we didn't put restrictions on after-hour visits. We both know it would be unethical for me to discuss testimony of other witnesses with Charlie and it's an unspoken agreement that we steadfastly adhere to. If asked, we can both deny any allegation of collusion without perjuring ourselves.

As soon as I arrive home, I telephone Charlie.

She answers, "Tony?"

"Yes, it's me," I respond.

"Thank God. I've been anxiously waiting for your call. How's selection going?"

"Well, Theo is confident and pleased with the jury pool as a whole. I have too much at stake to be objective so I just let him and Ray do the heavy lifting."

"Jury selection is always tedious." Slight pause. "Can you come by this evening? I'll make dinner."

I don't even have to think about my answer. "Yes. Thirty minutes. I want to change."

"Hope you're referring to clothing, I wouldn't want you to change anything else."

My heart skips a beat. *This woman gives me more than hope, she keeps me going.* I finally have to admit. it if only to myself, I'm in love with her. *Now I have to see if I'm going to prison before I declare my feelings. How can I ask her to wait?*

◆◆◆◆◆

CHARLIE HAS A fire, or simulated fire, in the fireplace when I arrive. The room is warm and cozy and I immediately relax in this environment. Charlie greets me at the door and takes my coat, hanging it in the closet. She turns and I enfold her in an embrace—gardenias. I love the way she smells. The scent is distinctly her. She hugs me back and after a quick kiss, she goes into the kitchen, returns with two drinks and motions for me to sit next to her on the sofa. I comply. *Nowhere else on earth I'd rather be. It's my favorite time of the day.* She lovingly pats my thigh and I tingle from head to foot.

"Are you as tired as you look?" she asks.

"H-m-m-m, yes and no. I'm tired of fighting each day for my survival but I'm not tired of the new chapter that has just recently been added to my book."

"And, that would be…"

"You!"

"Un-huh. Be sure to remember the chapter in case we want to reread it sometime soon."

"No need. I have it memorized."

"As do I." She takes my hand and kisses my knuckles. There goes the tingling again.

"Wow, you know how to warm a fellow up."

"How 'bout I feed the fellow before we both collapse from hunger? How does beef stroganoff with a side of fresh green beans seasoned with bacon and caramelized onion sound to you?"

"Wonderful! I'll put the warming up on hold until after the filling up."

"You're so romantic. Did you go to charm school?"

"Never had to. Women just fell at my feet. Besides, you little vixen, everything I know, you've taught me."

"If that's the case, you're still in kindergarten."

"Oh no. If I'm still in kindergarten, I doubt I can survive first grade."

Charlie rolls her eyes and heads for the kitchen. I lean back on the sofa cushions and must have fallen asleep because the next thing I know Charlie is shaking me. "Hey, Slugger. Wake up! Dinner is served."

"Oh my gosh. I'm so sorry. Guess I am as tired as I look." I rub my face with my hands.

Charlie pulls me up and points me toward the bathroom. "Go wash and after we eat, you're going home and to bed early. You need to be awake and alert in court."

Nodding my groggy noggin, I say, "Agreed! Home it is."

◆◆◆◆◆

THEO AND RAY are positioned at the defense table when I arrive the next morning. They look up as I approach and Theo smiles at me, "Tony, glad you could make it."

"Am I late?"

"Naw. I'm just giving you grief. Ray and I have been going over the questionnaires submitted by the potential jurors. We think we have a good idea of who we don't want."

I slip into my appointed chair at the defense table and say, "Hopefully there will be enough left to complete the fourteen we need to seat the jury after you and Ray cull them out."

"Just making sure we have all the bases…"

Before Theo can complete his thought, the bailiff calls the court to order. Ducky makes his grand entrance and its *déjà vu* all over again. The process continues.

By lunch break, we have seated twelve jurors and we need only two more to serve as alternates. Theo and I decide to go to a local deli for lunch. *Wilma's* is a small diner situated close to the courthouse and a favorite of judicial personnel. The food is quick and sometimes even good. Ray is otherwise indisposed and agrees to meet us back at the courthouse at 1:30.

"I'm pleased with our progress thus far. We should have a panel by late afternoon," Theo says through a mouthful of hot pastrami on pumpernickel. I toy with my fries. Lately, I don't have much of an appetite. As we sit there, I look around at the lunch crowd and notice an odd looking woman seated at the counter. Something about her seems familiar but I can't place her. My thoughts are interrupted when Theo asks for the check.

"It's time to head on back, Tony. You ready? You didn't eat much."

"Guess I'm too anxious to eat. When we get going in trial, I'll feel better."

We stand, slip our coats on, and head for the exit. "Yeah, me too. Relax, our case is moving smoothly and I have no doubt it will continue to do so. We may have to adjust the order of our witnesses. That, of course, depends on how the prosecution presents its case." Theo becomes distracted. He is mentally rehearsing our presentation. As we walk past the counter, I notice the woman is gone. That niggling persists but I still can't connect the dots.

◆◆◆◆◆

I GENUINELY LIKE Theo. He has earned his reputation as the best defense lawyer money can buy. His demeanor and appearance generate confidence. He wears expensive three-piece suits tailored to perfection to fit his six-foot-two-inch trim frame. I guess he must be close to my age, somewhere in his late fifties, early sixties. He sports a trim mustache, his thick salt-and-pepper hair is styled, not just cut, and his blue eyes are clear and probing.

The weather hasn't warmed up much and I'm relieved to be back in the warmth of the courthouse. Ray meets us in the lobby, and together, we walk up the three flights of stairs to the courtroom. The spectators have dwindled—apparently jury selection is not all that seductive.

The bailiff calls the court to order, and once again, we proceed with empaneling a jury. I am being tried before a twelve-person jury. However, two extras, or alternate jurors, are seated in the event one or two of the actual jurors cannot make it through the anticipated eight-week trial and are unable to participate in the deliberation. If one or both of the substitutes are not needed at the time the jury is sent out to deliberate, they will be excused.

Time drags on, but by three in the afternoon we have our jury. It's a mixed-bag. We have eight females, two of which are designated as alternates, and six males representing various races and stations in life. Ducky swears in the jury panel and instructs the fourteen selected members as to proper juror conduct.

"You will not talk about this case to anyone, not even your spouses. If anyone harasses you regarding your silence, please inform the bailiff. You will not read, watch or listen to anything presented in any form by the media concerning this case. You are expected to be prompt at all court proceedings." Ducky pauses and looks at all fourteen members then asks, "Are there any questions before we adjourn?" No one speaks so Ducky raps his gavel and announces, "Court will reconvene at eight o'clock tomorrow morning. You are excused and may now leave for the day. Those who were not selected are excused from further jury service for the remainder of our court term."

Everyone stands and waits for the newly-empaneled jury to file out of the private entrance they will use until the conclusion of the trial. Once the jury and the judge have gone, Theo asks Ray and me to join him in his office.

Upon arrival at Theo's office, we gather around his conference table. "We will meet here in my office every day after court and review our strategy for the next day. As you both well know, our plans are subject to change on the spur of the moment depending on the current day's presentation by the prosecution."

Ray and I nod. Esther Raddison joins us. She is Theo's wife and one hell of a paralegal. They have been together over twenty years, and Esther is almost as good as Theo — she just doesn't have the sheepskin.

"Ray, I want you and Esther," his eyes move to include Esther into the conversation, "to keep in close contact with our witnesses. It's crucial we know how to reach them at any time of the day for the duration of the trial."

Esther has been taking notes of the meeting, and as she writes in her spiral notebook, she nods.

"You boys have anything you want to bring up regarding the jury?" Theo asks.

Ray and I both shake our heads.

"Okay then. Now it's just wait and see where the prosecution takes us. Let's call it a day. We'll meet in the courtroom around seven forty-five tomorrow morning."

Ray audibly sighs. We are all physically, mentally and emotionally drained, and appreciate the reprieve of ending the day early.

I stand and extend my hand to Theo. "Thanks, Theo. Your zest and attention to detail have encouraged me and I'm grateful to have someone of your caliber at the helm."

"Thank you for the confidence. I assure you it is not misplaced. We have the best defense team in these parts and the facts are on our side. Try not to be tense in front of the jury, Tony. They pick up on every little thing."

"How well I know." I retrieve my overcoat from the coatrack, and after I slip my arms into the sleeves, I wave goodbye to Ray and Esther. "See you tomorrow." Esther waves back and Ray says, "You bettcha, Tony."

Theo walks me to the door. "Remember, Tony, Confucius say, 'Thousand mile journey begin with single step,' or something like that." Theo's Chinese could use some work. but point well made.

"You been eating Chinese fortune cookies again?" I joke.

"Yep, since I broke my crystal ball and have to resort to something for inspiration."

I step out into the corridor and Theo closes the door behind me. Buttoning my coat and pulling up the collar, I take a quick look around before proceeding to the exit. *Now, for the best time of the day. I can hardly wait to call Charlie.*

♦♦♦♦♦

"HEY, SLUGGER. DID you get a jury?"

"Finally. We were finished by three. The rest of the day we spent in Theo's office going over strategy. Apparently that will be the routine during the duration of the trial."

"It certainly pays to be prepared." Charlie pauses, then adds, "I've a meatloaf in the oven and I'm peeling potatoes…"

"If that's an invitation…"

"It is…"

"I'm on my way."

♦♦♦♦♦

CHARLIE SWINGS OPEN the door and the aroma of home cooking floods my nostrils. My mouth begins to water and suddenly I'm ravenous.

"My God, how many ways do you have to drive a man wild in your little bag of tricks?" I ask.

Charlie grins. "If you stick around long enough, you'll find out."

Charlie hangs my coat in the hall closet, takes my hand and leads me toward the kitchen. As we pass the dining room, I notice she has the table set for two with a single lit candle in the middle. I'm touched by the romantic ambiance. When we reach the kitchen, Charlie opens the oven and checks the meatloaf.

"Tony, dinner is almost ready. Would you pour us a glass of wine while I put on the finishing touches?"

"Indeed I will," I say, eager to be of assistance. "What else can I do?" I ask as I retrieve a chilled bottle of wine from a bucket of ice on the kitchen counter, pop the cork and fill two crystal goblets.

"That's it. I've got the rest covered," Charlie says. She squeezes past me transporting a platter of meatloaf to the dining room.

I like it when our hips rub together, so I say, "H-m-m, small kitchens certainly have their advantages." She rewards my smart-ass remark with a quick hip bump. I like that, too.

We take our usual seats, Charlie with her back to the wall. I toast her beauty; she my "charm." Dinner is delicious and the company delightful. I gobble down two full servings.

"My, you were hungry. What did you have for lunch?"

"Ah, Theo and I went to *Wilma's*. I had a burger but didn't finish it. I've been pretty tense…" Then it suddenly hits me and I pause midsentence. Fear crawls up my spine when I realize the woman at the lunch counter was the same one Charlie had seen at Emory's funeral. It was Willy. I grab Charlie's hand. She jerks her head up and frowns as she looks at me.

"What is it, Tony?" she asks still frowning.

"Do you still have the picture you took on your cell phone of the weird woman at Em's funeral? The one we believe was Willy in disguise?"

"Yes, but why?"

"I think I saw 'her'. She, or he, was sitting at the counter when Theo and I had lunch at *Wilma's*."

Charlie quickly rises and retrieves her cell phone. She scrolls through the pictures with her thumb. Suddenly she stops scrolling and turns the screen toward me, "Is this the woman you saw?"

"Yes…Oh, my God! She even had on the same outfit. Now it appears Willy is stalking me." I bury my head in my hands. *Oh, God, is there any end to this nightmare?*

Charlie puts her hand on my arm and I look up. "If I wasn't sequestered, I could sit in the courtroom and keep an eye on him," she says. "Not that it would do any good—but it may make him uncomfortable knowing that we see through his disguise."

"You're correct; you can't be in the courtroom. And I'd rather he didn't know that we're on to him, at least not right now. Let him play out his hand. We'll wait and see what he has up his sleeve. He's basking in the misery he's causing me, and from the looks of things, he intends to inflect more—much more."

Charlie picks up our dinner plates and heads toward the kitchen. "We have chocolate mousse for dessert. Would you like some coffee to go with it?"

"CHOCOLATE MOUSSE! One of my favorites."

"I know."

I'm surprised so I ask, "And just how did you know that?"

"I have my ways." Charlie whispers looking over her shoulder as she ducks into the kitchen carrying the leftovers.

I'm confused. Who would she know that knows me intimately enough to know my likes and dislikes? Dad! "I'll pass on the coffee. Keeps me awake if I drink any past three o'clock. What can I do to help?" I ask, clearing more dinner dishes from the table following Charlie into the kitchen.

"Nothing, thank you anyway. Just go relax and I'll bring dessert into the living room."

I comply and settle onto one of the sofas, turning on the national news. I purposely avoid the local news. They seldom get it right anyway. Charlie follows a few minutes later, carrying a tray with two parfaits brimming with chocolate mousse and whipped cream. She sits down beside me and hands me a napkin, a spoon and one of the parfaits. She takes the other, and clicking her parfait against mine, says, "Here's looking at you, kid," and wastes no time digging in. I follow suit. It's the best mousse I've ever had and I tell her so.

"Thank you, kind sir. Now, I'm awash with guilt and must confess, I bought the dessert at the deli so, I'm a fraud. I can't take credit for it."

"Yes, you can. You had the insight to purchase it. That's almost as good as creating it."

She smiles at my complement. "Not really, but I'll take it." Then she puts her hand on my thigh and my nerve endings go nuts. "You probably want to get home early to be refreshed for opening statements tomorrow."

"Want to go? No, I do not *want* to go."

The moment escalates from there and I leave for home a couple of hours later — ready to face the world and savoring the memories of my time with Charlie. There is no room to ruminate about my trials and tribulations. My cup is way more than half full. It's overflowing!

PART THREE

THE
GAME

CHAPTER

9

The courtroom is packed once again even though there's a blizzard raging outside. The wind pounds at the windows and snow is rapidly piling up on the streets and walkways. In the distance, I hear the scream of an ambulance and I shudder. The day adds to my gloomy spirits but I try to look as normal as possible.

All of the players are present and the jurors look as though they're eager to begin. Edison Hammond, the District Attorney, is lead prosecutor and Assistant District Attorney Adam Farnsworth is second chair. Sgt. Gary Slater is seated at the prosecution table in the capacity of advisory witness. My team, consisting of Theo and Ray, are refreshed and ready to proceed.

Court is called to order and Ducky asks the prosecution if they are ready with their opening statements.

"Yes, Your Honor, the People are ready," Farnsworth states.

"Then, do so," the judge says as His Honor leans back in his chair, and looking thoughtful, places one earpiece of his glasses between his teeth.

Farnsworth stands, buttons his jacket, and struts to the podium. He looks at each of the jurors individually before beginning. Some of the jurors shift in their seats under his gaze. Farnsworth's glare is unnerving and I'm sure they're feeling uncomfortable. *Good! Let him alienate the jury. First impressions are the most lasting.*

Farnsworth takes a moment to shuffle papers around and then positions a legal pad on the podium before he begins. Looking up, he addresses the jury:

"Ladies and gentlemen, thank you for your willingness to serve as jurors during what is anticipated to be an eight-week trial. We understand you have lives outside the courtroom and we will try to minimize the inconvenience and not disrupt your private lives any more than necessary.

"This is a complicated case. There is much evidence to present and many witnesses to be heard. I believe the court provided you with a tablet so you are free to take notes as the trial progresses."

Farnsworth takes a sip of water from the glass positioned on a small shelf under the top of the podium. He turns and points in my direction. I flinch when I hear him mention my name.

"Antonio Facinni is charged with three counts of First Degree Murder and one count of Cruelty to Animals. The prosecution will show that the defendant, a retired judge, purported to be close friends with the three victims and a pet by the name of Karma. This charade gave the defendant the advantage of surprise. His victims would, quite obviously, be comfortable in his presence. Who would suspect a close friend would stoop to poisoning, shooting, stabbing or plotting your death?"

"OBJECTION! Your Honor," Theo shouts and jumps to his feet. "This is not final argument."

"What say you?" Ducky asks Farnsworth.

"It's just part of what we expect the evidence to show," Farnsworth replies.

"Save it for final argument," Ducky orders.

Farnsworth stops and looks toward the defense table with what I interrupt to be contempt and disgust. It's obvious he dislikes Theo and that he's out to get me.

"The People intend to prove that the defendant, Antonio Facinni, indeed committed the crimes charged in the Information and that his motive was greed, and of course, an ego trip. We will also prove that the defendant not only had the motive but the means and opportunity to carry out his devious plans.

"On the surface, the defendant looks like what he purports to be: a retired judge who is now writing mystery thrillers. Beneath that façade, ladies and gentlemen, lies the real Antonio Facinni. One who would stop at nothing to promote his novels, even duplicating his imaginary crimes to garner publicity.

"The People will present evidence that conclusively places the defendant at each of the crime scenes. This evidence consists of fingerprints and personal items belonging to the defendant that were left at the various crime scenes."

Farnsworth turns around and glares at me. I resist the urge to reciprocate. He then drones on another forty minutes dwelling on minutia. I notice the jurors are growing restless and most are no longer focusing their attention on Farnsworth. Even I'm becoming bored. Finally, Ducky intervenes, "Mr. Farnsworth, you're becoming redundant. Can't we speed this up?"

"Yes, Your Honor," Farnsworth says sheepishly. Then finding his place in his script, he continues:

"Now, you ask yourselves, why would someone who is a writer and former judge do that? His novels have been on the best seller list for months. And that's a fair and logical question, but as they say in the trade, 'Any publicity is good publicity.' There is another saying to keep in mind, 'Arrogance produces fools.'"

I resist the urge to shake my head. Theo observes my reaction and nudges me with his knee, whispering, "Stay calm, Tony, stay calm."

Needing a distraction, I take a quick glance around the courtroom and notice Willy, in his now-recognizable disguise, sitting in the front row of the balcony. He has a smug look on his face and seems to be enjoying the opening statement. I turn my attention back to Farnsworth.

"If the evidence presented at trial is as the prosecution anticipates," Farnsworth says in a hushed tone, "we will have no hesitancy in asking you to return guilty verdicts against Antonio Facinni on all counts — not because we are asking you to do so but because we will have proven the defendant's guilt beyond a reasonable doubt."

Farnsworth resumes his seat at the prosecution table. Slater smiles at him. *That bastard....* My thought is interrupted by Ducky. He addresses Theo.

"Is the defense ready with its opening statement?"

"Yes, Your Honor, but may we take a short recess before I begin?"

"Yes, of course. That's a good idea. We all need to stretch. We'll take a fifteen minute break." He looks at the jury. "You may leave to use the facilities if you wish, but be back here by," Ducky looks at the large oak-framed antique clock hanging above the rear exit, "10:20." He raps his gavel and we all stand as the jury files out. Ducky then leaves the bench.

"What's up, Theo?" I ask.

"I just want the jury to have a break before I begin. They were looking pretty bored there towards the end of Adam's opening. He really didn't put much fire into his remarks."

"Un-huh. If their evidence is that good, they don't need much fire." I mumble.

"Ah, patience, Grasshopper. Watch and learn."

I take advantage of the break and head for the john. *At least Willy won't be in here,* I muse. I look at myself in the mirror above the sink. *Gad. I look awful. You'd never believe I'm only fifty-eight. I must have aged twenty years since this ordeal started.*

I get back just under the wire. The jury is seated and the courtroom has settled down from the fifteen minute reprieve.

Ducky looks refreshed as well. "Ready, Mr. Raddison?"

"Yes, thank you, Your Honor."

Theo is slow and deliberate as he walks to the podium. He exudes an aura of confidence I've seen in very few men. Once again, I'm buoyed by his demeanor and attitude. He doesn't bother to make a show of shuffling papers around. In fact, he approaches the podium with not so much as a pen or pencil.

"We, the defense, also thank you for your service," he begins. "Being a juror is an honor and a privilege. Due process and trial by jury is an integral part of our American system of justice. Not too many countries afford their citizens this right. We are truly blessed to be Americans.

"You will determine, as the case unfolds, how evidence can be misleading. Our experts will testify that evidence appearing to be indisputable, can oftentimes be contrived, fabricated or concocted. And to what end? To shift the blame, perhaps, or maybe to make it appear that a target of someone's wrath is the culprit. How can that occur? Easy. By taking someone's readily identifiable personal items and leaving them in a conspicuous spot at the scene of the crime. The evidence will show that even fingerprints can be lifted and transferred onto incriminating items."

"OBJECTION!" Farnsworth wails. "What's good for the goose is good for the gander. Mr. Raddison objected to parts of the prosecution's opening as being argumentative, now we have the opportunity to reciprocate."

"Sustained," Ducky says emphatically. "Mr. Raddison, please make a conscious effort not to do what you objected to during Mr. Farnsworth's opening."

"I apologize." Theo takes a sip of water before continuing. "The prosecution asserts that they will prove that Judge Facinni murdered three innocent people in cold blood to promote the sale of his novels. The evidence presented at the trial through the witnesses for both sides will show Judge Facinni's novels were already best sellers. The evidence will show that as a sentencing judge, Judge Facinni made enemies who vowed, upon their release from incarceration, that they would even the score. Other than the bogus motive asserted by the prosecution, the evidence will show that Judge Facinni had absolutely no motive to end the lives of his three cherished friends and a pet that had shadowed him and was his constant companion for ten years or more.

"When the case has been concluded, you will be able to determine whether the prosecution has kept their promise to prove each and every element of the crimes charged beyond any and all reasonable doubt. Mr. Farnsworth has promised to prove motive, opportunity and means 'beyond a reasonable doubt.' Actually, Mr. Farnsworth has promised what is already required by law. The defense submits that the evidence to sustain a conviction is deficient, and that the prosecution will neither keep its promise nor meet its burden. If the evidence, or lack thereof, is as the defense anticipates, it will by the end of the case have no hesitancy in asking you to return 'not guilty' verdicts on all counts. Thank you."

Theo comes back to our table. After he is seated, Ducky looks up at the clock and says, "It's close enough to noon to break for lunch." He then addresses the jury. "You will all stay together for lunch. The bailiff will escort you and bring you back here after lunch. We will reconvene at one-thirty. Bailiff, you may take the jury out now."

♦♦♦♦♦

THEO AND I opt to go back to *Wilma's*. Ray accompanies us this trip. When we enter, I automatically glance at the counter. Willy is not there. I breathe a sigh of relief. We take a booth in the back where it's relatively quiet. Sonya brings us water, takes our orders and heads back to the kitchen.

"That was some opening," I say after we're settled. "I'm impressed."

"That's just the beginning, Tony. I've locked horns with Hammond and Farnsworth before. They're good, but we're better." Theo looks at Ray. "Let's go over the list of prosecution witnesses one more time. I don't want any surprises."

"Sure." Ray takes a small note pad from his breast pocket. "If they call them in the order we discussed previously, their first witness will be Sgt. Gary Slater, followed by Detective Charlie Whitaker. I look for her testimony to take one to two hours depending…"

Charlie! I'm suddenly fearful as reality slaps me in the face. *What will Charlie testify to? We never discuss the trial.*

"Are you all right, Tony," Ray asks. "You look pale."

I take a long drink of water before answering, "I'm okay, Ray. Just anxious."

Theo squeezes and shakes my arm. "It's going to be all right—just keep the faith, baby."

I smile. *Keep the faith? I'm trying.*

◆◆◆◆◆

COURT IS BACK in session and the prosecution is ready, able and willing. In fact, it looks like they're chomping at the bit.

"Mr. Hammond, you may call your first witness."

"Thank you, Your Honor." We call Sgt. Gary Slater. Slater stands and walks to the witness stand, and raising his right hand, is sworn in by the judge.

Hammond has Slater detail his police credentials which highlight his training, education and experience.

"Thank you, Sgt. Slater." Hammond says, and continues reading from a script. "Please describe to the jury your involvement in the events leading up to the arrest of Judge Facinni."

Slater shifts in the chair and crosses his legs. He looks at me with a smug expression and begins.

"Judge Facinni called 911 on the night of October 13 reporting a missing person."

Hammond leads Slater through all of the contacts he had had with me during mid-October. I find no fault with any of his testimony. He is forthcoming and truthful.

At the conclusion of Slater's testimony, Hammond says, "Thank you, Sgt. Slater." He then turns to Ducky. "The people have no further questions at this time, but reserve the right to recall this witness for rebuttal if need be."

Ducky nods and says to Theo, "Your witness, Mr. Raddison."

Theo, again without notes of any sort, begins his cross-examination of Sgt. Slater.

"Sgt. Slater, didn't you find it odd that, at each crime scene, some item that would implicate Judge Facinni was found or intended to be found?"

"What exactly do you mean?" Sgt. Slater asks with a smirk.

Slater will be sorry he's playing the ignorance game with Theo. There's no way he can outfox the fox.

"Well, wasn't Leonard Wycowski killed with a .22 caliber weapon, the same caliber weapon that was described in one of Judge Facinni's novels and the same caliber as the gun Judge Facinni reported missing from his apartment?"

"Yes, but…"

"I don't mean to be rude, Sgt. Slater, but that question can be answered with 'yes' or 'no.'"

"Yes," Slater says defiantly.

"And, when the body of Doreen Lancaster was found, wasn't a tie tack, later determined to belong to Judge Facinni, found wedged in one of her hands?"

"Yes."

"And wasn't the murder weapon determined to be a hunting knife with a six inch blade with an elk's head etched into the ivory handle?"

"Yes."

"And, am I correct in assuming that the murder weapon was identical to the murder weapon described in another of Judge Facinni's novels?"

"Yes."

"Now, with regard to the tie tack found at the second crime scene: didn't Judge Facinni tell you that a similar tie tack belonging to him had also been removed from his apartment?"

"Yes, but…"

"Ahhh! Sgt. Slater. Can't that question also be answered with a 'yes' or 'no'?"

"Yes, but I have an explanation."

"I'm not asking for an explanation. If I need one or your attorney needs one, we can ask for it. Right now, I'm trying to stay on track and am asking you to do the same. Understand?"

"Yes."

"Do you want me to repeat the question?"

"Yes."

"With regard to the tie tack found at the second crime scene involving the murder of Doreen Lancaster, didn't Judge Facinni tell you it, like the .22 caliber handgun, had also been taken from his apartment?"

"Yes."

"Didn't all the crime scenes we've discussed thus far make it appear that Judge Facinni was somehow involved?"

"Well not at first, that is not until we found Judge Facinni's tie tack at the second murder."

"Wait a minute, Sgt. Slater. Didn't Judge Facinni call the 911 dispatcher and inform her that his friend had not shown up at the appointed time and that he was worried because a convicted felon who had threatened revenge had just been released from prison?"

"Yes, but I don't see your point."

"Well, let me draw you a picture…"

"OBJECTION; ARGUMENTATIVE," Hammond shouts.

"Sustained," Ducky says without hesitation.

"Let me rephrase that, Sgt. Slater. It was Judge Facinni who called the dispatcher to report a missing person. That person was Leonard Wycowski, a retired NYPD detective. Correct?"

"Yes."

"Judge Facinni is a retired judge. Correct?"

"Yes."

"Didn't your investigation disclose that a convicted murderer had been released from prison the day before Leonard Wycowski was murdered?"

"Yes."

"Didn't your investigation also disclose that the key witness in the prosecution of that convicted murderer was Leonard Wycowski?"

"Yes."

"Did your investigation disclose that both the key prosecution witness, Leonard Wycowski, as well as the sentencing judge had received death threats from the convicted murderer?"

"Yes."

"And didn't Judge Facinni's call to 911 indicate that as well?"

"Yes."

"By the way, Sgt. Slater, what was the name of the sentencing judge, who along with the prosecution's key witness, was threatened by the recently-released, convicted murderer?"

"Judge Facinni," Slater said, squirming in his chair and glancing in the direction of Messers Hammond and Farnsworth.

"The same Judge Facinni who is on trial here and the man seated at the defense table?" Theo points at me.

"Yes." For the first time in his testimony Slater looks down.

"Now, going back to what I was asking you before, wasn't Leonard Wycowski killed outside Judge Facinni's building?"

"Yes."

"Did your investigation disclose why Leonard Wycowski was in the vicinity of Judge Facinni's apartment building?"

"We learned later that he was going to watch a football game with Judge Facinni at Judge Facinni's apartment."

"And, when Leonard Wycowski didn't show up, Judge Facinni called 911. Right?"

"Right."

"Do you know whether Judge Facinni's name, phone number and address are listed in the telephone directory?"

"Yes."

"How do you know?"

"We looked at the directory before we contacted Judge Facinni to verify that he was the one who telephoned 911, and to verify his address as well."

"Would it be fair to say that anyone who wanted to ascertain Judge Facinni's address could do so by just looking in the telephone directory?"

"Yes."

"Now, you considered all possibilities before you concluded Judge Facinni was 'your man,' so to speak. Correct?"

"As I said, we didn't zero in on him right away. We ran checks on the recently-released convict, and others, to make sure we had 'our man.'"

"When you checked out the convicted murderer, who had the day before Leonard Wycowski's death, been released from prison, did you also check his rap sheet?"

"Yes."

"Did you discover that he had several burglary convictions?"

"Objection, Your Honor. Irrelevant." Hammond interjects.

"Mr. Raddison?" Ducky says as he peers over his glasses and looks at Theo.

"Your Honor, Judge Facinni reported his .22 caliber handgun, box of shells, tie tack and other items were missing from his home; Judge Facinni obviously having been the victim of a burglary. This line of questioning will reveal that the alternate suspect was not only a convicted murderer but a convicted burglar and that he had the motive, means and opportunity to have burglarized Judge Facinni's residence and committed the crimes for which Judge Facinni has been charged."

I watch as the prosecutors both squirm along with my nemeses, Sgt. Gary Slater.

"Very well," Ducky says. "Mr. Raddison, you may proceed but only in the confines of your offer of proof."

"Understood," Theo says to Ducky. Turning to Slater, he asks, "Do you wish for me to rephrase the question?"

"Please," Slater replies, a little more conciliatory.

"Was the convicted murderer you checked out also a convicted burglar?"

"We found two convictions for burglaries on his record."

"By the way, Sgt. Slater, you never recovered the .22 caliber weapon that caused Leonard Wycowski's death, did you?"

"No."

"Then you don't know whether the .22 caliber handgun Judge Facinni reported missing was the same on used to kill Leonard Wycowski, do you?"

"No."

"And with respect to the hunting knife used to kill Doreen Lancaster, you don't know whether that ever belonged to Judge Facinni, do you?"

"No, only that it was similar to the one described in one of Judge Facinni's novels."

"By the way, Sgt. Slater, was any attempt made to remove prints from the knife?"

"We were unable to remove any. The knife was wiped clean.'

"Other than the tie tack that was found at Doreen Lancaster's crime scene, the one that Judge Facinni reported missing, did you find anything else at the crime scene that pointed the finger at Judge Facinni?"

"No, only the reference in his novel."

"I assume you read all of Judge Facinni's novels, correct?"

"Yes, otherwise I wouldn't have known what was in them."

"Where did you obtain those novels?"

"We purchased them at the bookstore."

"Did you have any trouble obtaining them?"

"No. The bookstore was well-stocked."

"So, would it be fair to say that anyone who wanted them could purchase them and expect immediate delivery?"

"Yes."

"Going back to Doreen Lancaster's crime scene, didn't it appear odd to you that someone who would have been thorough enough to wipe the knife handle clean of any fingerprints would have carelessly left an easily traceable tie tack behind?"

"Everyone makes mistakes."

"Come now, Sgt. Slater. When I interviewed you after Judge Facinni was arrested you were asked by me what motive Judge Facinni would have to commit the crimes with which he is now charged. Do you remember telling me 'He did it to attract attention to himself and his novels so he would sell more books?"

"Yes, I remember."

"Do you still believe that?"

"Yes."

"Then, if that were the case, wouldn't fingerprints left at the scene be more convincing than items left at the scene that arguably could have been placed there by anyone bent on framing him?"

"Yes, but remember, his fingerprints were found on the undercarriage of Jeffery Wilkinson's vehicle whose death was caused by a severed brake line."

"Sgt. Slater, if Judge Facinni was the one who cut the brake line, why would he leave his prints there and not wipe them clean as you contend he did at Doreen Lancaster's crime scene?"

"You'll have to ask him; I don't know the answer."

"Sgt. Slater, let me ask you this. You are a seasoned crime scene investigator. Isn't it possible to lift someone's fingerprints from an item that he or she has touched and transfer them onto another surface such as the undercarriage of a car?"

"Absolutely, but they would have to know what they're doing."

"You, as a seasoned investigator, could do it, right?"

"Yes."

"Then how about a seasoned criminal? Could he or she do it?"

"Possibly."

"Let me ask you one further question. Who would more likely eliminate those near and dear to Judge Facinni? Judge Facinni himself, or someone seeking revenge, who threatened vengeance, and who has had the motive, means and opportunity to do so?"

Hammond springs to his feet. He is livid. Farnsworth tries to restrain him.

"OBJECTION! The question is designed to inflame the minds of the jury. Prosecution moves for a mistrial."

Ducky removes his glasses and glares at Hammond, "Your motion for a mistrial is denied. I am going to sustain your objection, Mr. Hammond, only because it calls for speculation." Turning to Theo, Ducky asks, "Any further questions of this witness, Mr. Raddison?"

"No, Your Honor. I have no further questions," Theo replies. He then resumes his place at the defense table.

After Theo's cross, the judge looks at the clock and announces it's lunch time. Court will adjourn until one-thirty.

◆◆◆◆◆

WHEN WE RECONVENE, Ducky invites the prosecution to call their next witness.

Hammond stands and announces, "The people call Detective Charlie Whitaker."

I tense as I watch the bailiff go to the door of the courtroom and call out, "Charlie Whitaker."

When Charlie enters, I find it hard to breathe. She looks lovely. The judge forbids law enforcement officers to wear their uniforms during testimony, so Charlie has on a striking navy blue suit underscored by a snow white blouse. Her hair is in an up doo and her makeup is impeccable. Her black patent leather high heels accent the shapeliness of her amazing long legs. She has combined professionalism with beauty and succeeded marvelously. She gracefully takes her place on the witness stand.

"Please state your full name for the record." Hammond says.

"Detective Charlie Whitaker."

"And, Detective Whitaker, what is your occupation?"

"I'm a detective with the New York City Police Department."

"How long have you been employed in that capacity?"

"Twenty years, give or take a month or so."

"Thank you, Detective Whitaker." Hammond pauses and rearranges his notes on the podium, then asks, "Where were you on the afternoon of October 14 of last year?"

"I was on duty at the forty-second, getting ready to go on a ride-along with a couple of rookies."

"Did you go on that ride-along?"

"No."

It's obvious Charlie isn't going to give up much without them asking.

Hammond moves away from the podium and approaches Charlie. "Why not? Why didn't you go on the ride along...NO, wait. Let me rephrase that question. Tell the jury exactly what happened that night."

Charlie shifts in her chair, adjusts her jacket and raises her chin looking somewhat defiant before answering. "Sgt. Slater directed me to accompany Judge Facinni to his home to retrieve his firearm."

"Did Sgt. Slater indicate why?"

"Judge Facinni reported a missing person who was later found dead in close proximity to Judge Facinni's apartment building. The victim was shot with a .22 caliber handgun. During an interview with Sgt. Slater, Judge Facinni, stated he had a .22 caliber handgun. When asked, he gave Sgt. Slater permission to examine the weapon."

"Okay, continue." Hammond throws Charlie a furtive glance.

From his look, I could almost read his mind. Hammond was thinking Charlie is a prosecution witness but acts more like a defense witness. I scoot my chair closer to the table hoping the movement will get Charlie's attention. When she looks at me, I gently shake my head hoping Charlie would take the hint not to be so evasive. She did. When she continued, she was more forthcoming.

"When we arrived at Judge Facinni's apartment, he went straight to his walk-in closet and ran his hand across the top shelf, searching for the weapon. Not finding it, he moved an ottoman into the closet and stood on it, doing a more thorough search. He seemed stunned that the gun was missing. I asked when he last saw it. He told me that it had been a few years. He said the only time he used it was when he and his father went target practicing and that was before his father had been placed in a retirement facility over five years ago."

"What happened next," Hammond persisted.

"I stood on the ottoman and conducted a thorough search of my own. After we both searched for the gun, and not finding it, Judge Facinni scratched his head looking as though he was trying to remember something. After a few moments, he told me he was thirsty and asked if it would be all right for him to get a drink. We went into the kitchen and found Karma, Judge Facinni's cat, lying dead on the floor in the laundry room. Judge Facinni rushed to her but it was apparent she was beyond help. We both detected the odor of almonds and determined she had been poisoned with cyanide. Judge Facinni was quite obviously unnerved by the discovery."

"At what point did you summon the crime scene investigative unit?"

"Because of the burglary and an obviously-poisoned pet, I called Sgt. Slater and informed him of the situation. Later I requested the captain to dispatch the CSI team."

"Ah, excuse me, Detective Whitaker. Please explain to the jury what a CSI team does. Not everyone watches television." Hammond grins, looking pleased with his editorial comment.

I rear back in my chair. *What a dumbass. He's determined to alienate the jury one way or another. By flaunting his cleverness, he's insulting their intelligence.*

"Oh, sorry. CSI is the acronym for crime scene investigation. It is their job to preserve and catalogue the evidence."

"Thank you. Go on…"

Charlie continues, "Judge Facinni was never out of my sight during the time we were in his apartment. The CSI team arrived and performed their function. The cat's carcass was placed in an evidence bag and taken to the morgue. The coroner later confirmed our assessment of the cause of death as cyanide poising. After the team left, I took Judge Facinni to the stationhouse so he could pick up his car. The next day, I prepared my report and gave it to Sgt. Slater."

Charlie stops and waits for Hammond to find his place in the script.

"The defendant is charged with three homicides. Were you involved in the investigations of the other two?"

"Yes. Judge Facinni's former clerk was found murdered. The crime mirrored a crime committed in one of Judge Facinni's novels — as did the other three."

"Other three? The people charged only three homicides."

"Yes, I know. Len Wycowski is considered the second victim and Karma the first as both were killed as depicted in *Fair Game and Fool's Game,* Judge Facinni's first two novels. I include Karma to establish a pattern."

"Oh, I see." Hammond said. "Please continue."

"Doreen Lancaster and JefferyWilkinson mirrored murders committed in novels three and four, *Skin Game and End Game.*" Charlie pauses waiting for Hammond to continue.

Hammond cups his chin with his thumb and forefinger and leans on the podium. "Can you tell us what the defendant's relationship was with all of these victims?"

Charlie glances at me before answering. "Leonard Wycowski had been a friend of Judge Facinni's since their school days; Karma, of course, was his pet cat; Doreen Lancaster was his clerk during the time he served as judge, and Jeffery Wilkinson was his attorney."

"I see. And what was your involvement in the investigation of the last two homicides?"

"I was on call when Doreen Lancaster's body was discovered, so I was among the first responders."

"Un-huh. Was there any evidence at the scene that would point to who the perpetrator might have been?"

Charlie does not hesitate. To falter would send an inappropriate message to the jury. "Yes. We collected samples, including hair and fiber, just as we would any other crime scene. We also discovered a tie tack lodged in the victim's hand. It had the words 'New York State Judicial Branch' embedded in the metal."

"And how does that piece of evidence point to anyone?" Hammond turns slightly and looks in my direction.

"That particular piece of jewelry is exclusive to the judiciary, and more particularly to judges, which narrowed the field down considerably."

"So then, Detective Whitaker, after discovering the tie tack, what did you do?"

Charlie shifts again in her chair. It's obvious she is becoming weary. However, her answers are still strong and clear. "I bagged the evidence, and knowing Judge Facinni had been a judge, I took two other officers with me and went to see him. When I showed him the tie tack, he stated he had one exactly like the one I had in the evidence bag. I asked him if I could see it."

"Your Honor, may I approach the witness?" Hammond asks. "Yes."

Hammond walks to the witness stand and hands the evidence bag containing the tie tack to Charlie. The red tape seal has the date and time of collection along with initials of the collector. It also has a red sticker with People's Exhibit #14 written on it. "Is this the tie tack you collected at the scene of Doreen Lancaster's murder?"

Charlie inspects the bag and hands it back. "Yes. I wrote my initials on the seal and these are my initials."

"Thank you." Turning to Ducky, Hammond continues, "Your Honor. The prosecution offers in evidence what has been marked for identification as People's Exhibit #14."

"Any objection, Mr. Raddison?" Ducky asks.

"May I question the witness before responding?" Theo replies.

"You may."

"The tie tack is not something you took from Judge Facinni or his residence, is it?" Theo asks.

"No," Charlie replies.

"Did you say you showed Judge Facinni the tie tack that was found at the crime scene?"

"Yes."

"Did he say it was his or only that it looked like one he had?"

"He only said he had one that looked exactly like it and offered to show me the one he had."

"Then I take it you are not saying the tie tack found at the crime scene was his, are you?"

"No."

Turning to Ducky, Theo says, "In light of the limited purpose for which it is offered, Your Honor, we have no objection."

"Very well," Ducky says, "People's Exhibit #14 will be admitted in evidence."

Hammond immediately seeks Ducky's permission to circulate the exhibit among the jurors. Ducky gives his permission and the tie tack is removed from the evidence bag. Hammond approaches the jury box and hands the tie tack to the first juror who inspects it and passes it on to the next juror and the next to the next and so on.

Hammond is back at the podium. "Then what happened?"

"I accompanied Judge Facinni to his bedroom where he went immediately to a small wooden jewelry box on top of his dresser. When he opened it, he looked stunned. He exclaimed that all of his jewelry was missing."

"Stunned? How do you determine stunned?"

"Well, by the look on his face."

"Are you qualified to interpret 'facial expressions?'" Hammond looks at the jury and smiles.

"Objection, Your Honor," Theo interjects. "The prosecution is attempting to impeach its own witness."

"Overruled," Ducky responds. "Let's get on with this," he tells Hammond. Ducky then tells Charlie she may answer.

"If you're asking do I have a degree in assessing facial expressions, the answer is no. I don't even think there is such a thing. However, I do have life experiences that equate to being able to tell if someone is, let's say, happy, sad, excited, surprised, horrified, yes, and even stunned." Charlie looks at the jurors, "And I'm sure all of you do as well."

"Detective Whitaker! Please confine your answers to the questions asked," Hammond instructs.

"Excuse me. I thought that was what I was doing," Charlie says and hangs her head.

The courtroom erupts with laughter; the judge pounds his gavel in an effort to restore order.

Hammond, visibly embarrassed, clears his throat and continues, apparently trying to defuse his blunder by rushing forward. "Then what happened?" he asks.

"I asked Judge Facinni to accompany me to the stationhouse, which, incidentally, he did without hesitation."

"And…"

"When we arrived at the stationhouse, apparently Sgt. Slater had already been briefed and was waiting for us. He took Judge Facinni into an interview room. I was not privy to that conversation."

"Okay, please continue with what you were privy to."

Charlie pauses and takes a sip of water, a brief hesitation often used to allow the witness time to consider the answer. She then continues. "The next thing I know, JefferyWilkinson arrived at the station and requested to talk to his client, Judge Facinni. Sgt. Slater left the interview room while they met. After a brief time, Mr. Wilkinson and Judge Facinni came out into the corridor where Sgt. Slater was waiting. Mr. Wilkinson told Sgt. Slater that they, Mr. Wilkinson and Judge Facinni, were leaving. Sgt. Slater seemed to be angry and said something to the effect that Judge Facinni was not free to leave. Mr.

Wilkinson told Sgt. Slater, if he intended to hold Judge Facinni, he would…"

"OKAY! That's enough. You can stop there," Hammond said trying to filter the anger from his voice.

"Oh. I was under the impression you wanted to know everything that happened, not just bits and pieces." Charlie says.

Hammond slammed his legal pad down on the top of the podium, "Your Honor, would you please instruct the witness to answer only the questions asked?"

"Mr. Hammond," Ducky sighs. "It appears to me as though the witness is trying to answer your questions thoroughly and truthfully. Your questions are very broad. It is up to you to confine your questions not up to the witness to determine what type of answer you're trying to elicit. Please continue or take your seat and let the defense cross."

Hammond is enraged. He is unable to disguise his anger and his reaction is obvious to everyone in the courtroom. He fumbles around with items on the podium, apparently trying to collect his thoughts. Finally, he asks, "How is it you were involved in the investigation of Mr. Wilkinson's death?"

"I was engaged in a ride-along with one of the rookies I mentioned earlier. We were at the end of our shift when we heard the accident call. Since we were close to the scene, I told dispatch we would cover."

"And what did your initial investigation reveal?"

"The wreck was too far down the mountain side and inaccessible at that time. Officer Masters and I cordoned off the scene and took photos of the roadway and the point where the automobile went over the cliff. We waited for the ambulance and backup. The EMTs arrived at the scene, scaled the cliff side, and upon examination, determined the driver was deceased. They didn't try to remove the mangled body. Instead, they suggested we call the county coroner and have a tow truck pull out the wreckage. Officer Masters called the accident in while

I took photographs of the roadway and the damaged vehicle from the top of the cliff."

"You were among the first responders, were you not?"

"Yes."

"Was the roadway wet or were there other dangerous conditions?"

"No. None that we could see."

"Were there skid marks indicating the driver tried to avoid the accident?"

"No. That was very unusual, unless the driver had fallen asleep. My first instinct was that he had. It was a beautiful sunny morning and there was no apparent reason for the accident."

"I see." Hammond appeared to have recovered and was hitting his stride. "After the car was towed to the impound lot and examined, was a cause for the accident determined?"

"Yes. It was determined that the brake line had been severed."

"What other evidence was collected at that time?"

Charlie looks at me then continues, "It was obvious the wreck was not an accident. The vehicle was examined thoroughly and fingerprints were collected."

Hammond looks around with a smug expression on his face. "Were you able to identify any of the prints?"

"Yes. There were a multitude of prints on the inside of the car itself; however, a single thumb print on the undercarriage, in the proximity of the severed brake line, was identified as belonging to Antonio Facinni."

I knew that was coming, but it hit me hard anyway. I just sat there, stone-faced, while chaos explodes behind me in the courtroom.

Once again, Ducky has to restore order. After the courtroom quiets down, he says, "Any more outbursts and I'll have the courtroom cleared—for the duration of the trial!" Waiting for a brief moment, he asks, "Are you finished with this witness?"

"Yes, Your Honor, at least for now. We reserve the right to recall this witness in rebuttal if need be."

The judge looks at the clock on the courtroom wall. It's 3:15. "We will recess for 15 minutes and reconvene at 3:30 sharp." He stands, waits for the jury to file out, and then makes a break for his chambers.

◆◆◆◆◆

IT'S 3:30 SHARP. Everyone is back in place and court has reconvened. The judge has the bailiff recall Charlie to the witness stand.

"Remember, Detective Whitaker, you're still under oath. Mr. Raddison, are you prepared for cross-examination?" Ducky asks.

"Yes, Your Honor, we are." Theo stands and approaches the podium without crib notes or script of any kind.

"Good afternoon, Detective Whitaker," Theo says.

"Good afternoon," she replies.

"It hasn't been established yet so I'll ask you, had you met Judge Facinni previous to that afternoon at the stationhouse?"

"No. I had not."

"That was when Sgt. Slater conducted the first interview with Judge Facinni, is that correct?"

"Yes, like I said, I was at the stationhouse when Judge Facinni was asked to come in for the interview. After he met with Sgt. Slater, Sgt. Slater instructed me to accompany Judge Facinni home to retrieve his firearm."

"When you discovered the gun was missing and Judge Facinni's cat had been poisoned, what was your initial reaction?"

"Well...," Charlie pauses apparently thinking. "Well, I had read all of Judge Facinni's novels and my first thought was the events sounded vaguely familiar."

"Un-huh. Familiar, in what way?"

"They seemed to mirror the murders in the novels."

"I see. I believe you stated that the succeeding murders were duplicates of the other two novels as well. Is that correct?"

"Yes."

"You were the lead investigator on the first two crimes; that is, the murder of Leonard Wycowski and the burglary of Judge Facinni's apartment, is that correct?"

"Yes."

"At this time, Judge Facinni was not a suspect, I assume, and it was not apparent that the crimes were associated with the novels in any way. Is that also correct?"

"Yes."

"The defendant is charged with three homicides. Were you involved in the investigations of all three?"

"No, only the ones involving Doreen Lancaster and Jeffery Wilkinson, and that is because I was a first responder on both."

"I see. Now, Detective Whitaker, you're an experienced investigator. In your opinion, other than the personal items left at the various crime scenes and the lone thumbprint on the undercarriage of Mr. Wilkinson's vehicle, did you believe Judge Facinni to be the murderer?"

"No. It was much too obvious to me that he was being framed for the crimes."

"OBJECTION! Your Honor, I move to have the answer stricken from the record and the jury admonished to disregard it," Hammond says as he jumps up, knocking his chair over in the process.

"On what grounds?" The judge adjusts his eye glasses as he glares down at Hammond.

"On the grounds that the witness is not qualified to render such an opinion. Besides, the question calls for speculation and conjecture on the part of the witness."

"Really, now. Detective Whitaker is a detective employed by the homicide division at the NYPD and has been for two decades. How is it you do not feel she is qualified to make such a determination?"

Hammond blanches, then says in a more civilized tone, "Isn't that up to the jury?"

"Precisely," Ducky says. "But in order to make the determination and return a just verdict, the jury must be provided with all the relevant evidence in the case including both facts and opinions from experts. I believe you would agree that it's just as important to exonerate an innocent man as it is to convict a guilty one. Now, if the lead investigator does not believe that the so-called evidence is what it purports to be, and that an innocent person may be convicted because of it, then a defendant's right to a fair trial guaranteed by the Sixth Amendment to the United States Constitution requires disclosure. Remember, Mr. Hammond, this is your witness, and since it is the prosecutions' duty to seek justice and not necessarily a conviction, I would expect you to welcome such a candid opinion."

Hammond was spent. "Yes, sir," he mutters and flops back down in his chair which had been righted by Farnsworth.

Theo briefly takes Charlie through her testimony shoring up any trouble spots. When he is satisfied he has firmed up defense's theory of the case, he tells Ducky, "We have no further questions for this witness."

"Thank you. Detective Whitaker, you may step down. You are not excused at this time upon the request of the prosecution, and may be called as a witness again on rebuttal."

"Thank you, Your Honor," Charlie says, and gracefully steps from the witness box and exits the courtroom. All eyes in the courtroom continue to be glued on her until the doors slam behind her.

At the end of the cross examination, Charlie would have been on the stand for about three hours and is showing signs of stress by the time Theo releases her. I watch her as she leaves and wish I could take her in my arms. She throws a furtive glance in my direction, then she is gone.

◆◆◆◆◆

THE REST OF the week is filled with expert witnesses' testimony. The prosecution calls experts in the fields of crime scene investigation, forensics, blood splatter, poison, and fingerprinting.

Theo does not attempt to impeach the experts with one exception. They are knowledgeable in their fields and their testimony is accurately based on scientific evidence. Theo asks a few questions of each witness, but nothing that would alter their findings. "Just for clarification," he would preface his questions.

The exception occurred when the prosecution called Teri Parker, their fingerprint expert, to the stand. Ms. Parker is led though the process of swearing in and reciting her credentials. After the formalities, Ms. Parker testifies that the thumbprint found on the undercarriage of Jeff Wilkinson's Lincoln in close proximity of the severed brake line was determined to be mine. Ms. Parker walks the jury through the identification process and explains how prints are collected, compared and identified. When Farnsworth finishes his direct examination, he turns to Theo. "Your witness," he says. Apparently, from the look on his face, he is confident that their case is airtight.

Ducky appears to be agitated at Farnsworth for overstepping his bounds and directing Theo to begin the cross-examination. He shoots Farnsworth a menacing glance as he asks, "Mr. Raddison, are you ready with your cross?"

"I am, thank you, Your Honor," Theo replies.

By this time the testimony is becoming boring and the jury looks as though they may be nodding off. Theo makes a show of rising by scooting his chair back across the wooden floor making an obnoxious noise that snaps the jury back into the moment. He buttons his suit jacket and takes his position behind the podium.

"Good afternoon, Ms. Parker," he says and smiles broadly at the witness.

"And to you, sir," she replies. I genuinely like Parker. During my time on the bench, she had testified in my courtroom several times and I found her to be professional all the way. No tricks, this one.

"FINGERPRINTS!" Theo shouts. I notice the jurors jump in their seats at the unexpected outburst. Parker, too, is shocked from the look on her face.

"What an amazing concept. When you think of all the fingers on this planet and that no two sets are the same, well, its mindboggling."

Parker nods her head. I notice Theo has the jury's attention again. What a lead in, I think, and I become absorbed in Theo's strategy.

"Tell me, Ms. Parker, are you familiar with the concept of fingerprint forgery and fabrication?"

"Yes, I've attended several training seminars on how to ascertain if fingerprints have been forged or fabricated. I've also read many newsletters and articles regarding the same."

"Would you be so kind as to explain to the jury how fingerprints can be fabricated?"

"Of course." Parker turns to face the jury. "Fingerprints can be lifted from a surface by using tape. You may have noticed, if you use packing tape, that your prints stick to the tape when you touch it as you seal your packages. If these prints are carefully preserved, they can be reapplied to another surface."

"And, Ms. Parker, can these fabricated prints be detected by expert examination?"

Parker frowns, apparently thinking her answer through. "Well, fabricated prints are not readily detectable. If they are applied to the receiving surface haphazardly, yes. Otherwise, not so much unless you're looking for them."

"I see." Theo furrows his brow and looks thoughtful as he ponders his next question. "In the case at bar, is it possible the print found on the undercarriage of the Lincoln could have been fabricated?"

Parker doesn't even have to think about it; she answers immediately. "Yes, it is possible."

"So, for clarification, Ms. Parker, could someone have lifted fingerprints from a surface, say in Judge Facinni's home, preserved them and then later transferred one, say a thumb-print, to the undercarriage of the Lincoln?"

"Yes."

I steal a glance at Hammond. He does not look happy.

"Thank you, Ms. Parker. No further questions," Theo says.

The judge looks at Hammond and asks, "Redirect?"

Hammond stands, "No, Your Honor."

Ducky turns to Parker. "You may step down."

After Teri Parker leaves the courtroom, the judge address-es the jury.

"We are going to adjourn for the day. I remind you that you are not to talk to anyone about this case. You are also not to read or listen to any news about this case. We will reconvene at nine o'clock tomorrow morning. Bailiff, escort the jury to the jury room."

The next morning we are back in court. All of the witness-es have testified and we are ready for closing argements. My gut tells me this could go either way. Depression haunts me. *If I'm convicted, what will become of Dad?* I clear my mind trying not to think negative thoughts. As we sit waiting for the judge to reconvene, Theo is thumbing through the photos he wants to use during his closing. His file is open on the table and I absently look at a picture of Karma that has partially slipped out of the folder. *Karma!* I pick up the picture and examine it more closely. *Karma was a scratcher. If anyone tried to pick her up, even me, she would scratch the hell outta them.* In the picture, she is lying on her side with her paws extended. *My God! That's it! She probably scratched her killer and there could be DNA evidence embedded in her claws.*

"Theo, we have to talk!" I say, grabbing his arm.

"Now?" he replies. I notice the agitation in his voice.

"Yes, it's urgent!"

Theo looks around the courtroom. The judge hasn't appeared nor has the jury. "Okay, let's go into the conference room," and Theo points toward the rear of the courtroom.

Once we're in the conference room, Theo asks, "What is it, Tony?" I hear his irritation at having been pulled away from concentrating on his final argument.

"Theo, Karma—Karma was a scratcher. She would have scratched her killer."

"Okay...so?" he says.

He still doesn't get it. I continue, "Don't you see? She would have her killer's DNA embedded in her claws. It's simple. The killer would have been the last person Karma interacted with while she was alive. Her carcass was confiscated and has been held in evidence from the time Charlie and I discovered her. The chain of custody has been preserved. Even if Karma had used her litter box before she died, the DNA evidence would still be embedded in her claws. If we can get the DNA examined, and if it matches that of Wilber McCrombie, then BINGO! Our case is significantly better. In fact, because of newly-discovered evidence, charges may even be dismissed. We have maintained that there is an alternate killer from the start. Now we can prove it."

"BY GEORGE! I think you may have something. How did you come up with that?"

I'm flattered at Theo's compliment and a broad smile spreads across my mug as I answer, "From looking at the photos you had spread on the table."

"Come on, let's get a continuance." Theo grabs my elbow and ushers me back into the courtroom.

"Well, Mr. Raddison, so glad you could join us," the judge says sarcastically as he strums his nails on his glass desktop.

Theo shrugs off the insult. "Your Honor, may we approach?"

"This better be good," the judge says as he beckons Hammond and Farnsworth to the bench along with Theo for a sidebar.

I'm positioned close enough to hear what transpires. The jury is not. "Your Honor, the defense has newly discovered evidence. We are requesting time to get the evidence tested," Theo says. "We will need at least two days..."

"TWO DAYS!" Hammond says in a loud voice.

The judge holds up his hand to quiet Hammond's outburst, then looks at Theo. "What's this newly-discovered evidence that has suddenly risen in prominence?"

Theo explains our suspicions regarding the DNA embedded in Karma's claws to the judge and prosecution. Hammond violently shakes his head. "None of that, Mr. Hammond," the judge admonishes with a stern glance.

Theo continues explaining, "Your Honor, it has been our position from the beginning that Wilber McCrombie, the murderer that Judge Facinni sentenced to prison twenty years ago, is the perpetrator responsible for the crimes charged in this case. McCrombie vowed revenge at the time of his sentencing. The murders with which my client is charged were committed after his release. Because of his conviction, McCrombie's DNA is on file with the FBI. If indeed we are able to extract DNA samples from Karma's claws, and if that DNA matches McCrombie's, then I believe we have substantial evidence to request dismissal of the charges against Judge Facinni."

The judge scratches his head. Having been in that situation, I believe he is thinking of the possibility of being overturned on appeal. Then he asks, "Mr. Hammond?"

"The people do not object," Hammond responds. I have to give him credit. For all that he isn't, it appears to me that he would seriously not want to convict an innocent man. More importantly, not to have collected and tested obvious evidence, or possible evidence would undermine the whole goal of the criminal justice system — that is to seek justice, not obtain convictions, especially unwarranted ones.

"In that case, Mr. Raddison, you may have two days. Get the process started as soon as possible. I will issue an order for the evidence custodian to release the carcass of the cat to the laboratory and an order for the laboratory to expedite the testing." He looks at Theo and Hammond. "Anything else?"

Both attorneys shake their heads. "Thank you, you may take your seats." After everyone is back in place, the judge addresses the jury, "Ladies and gentlemen, due to recent developments and due to circumstances beyond anyone's control, we are continuing this trial for a period of two business days."

I watch the jurors look questioningly at each other, apparently wondering what happened.

Ducky looks at his clerk, Thelma Davis. "What's the date two days from today?"

"February 22nd," Thelma replies.

Then, refocusing his gaze, he addresses the jury. "You are excused until 9:00 a.m. February 22nd, but remember, YOU ARE STILL under the strict rules established by the court. You are not to talk about the case or read, watch or listen to any media reports of any sort from any source." Closing the court file and gathering up his assortment of legal paraphernalia, he announces, "We will reconvene in this courtroom on February 22nd at 9:00 a.m. Court adjourned." Ducky smacks his gavel for emphasis and rears back in his chair. "Bailiff, escort the jury out."

As soon as the jury files out, Theo hastily gathers up his files. "Meet me back at my office, pronto!" he commands Ray and me, then he's gone. Ray and I follow suit. The courtroom is still crowded, and as we approach the exit, I see Willy. Even with his disguise, I can see the stunned expression on his face. *You murdering bastard. It isn't over yet!*

Reporters clog the corridor. We push through on our way to the exit. "Hey, Facinni, what's going on?" I hear Jason Buchanan, a writer for the *Times Reporter*, shout after us as Ray and I rush past. I, of course, ignore his question, but give him a wave of acknowledgment.

◆◆◆◆◆

WHEN WE ARRIVE at Theo's office we find him explaining to Esther what happened in court. I notice the stunned look on her face but she manages a smile as we enter.

"…and, Esther, please prepare a motion dismissing all charges with prejudice. I want to have it ready to take with me next week."

My heart races. *Could it be? Could this really be happening? I need to call Charlie…*

"Theo, may I use your phone?"

"Of course — use that office." He points to an empty office.

I close the door and dial Charlie's cell number. She doesn't answer, so I leave her an abbreviated message regarding what happened in court this afternoon. I tell her I'm meeting with Theo and will call her as soon as we are finished. I drop a hint that there may be light at the end of the tunnel after all and ask that she cross her fingers.

CHAPTER

10

When Willy observes the side bar at the bench and the events that follow, he knows something monumental is occurring. His intuition tells him, whatever it is, it won't be in his favor. *But what? So far, even I'd convict the SOB. And I know who done the deed. Guess I'll just wait it out. Maybe I should just blow this popsicle stand — but then, I'd miss the look on Facinni's face when the jury comes back with guilty verdicts.*

◆◆◆◆◆

THE NEXT DAY, the evidence custodian delivers Karma's carcass to Kingsley Laboratory, an independent facility, to conduct the DNA testing. Both the prosecution and defense had designated an agent to be on hand to view the process to ensure it was done properly and that the evidence was not tainted in the process. The laboratory was in possession of the hand-delivered court order directing them to do the testing immediately as the case at bar was awaiting the results in order to continue with the trial.

Police Lab Technician Mitchell Keeler, accompanied by Officer Larry Branson, stands in the lobby of the laboratory waiting for an agent to accept the evidence and sign the chain-of-custody form. This process is an absolute necessity every time the evidence is transferred from one place or individual to another, in order to precisely track where the evidence goes and who accepts it. If the chain is broken, either side could argue that the evidence could have been tampered with, making it unreliable and thus unacceptable as a court exhibit.

Loraine Desmond, wearing a white lab coat which does little to disguise her curvaceous figure, enters the lobby and greets the two officers. "Good morning, Mitch," she says and extends her hand toward Mitchell Keeler.

"'Morning, Loraine," Mitch replies then gestures toward Larry Branson who is holding the plastic evidence bag containing Karma's carcass. "This is Officer Branson...and of course, Karma," he says with a broad smile. Officer Branson nods toward Loraine as Mitch continues, "We have the chain paperwork ready for you to sign, then we'll transfer the evidence."

"Nice to meet you, Officer Branson. Let me see the release, Mitch. There seems to be some urgency surrounding the examination of this feline."

"For sure. Judge Duckworth has the jury on hold waiting for the results," Mitch says as he hands Loraine a clipboard.

Loraine examines the proffered form attached to the clipboard and then hastily signs it. "Since we're in possession of a court order to expedite the testing, I'll just take the kitty and bid you two adieu."

"Sure thing." Mitch gestures to Branson to give the remains to Loraine. Then he says, as he tucks the clipboard under his arm, "Nice seeing you again, Loraine." The officers turn and head toward the exit. As soon as they are out of earshot, Mitch whispers, "Yes, very nice, indeed!" Branson nods.

Loraine, holding Karma's remains, carefully makes her way back to the laboratory.

Senior Tech Autumn Walters had set up the lab for a DNA examination as soon as they were informed the evidence was on its way. Present with her in the lab are James Chesterton, the defense expert, and Victor Franklin, the prosecution expert. All gather around the table as Autumn carefully removes the carcass from the plastic bag. She then extends Karma to her full length and takes the cat's paws, one-by-one, in her hands and gently extracts the material embedded under the claws with a sterile pick.

◆◆◆◆◆

THERE ARE BASIC steps that are followed in the testing regardless of the type of material being tested. These include: isolating the DNA collected from the evidence sample; processing the DNA to obtain test results; determining test results, and comparing and interpreting the results with known and/ or unknown samples.

Because of the circumstances surrounding the crimes I had been charged with, Ducky included in his order that the lab be provided with a profile of Wilber McCrombie's DNA which was collected when he was sent to prison. If the defense's theory that McCrombie could be, and most likely was, the perpetrator, then having McCrombie's DNA profile on hand for instant comparison would save many hours of running comparisons through the FBI database. The highest probability on a DNA test is 99.99%. After the samples were collected from Karma's claws, tested and compared, it was determined that the DNA collected was a 98% match to that of McCrombie's DNA profile. The results were conclusive and both the defense and prosecution experts were satisfied to a "reasonable degree of scientific certainty."

◆◆◆◆◆

THE REPORT WAS delivered to the court, the defense and the prosecution the same day it was generated. Theo told me that Ducky, after reviewing the report, instructed his clerk, Thelma, to arrange a meeting between himself and both Edison Hammond and Theo in the judge's chambers as soon as their schedules would allow. Theo said they met that same afternoon. Afterward, Theo gave me a blow-by-blow recitation of how the meeting went. He said that Hammond told them after he read the report, he instructed Slater to have McCrombie immediately picked up for questioning. Theo went on to relate:

"That was going to be my first suggestion," Ducky said. Then, "Gentlemen, since you've had time to read the report, I'm open for discussion."

"Thank you, Your Honor," Theo responded. Handed his motion to dismiss to the judge with a copy to Hammond. "In light of the DNA results, I am asking that you forthwith dismiss all charges against Judge Facinni with prejudice." (*With prejudice* means the charges can never be resurrected.)

"I OBJECT!" Hammond shouted as he rose, and according to Theo, knocked his chair over. Knocking chairs over seems to be his method of expressing displeasure.

Theo said that Ducky held up his hands, palms out, saying, "Calm down, Mr. Hammond. You'll have a chance to respond."

"Yes, sir," Hammond said as he picked up his chair, slid it back into place and sat down.

"Now, Mr. Raddison, continue…"

"Thank you, Your Honor. The defense has asserted all along that Judge Facinni did not commit the crimes charged. Our defense is that an unknown intruder broke into his apartment, poisoned his cat, stole his revolver and jewelry—jewelry items that were left at the various crime scenes, and incidentally, that were instrumental in the ensuing arrest of Judge Facinni." Theo paused to organize his thoughts, then continued. "The only other piece of evidence that implicates my client is the thumbprint lifted from the undercarriage of JefferyWilkinson's vehicle. That evidence is now suspect in light of the proof beyond a reasonable doubt that Judge Facinni's home was burglarized thus providing the perpetrator the means, opportunity and motive to obtain Judge Facinni's fingerprints. The prosecution's own witness explained how fingerprints can be fabricated and forged. The thumbprint found on the vehicle could have been transferred by the actual perpetrator." Theo then leafed through the lab report before continuing. "Your Honor, it would be a travesty to continue this trial with so much evidence pointing in the direction of the alternate suspect."

Then, putting the report aside, Theo said, "Wilber McCrombie had the *means*. It is now apparent that he broke into Judge Facinni's home, and at the very least, poisoned his cat and stole the items he would later use to frame Judge Facinni. It would then have been an easy task to lift Judge Facinni's prints from almost any surface in his home. Wilber McCrombie had the *motive*. At the time Judge Facinni imposed sentence upon McCombie's conviction for murdering his girlfriend, McCrombie vowed he would seek revenge. If McCrombie could kill his girlfriend in cold blood for some ill-conceived reason, why is it so inconceivable he could not have also carried out the plot to kill those near and dear to Judge Facinni, the sentencing judge, and make it appear that Judge Facinni was the perpetrator? It was an ingenious plot that was hatched on the day McCrombie was sentenced, fine-tuned during his years of imprisonment, and carried out starting the day following his release from prison. McCrombie also had the *opportunity* to perpetrate the crimes and carry out his diabolical scheme. A convicted burglar and murderer, he had the skill, training and experience to execute his threat, which to date has been a work of art, and very effective in exacting his perceived pound of flesh. He was able to slink around, undetected, planning his heinous acts. We are requesting the court take into account all of the facts and sign the Order of Dismissal. By dismissing all of the charges against my client, Antonio Facinni, justice will indeed be served."

According to Theo, Ducky sat rubbing his chin. and then said, "Mr. Hammond…"

Edison Hammond, Theo said, stood and walked to the window overlooking the park surrounding the courthouse. After what to them seemed like forever, Hammond returned, and still standing, said, "A greater travesty would be a dismissal of this case. The People assert and all along have asserted that Judge Facinni is either very clever or very stupid…"

"Your Honor," Theo said, "I object to…"

"Mr. Raddison, this is not a courtroom. This is an informal meeting in chambers so the courtroom rules do not apply." The judge glared at Theo then turned to Hammond. "Mr. Hammond, please continue."

"Thank you." Hammond, according to Theo, sat down before continuing. "The people are not convinced by Mr. Raddison's flowery speech that Judge Facinni is innocent. We continue to assert that there is enough evidence to convict him of the crimes charged beyond a reasonable doubt. I do not, unless of course, the court orders it, wish to address Mr. Raddison's comments at this time. To do so, Your Honor, would be tantamount to giving away the people's strategy thus providing the defense with unwarranted ammunition to shore up their final argument." Hammond folded his arms across his chest and leaned back in his chair. "The people strenuously object to the granting of the defense's motion to dismiss."

Theo later told me that it was apparent, judging from the look on the judge's face, that Ducky was in a quandry. Theo said he could almost hear the wheels turning in Ducky's head saying, "No matter which way I go, there will be the inevitable appeal. If I rule for the defense, the prosecution will appeal on the legal issue, but even if the Appellate Court rules in favor of the prosecution, Judge Facinni cannot be retried because that would be double jeopardy. On the other hand, if I deny the defense motion and Judge Facinni is convicted, he will be able to appeal the ruling. If my ruling is wrong, Judge Facinni will receive a new trial. If I commit an error, it can be rectified by ruling against the defense — not the other way around."

I'm ready for my ruling," Ducky said. "You both have logical arguments. To that end, I'm declining to take the case away from the jury. After all, Judge Facinni has requested a jury trial, and it's the jury that should make the factual determination, not the judge."

"Your Honor," Theo said, "in that case, we request the court allow us to reopen our case and offer the DNA results into evidence. It is after-acquired evidence and evidence that could have a bearing on the outcome of the case."

Ducky looked at Hammond. Hammond sat tapping his pen against his copy of the lab report before declaring, "The people do not object."

Ducky then nodded and declared: "Since it's the end of the week, I will have Thelma contact the jurors and have them report for duty Monday at nine. Mr. Raddison, the defense will have the opportunity to present the DNA evidence first thing Monday when we reconvene. Please have your witnesses available to avoid any further delay. After you have concluded, we will proceed to closing arguments."

Theo rushed back to his office and had Esther prepare subpoenas for Mitchell Keeler, Larry Branson, Loraine Desmond and Autumn Walters for the following Monday at 9:00. He didn't think he'd need all four, but subpoenaed all of those involved in the chain of custody "just in case."

◆◆◆◆◆

NOT KNOWING HOW much longer I will remain a free man, Charlie and I plan our weekend. We are still very cautious about being seen together, so Charlie rented some movies, shopped for an assortment of delectable meal preparations and ensured we had enough wine to tide us over. All-in-all, it would have been a perfect weekend if not for the dark cloud of uncertainty looming over my head.

"Hey, don't be so glum, chum," Charlie teased. "With 'Karma's testimony', I don't see how the jury can convict."

"I do," I said. "I've spent enough time with juries to realize you can never predict what they'll do. It boils down to one's point of view. Kinda like having witnesses describe a suspect. If you have three witnesses, you will probably have three entirely different descriptions."

"I know that, silly. What I'm saying is your case has become much better with the DNA evidence." Charlie pauses. "Is Willy still making his courtroom appearances?"

"Yes. He's usually there every day, all day. I'm hoping the recent events didn't scare him off. If he shows up Monday, I'll let the guards know since there is an APB out for his arrest."

I've known Charlie long enough to recognize that mischievous glint in her eyes—I now detect her 'tell', as we say in poker. I love the way she segway's into whatever mischief she's planning and I wait in excited expectation until she finally says, "In the meantime..." She takes me by the hand and leads me to that other place. Charlie is sweet surrender. For the rest of the weekend, I shut out everything extrinsic. Charlie has become my only world.

◆◆◆◆◆

ANOTHER MONDAY DAWNED cold and dreary. I was eager to get to court to see if Willy would show up and was disappointed that he had not. Slimy bastard that he is, he probably figured something was going on and something not to his liking.

Theo's presentation of the DNA evidence was cut and dried. The witnesses were professional and believable. The officers testified to delivering the preserved evidence to the lab and the technicians testified as to how the test was conducted and what the results revealed. The jurors gasped when they learned the identity of the person to whom the DNA belonged. Theo, through his questioning, made sure the jury understood it was not my DNA.

When Ducky invited Hammond to cross examine each witness, Hammond responded, "We have no questions, Your Honor."

The judge looked at each of the attorneys before asking, "Are each of you ready to present your final arguments?"

"Yes, Your Honor," Hammond responded. "The prosecution is ready."

Theo answered, "Yes, Your Honor. The defense is also ready for final arguments."

Ducky looks at his watch. "Since it's close to lunch time, we will adjourn for lunch and reconvene promptly at 1:30 at which time we will proceed with the people's opening argument. Accordingly, we will adjourn for lunch and reconvene at one-thirty. Bailiff, please escort the jury to lunch and have them back in the jury room no later than one-fifteen."

When we leave the courtroom, Theo turns his cell phone on and looks at his messages.

"That's odd," he says. "I have a message from Detective Whitaker."

"WHAT!" I respond. "Maybe she has a lead on McCrombie."

Theo is a jump ahead of me and has the phone to his ear waiting for Charlie to answer.

"Yes, hello, Charlie. This is Theo."

He listens, then says, "That's fantastic. How soon can we…Oh, I see. You're already on it."

He listens again, then, "Charlie, we reconvene at one-thirty…Okay, I see. Keep me posted." He shuts his phone and tucks it in the inside pocket of his suit coat.

I can no longer stand the suspense. "WHAT? What did she say!"

"Well, apparently, Mrs. Rothburg was in court this morning. Probably waiting for you to get your ass kicked. However, after our DNA presentation, she left the courtroom and called Charlie."

"Okay, go on…"

"She told Charlie that Phillip suddenly had a recollection of the man he saw at the park and wanted to look at the pictures again."

"Un-huh…"

"Charlie said she was on her way to the Rothburgs' as we spoke. If the kid makes an ID, we'll seek the court's permission to have him take the stand. My fear is Ducky is going to get tired of our last-minute Perry Mason tactics."

"Too bad. You know full-well that in the judicial process, credible evidence is allowed at any juncture during the trial; even after the trial if crucial evidence becomes available and could not have reasonably been discerned previously."

"That's true." Theo pauses. "I may need a continuance to prep the kid. What time is it, anyway?"

"Twelve-o-five," I say. "We have almost an hour and a half before court reconvenes. Think Charlie can get the job done."

"Don't know. Hope so." Theo runs his hand through his hair. "Let's go to the office and make preparations—just in case. I'll call Esther and have her pick up some sandwiches."

Twenty minutes later, Charlie calls Theo once again.

"Hello."

"Theo, I'm at the Rothburgs'. Phillip identified Willy McCrombie as the man who put the handkerchief in the storm drain."

"Great news." Theo gives me the thumbs up. "Charlie, bring the kid and mom to my office, pronto!"

"Will do. We're on our way."

Theo, Ray, Esther and I are gathered in Theo's office. The wait is unbearable not knowing whether all of this will have been in vain. Every few moments I look at my watch. I wonder why it is taking them so long. Finally, we hear the clatter of heels clicking against the polished wood of Theo's outer office. Theo slings the door open and Charlie, Phillip and Helen Rothburg are ushered in. I glance once again at my watch: one-twenty. We have ten minutes.

"Good work, Charlie," Theo says with a twinkle. "Hello, Mrs. Rothburg. Thank you for coming forward." Theo extends his hand to Phillip. "And thank you as well, young man."

Charlie meets my gaze and smiles. I return the smile. To the trained eye, there were more than smiles transmitted across the room. I resist the urge to go to Charlie and embrace her, but realized that might be ill-advised.

"We don't have time to waste," Theo says. "We'll take my car, but Tony you drive. I want to prepare our witnesses for their testimony on the way."

Like bats outta hell, we all race out to Theo's Escalante and pile in. By the time we reach the courthouse, Theo has prepared Phillip and Mrs. Rothburg for their testimony. He requests that they wait in the corridor along with Charlie, who beat us to the courthouse. Theo and I enter the courtroom, albeit, just a bit late. The jury has not yet been seated, probably waiting for the go-ahead by the bailiff.

"Well, Mr. Raddison, what's your excuse this time?" Ducky demands as he folds his arms and looks sternly at us.

"May we approach?" Theo asks.

Ducky jerks his glasses from his face in a show of agitation. "If you must," he says in a snarky voice and gestures for the attorneys to come forward.

When they are all at the bench, the judge says in a condescending tone, "Okay…we're waiting,"

"Your Honor, we have additional witnesses. They have been endorsed, but because of extenuating circumstances, they were not called at our initial presentation."

"Be more specific, please."

Theo turns to Hammond. "You may remember the police report indicates that a five-year old boy, Phillip Rothburg, retrieved some items from a storm drain in the park. They turned out to have been stolen from Judge Facinni's home. The lad related that, while he was playing in the park, he watched a man secrete the items in the drain. After the man left, Phillip retrieved the items from the storm drain and later showed them to his mother." Theo paused, apparently thinking about his next statement. Then he continued. "A ring bearing the judicial emblem," Theo gestures toward Ducky's ring, "much like the one you're wearing, Judge, was among the recovered items. The ring had Antonio Facinni's name engraved on the inside. Mrs. Rothburg contacted Judge Facinni and invited him to come to her home to collect the items, which incidentally, have already been entered into evidence." Theo points to the table where all the admitted evidence is neatly and systematically arranged.

"Detective Whitaker accompanied my client to collect his belongings. She asked Mrs. Rothburg if it would be okay to bring back a photo lineup for Phillip to view in an effort to see if he could identify the person who had placed the items in the drain. Mrs. Rothburg gave her permission to do so. When Detective Whitaker returned, she said she felt hostility from the Rothburgs. At that time, Detective Whitaker was unable to get Phillip or his mother to cooperate. Detective Whitaker later said it was obvious that Phillip wanted to cooperate, but was prevented from doing so by his mother. Detective Whitaker said she was so convinced that she advised Mrs. Rothburg of the consequences of interfering with an official investigation."

"Okay," Hammond says, "how is that relevant at this point."

"Well, apparently Mrs. Rothburg was present today during our DNA presentation. When she realized that there possibly was another suspect, she became concerned that she had made a terrible mistake by encouraging Phillip not to attempt to identify the man in the photo lineup. Her conscience apparently got the better of her. She called Detective Whitaker and asked her to bring the photo lineup for Phillip to view. Although Mrs. Rothburg did not admit to interference, she said she is prepared to accept whatever punishment the court imposes for her role in causing a perceived court delay.

"This all happened during the lunch break. When Detective Whitaker showed Phillip the lineup, she was able to get a positive identification. The man he identified was Wilber McCrombie. She telephoned me and also attempted to reach Sgt. Slater in an effort to reveal the change of events. Although she left a message for Sgt. Slater, he never returned the call."

Hammond whips around and glares at Slater. Slater just shrugs his shoulders.

Theo continues, "Because of the time constraint, I asked Detective Whitaker to bring the witnesses in for an interview, which she did. Your Honor, I have both Mrs. Rothburg and Phillip waiting in the corridor. They are willing to testify. In the interest of justice, I request you allow them to do so."

Theo told me later that he saw that "overturned on appeal" look cross Ducky's face just before he said, "I'll allow it."

"Your Honor, all of these theatrics are…" Hammond interjected.

"I said I will allow it, Mr. Hammond: there is no reason not to."

Theo returns to our table with a broad grin on his face. I begin to think maybe we can win.

◆◆◆◆◆

MRS. ROTHBURG IS called to the stand first. After the swearing-in, she sits rigid in the chair on the witness stand. Theo begins.

"Mrs. Rothburg, will you explain to the jury exactly what happened to bring us to this time and place?"

Mrs. Rothburg is determined. She does not flinch. Her testimony mirrors what Theo had outlined to the judge and the prosecution. Hammond waives cross-examination.

Theo then calls Phillip to the stand, but, before Mrs. Rothburg is excused, Theo asks the court: "Your Honor, in light of our next witness' age, we would request that his mother be allowed to remain in the courtroom during Phillip's testimony so that he is less traumatized."

"Mr. Hammond?" the judge asks.

"The people have no objection," Hammond replies.

"Your request is granted. Mrs. Rothburg, please take a seat in the front row directly behind the defense table."

Mrs. Rothburg leans over as she passes Theo and whispers, "Thank you."

The bailiff escorts Phillip in. Mrs. Rothburg reaches out and touches his arm as he passes. I notice the jury is very attentive as the five year old enters the courtroom, takes the oath and sits on the edge of the chair on the witness stand. That's a plus. Usually by this time of day the jurors are anxious for the day to end.

Phillip is sworn in by using a simplified version of the oath. He holds his hand up high above his head mimicking Ducky and nods his head when asked if he will tell the truth. The judge is kind and says, "Phillip, you need to say your answers aloud so everyone can hear them."

Phillip responds, although in a weak voice, "Okay."

Theo had established a repport with Phillip on the ride to the courthouse, and Phillip seems to relax when Theo rises and approaches the podium. Mrs. Rothburg is sitting directly in the boy's line of vision and I sense this also comforts the child.

"So Phillip, do you like to go to the park with your mother?"

Phillip is direct with his answers.

"Yes."

"Do you go there a lot?"

"Sometimes."

"What is your favorite thing to do at the park?"

"Play with other kids."

"Okay. What games do you play with the other kids?"

"U-m-m, I like hide-'n-seek the best."

"Hide-'n-seek. Were you playing hide-'n-seek when you saw the man hide something in the storm drain?"

"Yes."

"Then what did you do?"

"Well," Phillip looks at his mother who nods slightly. "After the man left, I went to the storm drain and found the thing he was hiding."

"I see. And what was that thing?"

"A hanky."

"A hanky. Tell me what the hanky looked like."

"It was white with some writing on the corner."

Theo goes to the evidence table and picks up the plastic bag containing the handkerchief, ring and cuff links. He holds it up and asks Phillip, "Is this the hanky?"

Phillip adjusts his dark rimmed glasses and examines the handkerchief,

"Yes."

"Did you look inside the hanky after you took it from the storm drain?"

"Yes."

"And what did you find?"

"Some stuff."

"What kind of stuff?"

"A ring and some links."

"I see. What exactly are 'links'?"

"Mommy said men use them to keep their cuffs together."

"Un-huh. I had some of those once upon a time." Theo pauses. "You doing okay, Phillip? Need a drink or something?" Phillip shakes his head.

The judge says, "Please say 'yes' or 'no', Phillip."

Phillip looks up at the judge and says, "No."

Theo continues, "Okay, Phillip, then what did you do?"

"When we came home, I hid them under my bed," Phillip steals a quick glance at his mother before he continues. "After dinner I got scared I would be in trouble so I took them to Mommy."

"Is that when your mother called Judge Facinni and told him you had found some property that belonged to him?"

"Ye..."

"OBJECTION! Leading the witness." Farnsworth shouts. I watch Phillip shrink back further into his chair, his face wrought with fear. At the same time, Hammond shoots Farnsworth a scathing glance.

"Mr. Farnsworth, you know full well child witnesses are questioned differently, and some leading questions are permitted. Objection overruled. Continue, Mr. Raddison."

"Thank you, Your Honor." Theo looks at Phillip and asks, "Then what happened?"

Phillip squirms in the chair, probably still unnerved by Farnsworth's interruption. He is obviously on pins and needles anyway. Mrs. Rothburg nods at him and he seems to relax a bit. "Well, then Mr. Cinni came to our house and Mommy gave him the stuff. They asked if I would know the man if I saw him again."

"They? Who were 'they'?'"

"Mr. Cinni and the nice lady."

"Okay. What nice lady?"

"Charlie. She came with Mr. Cinni."

"Un-huh, I see. What did you tell them when they asked if you thought you could recognize the man?"

"I said I think so, but he was scary." Phillip's voice shakes as he asks, "Please, may I have a drink?"

The judge pours a half glass of water and hands it down to Phillip. "Here you go, young man."

"Thank you," Phillip takes the proffered glass and sips at it a couple of times.

"You okay, now?" Theo asks.

"Yes, sir." Phillip says as he stands and hands the glass back up to the judge. The judge nods to Theo to continue.

"Then what happened—after you said you thought you would know the man if you saw his picture?"

"Well, they left, and later Charlie came with some pictures."

"Was that the same day?"

"No. Two days after." Phillip fidgets again before saying, "Mommy told me she was coming and it would be best for me not to tell which one it was."

"I see. Then what happened?"

"When Charlie showed me the pictures, I fibbed and said I didn't know."

"Okay. Now, jumping ahead a few weeks, Phillip, what happened that you 'remembered' what the man looked like?"

"Well, today, Charlie came back with the same pictures. That's when Mommy said I could pick out the one I thought was the man."

"And did you?"

"Yes."

Theo walks back to the podium and picks up a file, "I'm going to show you the pictures again and ask that you point to the man you saw hide the stuff in the storm drain."

Phillip shifts in his chair, "He scares me."

Theo says, "I know, but he isn't here and he can't hurt you." Theo spreads the photographs that constitute the line-up on the railing separating the witness stand from the court-room and steps back. "If you see his picture, would you please point to it?"

Phillip looks at his mother for a brief instant and she nods her head. Phillip does not hesitate; he points to Wil-ber McCrombie.

"Let the record reflect that the witness picked photo num-ber three, that of Wilber McCrombie." Theo steps forward and collects the lineup and hands it to the clerk who in turn hands it to Ducky. "The defense offers Defense Exhibit #38 in evi-dence," Theo announces.

"Any objection?" Ducky asks Hammond.

"No objection," Hammond states in a shaky voice.

"Very well. Defense Exhibit #38 is admitted."

"We have no further questions of this witness," Theo announces.

Looking at Hammond and extending an open hand in his direction, Ducky asks, "Does the prosecution wish to cross-examine?"

"Yes, Your Honor," Hammond responds as he rises and adjusts his suit coat. "Good afternoon, Phillip. My name is Edi-son Hammond. I understand you like to play hide-'n-seek. Is that correct?" the prosecutor asks as he walks toward Phillip.

"Yes." Phillip scoots back further in his chair, apparently distancing himself from Hammond . His legs stick straight out in front of him emphasizing his smallness in comparison to the imposing, straight-backed oak witness chair.

"Do you wear your glasses when you're playing?"

"Yes," Phillip responds and awkwardly positions his glasses closer to his eyes.

"So, you were wearing your glasses on the day you say you saw the scary man hide the handkerchief? Is that correct?"

In my peripheral vision, I see Mrs. Rothburg fidgeting. She obviously does not like the direction this is heading.

"Yes."

"How close were you to the man when you observed his actions?"

Phillip looks around and then points to where his mother is sitting.

Hammond turns and steps off the distance before saying, "Let the record reflect approximately 20 or 25 feet away."

"It will," Ducky says.

"Now, tell me, Phillip, that man standing there in the back by the door," Hammond turns and points, "what color is his hair?"

"Objection," Theo interposes. "The distance to the door is more than double…"

"Overruled, I'll allow the boy to answer. Go ahead, Phillip, answer the question."

Phillip looks up and immediately says, "Brown."

I look back at the security guard standing by the door. His hair is brownish-blond.

"You're sure?"

Phillip looks again, "Yes."

I notice a smirk cross Hammond's face as he asks permission to see the guards' driver's license. It is granted and the judge instructs the guard to produce his driver's license. The guard, Randy Chase, comes forward and hands it to the judge. After Ducky inspects the license, he hands it to Hammond who examines the license, then blanches. Apparently the driver's license lists 'Bro' as the color of his hair.

Hammond seems to be at a loss for words. After a moment, he stammers, "Thank you, Randy," and hands the license back.

"Well," Ducky says to Hammond, "are you going to share the color of the deputy's hair listed on the driver's license with the jury?"

Obviously embarrassed, Hammond says, "Brown." Then he adds, "No further questions, Your Honor."

"Phillip, you may go sit with your mother," Ducky says with a smile and a bow.

Guess the DA forgot it's never a good idea to pick on kids. I'm buoyed beyond belief. *Maybe, just maybe... Thank you, God!*

"We'll take a fifteen minute break before proceeding," Ducky announces.

I can't remember how long we've been sitting, but my legs seem to have forgotten how to support me when I stand. I groan and stretch, then make a break for the men's room. As I exit the courtroom, I see Charlie standing in the corridor with Mrs. Rothburg and Phillip. I give Charlie a thumbs-up; she smiles and nods in reply.

PART FOUR

THE
NAME

CHAPTER

11

Before we left Theo's office on our mad rush to make it to court on time with our two witnesses in tow, Theo instructed Esther to prepare another Motion to Dismiss, with orders to deliver it to him at the courthouse. However, pursuant to the judge's orders, the security guards are required to exclude spectators from portions of the proceedings to protect the child witness. When Esther arrives, she is detained and now sits waiting on the wooden bench in the corridor. The jury has not yet been brought back into the courtroom from the break. Theo, realizing Esther has been waiting for him outside the courtroom with his second Motion to Dismiss, takes a quick look at his watch. "Your Honor, I'm expecting a delivery from my office. May I have a minute?"

"Yes—but just *one minute,*" Ducky answers.

Theo rises, strides to the rear of the courtroom and silently slips out. He is back in less than a minute. He pauses by the defense table just long enough to scribble his name on the motion and a copy.

"Your Honor, may I approach?"

"You may."

Theo steps forward and hands the motion to the judge. He then walks to the prosecution table and hands the signed copy to Hammond. I watch the judge glance at the motion and then set it aside. "Mr. Raddison," he says, "the court still maintains its position to let the jury decide the case. Your motion, therefore, is denied on its face."

Theo, still standing, appears as though he was expecting the ruling and responds, "Yes, Your Honor." As Theo takes his seat, I notice a smug look cross Hammond's face.

"Any more issues to address before I instruct the bailiff to bring in the jury?" Ducky asks.

"No, Your Honor," Hammond and Theo say simultaneously.

"In that case, we will begin final arguments as soon as I instruct the jury on the law and provide them with a written copy of the jury instructions."

I lean back in my chair trying to relax and prepare myself for the upcoming onslaught. *Welp, here we go, God help us.*

♦♦♦♦♦

AFTER THE JURY has been instructed, Ducky says, "Mr. Hammond, is the prosecution ready to present its opening argument?"

"Yes, Your Honor," Hammond replies.

Hammond appears to have recovered somewhat from his embarrassment as he rises and saunters forward. He briefly stops at the table displaying the trial exhibits and repositions several before continuing to the podium. He has with him a black three-ring binder. The podium, previously facing the witness stand, has been rearranged and now faces the jury.

"Ladies and gentlemen," he begins as he attempts to locate the right page in his binder, "eight weeks ago, I told you that the prosecution would prove to you, *beyond a reasonable doubt*, that the defendant, Antonio Facinni, is indeed guilty of the murders with which he is charged in this action." Hammond abruptly turns and jabs a finger in my direction. "And," he continues, "we are asking you to find him guilty of each and every count."

This time, however, I expect it so I remain stoic and do not react. Theo glances at me. I notice a trace of a smile on his face. Hammond looks disappointed as he turns back to the jury. "It is the prosecution that bears the burden of proof and the prosecution that is required to prove beyond a reasonable doubt that the accused is responsible for perpetrating the crimes charged in the Information. Now, it is your duty, if the evidence warrants it, to return four guilty verdicts." Hammond frantically searches for the right page in his binder, finally exchanges it for the binder handed to him by Farnsworth.

Theo scribbles on his legal pad which he pushes in my direction: *I've never seen Hammond so flustered. He's having difficulty finding his pace.*

Judging from the looks on his and Slater's faces, it appears they recognize they have a chink in their armor and realize they are prosecuting the wrong man. I scribble and push the legal pad back in front of Theo. Theo nods as Hammond finds the right page in the right trial notebook.

"We, the prosecution," Hammond plods on, "assert that we have proven our case beyond a reasonable doubt. It should be crystal clear to you, the jury, that the defendant had the motive, opportunity and means to carry out these heinous crimes." Hammond obviously borrowed a line out of Theo's earlier argument to Ducky. "Now, let's dissect each murder piece-by-piece in order to help you eliminate *any doubt*, much less *reasonable doubt*, you may be harboring concerning the defendant's guilt.

"As you are aware by now, Judge Facinni's novels were published in the following order: *Fair Game*, victim number one was poisoned with cyanide; *Fool's Game*, victim number two was shot multiple times; *Skin Game*, victim number three was stabbed with a hunting knife, and *End Game*, victim number four died after the brake line on his vehicle had been severed.

"Although the animal cruelty charge isn't on its face even close to the gravity of the three murders, it does, however, go to the mindset of the defendant. By comparing the murders with Judge Facinni's novels, my intent is to prove to you how Judge Facinni's arrogance emboldened him to move forward and commit these crimes. Once again, I remind you that the prosecution has argued throughout this trial that Judge Facinni's *motive* was to generate publicity and increase the sale of his novels—novels that served as a flowchart for his murderous actions.

"The defense argues that the defendant's novels have been on the best-seller list for weeks and it is, therefore, preposterous to suggest he would go to such lengths to promote greater sales. The opposite is true. A man with Judge Facinni's ambition is not content with staying at one level. He always has his sights on the next level and will do everything he can not only to reach that level but to stay there. What better way is there for a celebrity to remain in the public eye than to create the sensational. For Judge Facinni it was to transform his fictional crimes into the real thing."

◆◆◆◆◆

THE DISTRICT ATTORNEY drones on for over an hour explaining how I perpetrated the crimes. He clicks them off on his fingers one-by-one as he proceeds. In essence, his narration consists of:

"Next, we discuss the *opportunity* Judge Facinni had with each of the four victims named in the four counts. Victim number one, Karma, of course, was an easy target since she lived in the same household as Judge Facinni. The cause of death was cyanide, the same as that in Judge Facinni's first novel.

"Victim number two, Leonard Wycowski, a close friend of Judge Facinni's was lured to the Judge's home under the pretext of watching a football game. Guess *how* he was killed. He was shot multiple times with a .22 caliber handgun just like the victim in Judge Facinni's second novel. Guess *where* he was killed. Actually, you already know the answer: in an alcove just outside Judge Facinni's apartment building. How convenient was that? The judge didn't have to leave his property to commit the murder. If he was spotted at the scene, it was because he lived there. Again, how convenient! And wasn't it convenient that Judge Facinni owns a .22 caliber handgun but the gun mysteriously vanished just after Leonard Wycowski's murder?

"Victim number three was Doreen Lancaster, a court clerk who had worked for Judge Facinni for over twenty-five years. He, of course, knew where Doreen Lancaster lived and knew she lived alone. He would obviously have been deemed harmless and been invited into her residence without any hesitation. How was she killed? You heard the evidence. She was killed by a hunting knife with an elks head etched in the handle, just like the one in Judge Facinni's third novel. We will never know whether Judge Facinni deliberately or inadvertently left his tie tack at the scene of the crime. It is really unimportant why it was left at the scene; only that it was.

"Judge Facinni's fourth victim was his own attorney, Jeffery Wilkinson. Remember he was killed in an automobile accident shortly after leaving the parking garage at Judge Facinni's upscale apartment building. It was later determined that the brake line on Jeffery Wilkinson's vehicle had been cut, presumably while he dined with Judge Facinni in the judge's apartment. Do you think it's a coincidence that the manner in which JefferyWilkinson died is the same as that in Judge Facinni's fourth novel? Hopefully, that supposition was dispelled by the discovery of Judge Facinni's thumbprint on the undercarriage of Jeffery Wilkinson's vehicle.

"You've heard twelfth-hour testimony from Phillip, a five-year old boy, who says he saw a man hide items belonging to Judge Facinni in a sewer drain in the park many months ago." Hammond strolls to the evidence table and holds up the plastic bag marked Prosecution Exhibit #45. He turns it over in his hands examining the contents before replacing the bag on the table.

"Phillip had a fleeting glance at a 'scary man' over four months ago from a distance of more than twenty feet. Well, I ask you, how many of us would be able to identify a stranger we had a chance glance at from that distance four months after the fact? Toss in the boy's fear factor, that the individual was 'scary', and that leaves you to doubt that the identification was even close to being accurate." Hammond rubs his chin and pauses for a moment before continuing. "The defense's explanation for Phillip's delay in coming forward is that his mother didn't want him to become involved. Quite obviously, the person Phillip identified from the photo lineup is still out there. If his mother didn't want her son to be exposed to danger, then why would she have a so-called last-minute attack of conscience and put her son on the hot seat? I don't have a viable answer to that question. I leave it up to you to decide the truthfulness of the Rothburgs' testimonies. My mind is still boggled trying to figure it out.

"So you see, ladies and gentlemen, this isn't rocket science. Judge Facinni is either completely insane or very brilliant." Hammond turns to me and stares for what seems like an eternity. I watch the jurors' eyes follow his gaze. He turns back to the jury and states, "Judge Facinni, a retired lawyer and jurist, and of late, a best-selling author, it appears, has outwitted himself. He's tittering on the edge and the criminal justice system is not designed to provide him with the proverbial golden parachute."

Hammond then makes a show of gathering up his binder and other notes. "I promised you in my opening remarks that I would prove to you Judge Facinni's guilt *beyond a reasonable doubt.* I have fulfilled my promise. Mr. Raddison will now try to convince you otherwise. I know you're intelligent enough not to fall for the defense's distorted version of the facts. The burden of proof is on the prosecution, so at the end of Mr. Raddison's statements, we will be allowed rebuttal argument, at which time we will address and discredit the defense's theories. Thank you for your attention."

I notice, and I'm sure the jury does too, Hammond doesn't mention the DNA match nor does he offer an alternative explanation as to how Phillip was able to pick Willy from the lineup. And of course, he chose to ignore the embarrassing fact that Phillip could make accurate observations even at great distances.

As Hammond takes his seat, I check my watch. It's 3:00 o'clock. Ducky clears his throat before saying, "We will take a break and reconvene at 3:15 at which time we will continue with defense's final argument followed by the prosecution's rebuttal argument, if any." He looks at Theo for confirmation and Theo nods his head.

"The defense will be ready, Your Honor."

"Bailiff, escort the jury out. Have them back at precisely 3:15."

I involuntarily jump as Ducky bangs his gavel punctuating his decree. *Wish the judge wouldn't do that. I'm racked up enough without those sudden, irritating, loud noises.* Theo reaches over and squeezes my arm. "Hammond's argument was lackluster and packed the sting of a gnat." I nod but am not sure I totally agree.

Theo pushes his chair back and says as he stands, "Come on, Tony, loosen up. It's not over 'till it's over. Ducky instructed the jurors to keep an open mind and we have to do the same thing."

◆◆◆◆◆

WHEN THE ROTHBURGS finished testifying and Ducky released them, Charlie took them home. She did not make it back in time to hear Hammond's opening argument. She, however, was waiting in the courtroom when we returned from the break. We make eye contact but do not speak. It reassures me to just have her present.

After the formalities, the judge nods to Theo to begin his final argument. Theo rises, adjusts the jacket of, what appears to me to be at least a thousand dollar three-piece dark blue suit, and takes the podium. Every hair of his stylish cut is in place and his blue eyes sparkle with the hidden excitement he must be experiencing. Theo is truly in his element. This is now his show and he's the ring master. There is an aura of confidence surrounding him, and just watching him makes me absorb some of that confidence. I notice that some of the jurors are already leaning forward.

"Good afternoon," Theo begins, looking very relaxed as he flashes that winning smile at the jury. "Well, here we are at the end of the saga." Theo pauses for a brief instant and looks toward the prosecution's table, then says, "Mr. Hammond's statements were quite convincing. However, they were lacking."

I notice Hammond squirm in his seat.

"Reasonable doubt, ladies and gentlemen, means a *real* doubt, a doubt you may have based upon reason and common sense that arises from a careful review of the evidence or the *lack* of sufficient evidence in this case. It is such a doubt as would cause a reasonable person to hesitate and pause in important transactions in his or her life. As the jury instructions have indicated, there is a level of certainty you must reach in order to find Judge Facinni guilty. Now, I ask you, is it reasonable that a man of Judge Facinni's background and prominence would jeopardize all that and his future by engaging in the criminal acts charged? ABSOLUTELY NOT!" I watch several of the jurors jerk when Theo raises his voice. Now that he has their undivided attention, he continues, "Not only would he jeopardize his legacy, freedom and eternal salvation, but he also would have betrayed his innate personal convictions. In the immortal words of Shakespeare, 'to thine own self be true...'"

Pretty theatrical, but it appears to be working. The jurors began to lean forward, their eyes are riveted on Theo as he proceeds.

"Judge Facinni," Theo says sweeping his hand in my direction, "served the people of the state of New York for close to three decades. During that time, Judge Facinni was never overturned on appeal. What that means is that his decisions were informed, justified and fair. And when challenged, they were upheld by the appellate courts. My client would not compromise his integrity for a 'moment in the sun.' He would not throw his whole life away or sell his soul for a few months of publicity. And he certainly would not kill those whose lives he cherished."

I look back at Charlie. She does not see me; she is staring at Theo obviously caught up in the mood. That's a good sign, a very good sign. I direct my attention back to Theo as well.

"You heard testimony from experts regarding DNA collected from the claws of Karma and examined by an independent laboratory. The experts in the field determined that the DNA matched that of the alternate suspect, Willy McCrombie. Granted, finding the DNA of Willy McCrombie, a man who Judge Facinni sentenced for murder and a man who vowed vengeance, under Karma's claws isn't enough to link him to the actual murders of three human beings. However, it does implicate him as a burglar who had the means, motive and opportunity to steal Judge Facinni's gun and jewelry — jewelry that was recovered from the hand of Doreen Lancaster at the scene of her murder and from a sewer drain by five year old Phillip Rothburg. Didn't you find it odd that Mr. Hammond, the district attorney, failed to mention those very significant facts in his opening argument?"

Theo pauses a few moments, then continues, "I ask you to recall Detective Charlie Whitaker's testimony. Detective Whitaker is a seasoned investigator who has dealt with criminals from all walks of life during her stellar career as a law enforcement officer. Remember, she was a witness called by the prosecution and her testimony was unshakable, which is not surprising. We all store information we collect on our journey through life. For example, a mother instinctively knows when her child is lying — even if the child's hand isn't in the proverbial cookie jar. A wife can tell from her husband's face when he comes home what kind of day he's had — good or bad. A teacher knows, almost from the first day of class, how well a student is going to perform. It's innate. It's built into our psyche. So, when Detective Whitaker testified that seeing Judge Facinni's reaction to finding his dead cat, she was convinced his shock and horror were genuine."

Theo looks at each juror before continuing. "Now, ladies and gentlemen, we'll do what the prosecution did and analyze the murders piece-by-piece in an effort to determine whether it was likely the perpetrator was Judge Facinni.

"Victim number one." Theo gazes briefly in the direction of the prosecution table and then back at the jury. "When the prosecutor referred to Karma as the 'deceased,' remember him smiling? Did you notice Judge Facinni didn't find it at all amusing? In fact, he hung his head, didn't he? Virtually every juror nods. "How many of you have or have had a pet? Raise your hands, please." All twelve jurors raise their hands and I notice Theo has them in the palm of *his* hands. "Absolutely! So do I. We live in a nation of compassionate people and cringe when we see someone mistreating a pet, or for that matter, any animal. We even go so far as to call Animal Control to report the misconduct. When our pets become sick or injured and there is no hope for recovery, we do the humane thing and have them put down to alleviate their suffering. Right?" All of the jurors nod their heads.

"Cyanide poisoning is a terrible way to die. Some would say, 'what's the big deal, it was just a cat.' You know in your hearts that your pet is not 'just a cat or just a dog or just a canary.' Your pet is a member of your family and you love that creature. Now, I appeal to your common sense. Even though Karma was just a cat, do you believe Judge Facinni would deliberately poison his pet, a pet he has loved and cared for for twelve years, and subject her to a horrific death to generate publicity?" Theo slaps the podium, "Of course he wouldn't, nor would any of you."

Wow! What a great approach. My opinion of Theo shoots to the top of the respect meter. Theo grips the sides of the podium with his hands and leans forward. I watch the jury follow his every movement with their eyes. I, too, am mesmerized.

"That brings us to victim number two, Leonard Wycowski. Len, that's what Judge Facinni fondly called him. Len was a childhood friend. The two were classmates during their grade and high school years. After graduating high school, they continued to stay in touch even though they pursued different careers. Judge Facinni pursued the law eventually earning his *Juris Doctorate* while Len joined the New York Police Department and worked his way up the ladder eventually becoming the Chief of Detectives. Because they were both in the legal field, their paths crossed often. In fact, in the murder prosecution over which Judge Facinni presided involving Wilber McCrombie, Leonard Wycowski was the key witness for the prosecution.

"The day Len was murdered, he telephoned Judge Facinni and they talked about 'Willy' McCrombie having been released from prison. Their concern was that Willy had threatened each of them as he was being led from the courtroom some twenty years ago. Judge Facinni had imposed a twenty-to-life sentence on Willy after a jury found him guilty of first degree murder. Remember several prosecution witnesses testifying that that was what they were told when they interviewed Judge Facinni?

"During the call, Judge Facinni invited Len to join him for beer and football. Judge Facinni told the police officers, when he was interviewed, that Len excitedly accepted and said he would be there within twenty minutes or so. Judge Facinni waited, but when after a few hours Len hadn't shown up, he telephoned the police to report Len as a missing person.

"Once again, I call upon you to exercise your common sense. Would that have been the act of a person who had just shot and killed someone outside his own apartment building, someone he considered a lifelong friend? NO! Of course not!"

Theo is on a roll. I watch the jurors carefully. They barely move and appear to be hypnotized not just by what he says but by the tone of his voice.

"However, ladies and gentlemen, it is likely Willy McCrombie, a convicted burglar, was the one who burglarized Judge Facinni's apartment and stole his .22 caliber handgun. If Willy was intent on carrying out his twenty-year-old threat, wouldn't it be reasonable to assume he would be staking out my client's home and mentally cataloging his comings and goings? That would put him in the vicinity of the alcove where the body of Len Wycowski was later discovered, riddled with bullets — bullets later determined to have come from the same caliber weapon stolen during the burglary of Judge Facinni's apartment. Can you imagine Willy's excitement when his prey appeared at the scene of his stakeout? He would kill one of his avowed targets without much effort and pin it on his other avowed target at the same time."

As Theo previously pointed out, life's experiences contribute to our five senses. During my career on the bench, I learned to read people, especially lawyers, and I could tell by Theo's voice and mannerisms that he knew the jury was with him. Without pausing, he went right into his synapsis of the next murder.

"Doreen Lancaster, victim number three. Doreen was Judge Facinni's 'Girl Friday' the whole time he was on the bench. That would be over two and a half decades give or take a year or so. They were not only coworkers; they were friends. My client was a frequent guest at the Lancaster household for dinner and spent many holidays with the Lancasters. In fact, Doreen's daughters called Judge Facinni 'Uncle Tony.' That's how close they were. Thomas Lancaster, Doreen's late husband, played golf with Judge Facinni at the country club on a weekly basis. The Lancasters were Judge Facinni's extended family."

Theo pauses and takes a sip of water before he continues.

"At the risk of sounding monotonous, I'm tapping into your common sense once again and asking you to imagine Judge Facinni actually stabbing Doreen to death. I mean, in your mind's eye, can you visualize the scene? Do you seriously think Judge Facinni's alleged quest for publicity would prompt him to take a hunting knife with a six-inch blade and lay in wait for this helpless widow to come home? Then, when she enters and smiles recognition, do you believe he would grab her and viciously slash her time and time again until her life was snuffed out, then pry her dead fingers open in order to plant the tie tack—another item taken in the burglary of Judge Facinni's apartment—into her lifeless hand? That is unconscionable and too preposterous to even consider. Wouldn't it be more logical that a depraved mind, someone with a grudge to bare, would viciously attack, not only the police officer who testified against him, but the court clerk who was present during his trial, and particularly at his sentencing, and again pin it on the judge who it appears was his primary target? If such a person was bent on vengeance for being incarcerated and wanted the sentencing judge to squirm, what better way than to kill those closest to him, his longtime pet, his longtime friend and his longtime clerk?"

Theo goes to the evidence table and holds up the plastic evidence bags containing the knife and the tie tack. Traces of blood can be seen on both items. I watch some of the jurors blanch and look away.

Now back at the podium, Theo continues, "And ladies and gentlemen, last but certainly not least is victim number four, Jeffery Wilkinson. Mr. Wilkinson was not only Judge Facinni's attorney but also a close friend. According to the statement given to police authorities, when Judge Facinni called Mr. Wilkinson advising him of his situation, Mr. Wilkinson dropped everything to accommodate Judge Facinni's request that he meet him at the police station. When he arrived at the station, he met with Judge Facinni in the interview room. Upon hearing the facts relating to Judge Facinni's detainment, Mr. Wilkinson immediately demanded Judge Facinni be charged or set free. As you will recall from the testimony, Judge Facinni was released. However, Sgt. Slater was determined to build a case against him."

Theo looks again at the prosecution table where Sgt. Slater is seated. Slater does not react and remains stoic. Theo continues.

"Upon release from custody, as Judge Facinni would later tell authorities, and because Judge Facinni did not have his vehicle at the police station, Mr. Wilkinson offered him a lift home. When they arrived, Judge Facinni invited his attorney and friend to stay for breakfast; an invitation Jeff Wilkinson accepted. Over breakfast, the pair discussed the probability that Judge Facinni would be arrested and charged, and they proceeded to plan their strategy if that occurred.

"Now I ask you in all seriousness, do you believe Judge Facinni would excuse himself and race down to the parking garage, cut the brake line on his attorney's vehicle, then race back to his apartment and proceed as if nothing had happened? And don't you think Mr. Wilkinson would become suspicious at his host being gone for such a long period of time. After all, Judge Facinni's apartment is on the eleventh floor as the evidence shows."

Theo pauses. looking pensive, then raises his eyebrows and again gazes at the jury.

"I won't insult your intelligence by asking you to call upon your common sense again, but wouldn't it be more logical that someone who was watching Judge Facinni's comings and goings and seeing him arrive in his attorney's vehicle, and being bent on vengeance, would be the one who cut the brake line on Mr. Wilkinson's vehicle? Wouldn't that be still another way to make one's sentencing judge squirm even more?' One of the female jurors looks down and examines her fingernails. Another folds his arms and nods.

"It is not uncommon for new evidence to surface during trial as happened in this case. However, I'm going to let you in on a secret."

All the jurors strain to listen.

"We rested our case after all the evidence of which we were aware had been presented. At that time both sides had begun to prepare for final arguments. Fortunately, Judge Facinni remembered Karma was a scratcher. She didn't like to be picked up and she would scratch the devil out of anyone who tried — even her master. The material embedded in Karma's claws was then examined. The results were then revealed to you. They verified Willy McCrombie had not only been in Judge Facinni's apartment but that he was the one who poisoned Karma. It follows that the convicted burglar and murderer removed the .22 caliber handgun and personal items that identified their true owner. These he methodically placed so as to appear to have been left at the various crime scenes by his prime target, Judge Facinni."

The jurors eyes are still glued on Theo as he steps in front of the podium.

"The proof was in the pudding when five-year-old Phillip Rothburg testified he witnessed Willy McCrombie dump the unused items belonging to Judge Facinni in the sewer drain.

"We, the defense, get only one crack at final argument. Since the burden of proof is on the prosecution, they now have a second chance to convince you that despite the evidence, they are prosecuting the right man. Remember, it is their duty to seek justice and not a conviction. Fortunately, the criminal justice system has a safety-device in place to make sure an innocent person is not convicted. Ladies and gentlemen, that safety-device is you, the jury."

Theo returns to our table. He places his elbows on the table and rests his chin on his thumbs and index fingers. He glances straight ahead as if in a trance, oblivious as to what is going on around us. Theo gave it his all and I can see that he is calling on a greater power to assist the jury in seeing that justice is done.

The courtroom is still for a long moment. Glancing at the courtroom clock, Ducky finally says: "Mr. Hammond, it is now 4:30. I assume the prosecution's rebuttal argument will exceed thirty minutes. If so, we will adjourn for the day and you can present first thing in the morning." Ducky then lowers his glasses and peers at Hammond. Hammond stands, and shaking his head, responds. "We're estimating that our rebuttal will take more than double that amount of time. To be safe, we would suggest it be continued until tomorrow morning when everyone is fresh."

"Very well," Ducky says. "We will adjourn until 9:00 a.m. tomorrow morning at which time, Mr. Hammond, the prosecution will be prepared for its rebuttal argument. The jury is excused until that time with the usual admonition."

◆◆◆◆◆

WHEN THE COURT reconvenes and the jurors are once again seated, Ducky asks Hammond if he is ready to proceed with his rebuttal argument. Hammond replies in the affirmative and I steel myself for round two. Hammond's second closing is more of the same. It takes him over an hour to go back through and try to twist Theo's words to fit the prosecution's theory. The jurors fidget in their chairs and several are looking in my direction. I avoid eye contact but feel for the first time they are in my corner and are not paying a damn bit of attention to Hammond's rhetoric and speculative meanderings.

"...so in closing, I ask you, ladies and gentlemen, to carefully consider all of the facts presented to you during this trial," Hammond groans. "The real perversion of justice would be for you to acquit Judge Facinni. The prosecution has clearly proven to you, beyond a reasonable doubt, that Judge Facinni is guilty of each and every one of the crimes charged."

Hammond takes a quick look at his notes, and obviously satisfied he has covered all the bases, says, "Thank you again for your service. I trust you'll do the right thing and return verdicts as your consciences dictate."

After Hammond is seated, Ducky announces to the jury, "The case is now concluded and the bailiff will escort you to the jury room where you will deliberate and return your verdicts on the crimes charged. The bailiff will be seated outside the door of the jury room. If you are in need anything, please let him know. He will do everything possible to make sure you are comfortable. Remember, during deliberations you will not be allowed to communicate with the outside world. I would suggest you call your families to let them know you may be detained. The bailiff will then collect your cell phones. "Any questions?" All of the jurors shake their heads. "Good! In that case, the rest of you are asked to remain in the courtroom until after the last juror has exited." After the jury has filed out, Ducky bangs his gavel and says, "Court is now adjourned."

It didn't take long for the courtroom to empty. As Theo and I leave, I notice Charlie standing by the door waiting to hold it open for us. Both Theo and I have our hands full with the trial amenities. I always marvel at the weight of paper. Charlie's eyes transmit optimism as we pass. Instinctively, I wink, transmitting my own yearning, affection and appreciation for her being the glue that has held me together during this whole ordeal.

"Well, Tony, how'd you think it went?" Theo asks as we walk to our respective vehicles. We stop at Theo's Rolls and fill the backseat with our armloads. I know he is interested in my assessment of the case as well as his own performance. Trial lawyers sometimes have an inferiority complex particularly those who are the most gifted and most effective. They always strive to be the best and recognized as such.

Since the case is pretty much out of our hands and the outcome no longer in our control, I feel an indescribable relief and let emotions pent up inside of me find their release, much to my embarrassment. Theo puts his arm around me and I sob as I did the day of my mother's funeral. Then, it was not only for relief because her suffering ended, but of remembrance, resignation, regret, reconciliation and rebirth. In my case, it was only for relief.

Theo removes a monogramed silk handkerchief from his breast pocket, unfolds it and hands it to me. My embarrassment soon turns to humor, and I say, "Didn't know your representation included babysitting, did you? Now I suppose you'll bill me for 'hazard pay.'" We both laugh.

All this has not been easy for Theo either. He says, "I didn't think my question as to how you thought things went would cause my all-time-favorite judge, and now client, to shed tears. Your response is giving me a complex. Remember, you can even claim your Fifth Amendment privilege against self-incrimination as to my questions." Our laugh is now hardier and my tears have subsided for the most part.

"I'll have to revise my assessment of myself as a trial lawyer. After your performance on my behalf, I would have to say I am second best. You were superb. I am normally disappointed and seldom satisfied with outcomes. This is one of those rare times. Guilty or not guilty, I can't see anything we could or should have done differently."

"That's nice of you to say, as your trial skills were always something we fledglings sought to emulate. Your win-loss record speaks for itself."

I think back to numerous times I was in Theo's position. 'Eager' for a favorable verdict as the case went to the jury was not really an apt description as to how I felt. 'Anxious' was a more appropriate term to describe not only how my clients felt, but how I felt as well. A trial lawyer always feels responsible for the outcome — good or bad.

"I can see wheels turning," Theo says. "Are you rethinking our decision not to have you testify? I know you reluctantly agreed, claiming that only guilty men remain silent."

"I thought about that long and hard up to the time of the final arguments," I respond. "In retrospect, it was the right thing to do. Through the cross-examinations of the prosecution witnesses and the direct-examinations of our own witnesses, I told my story. There was little I could have added, other than that I didn't commit the crimes and that was already conveyed by my *not guilty* pleas and statements to the police.

"And, of course, the presumption of innocence," Theo adds.

"Yes, that, too," I say. "I think we caught Hammond off-guard when we rested our case without me testifying. He's known for trying to manipulate witnesses with his cross-examinations, and as you said during our strategy sessions, regardless of how I answered his questions, they would have had a questionable, if not negative, impact. They would have connected me to the incidents. By not testifying, I kept my distance. That also left Hammond without much ammunition in final argument such as challenging my credibility and claiming my statements were self-serving."

"Or impeaching you by prior inconsistent statements," Theo interposes.

"Another reason for me not testifying," I say. "All he could argue was his theory of 'who done it.'" I pause before asking, "Any idea as to how long the jury will be out?"

"Sounds like you're predicting not guilty verdicts," Theo says, raising his eyebrows.

"What do you think?" I ask.

"About your prediction or mine?" he responds.

"About yours," I answer. "You can never second guess a jury as you well know. The one's you think should go a certain way usually go another. If I were a betting man and watching from a distance, I'd say the jury will rule in my favor. The telltale signs were the reactions of the jury during closing arguments. They paid attention to what you had to say and fidgeted when Hammond spoke."

Theo looks thoughtful as he replies, "Several of the jurors made eye contact with me on the way out. That usually is a good sign. As for as my prediction as to when the jury will reach a verdict, I can categorically say it won't be tonight, but sometime close to lunchtime tomorrow."

As I head for my vehicle, I turn and say, "I can't thank you enough. I just hope someday I can return the favor."

"Go home and relax," Theo says. "There's nothing we can do about it now. My gut tells me we have nothing to worry about. I plan on getting a good night's sleep so I am fresh for the not guilty verdicts. Hope you do the same."

◆◆◆◆◆

AS SOON AS I'm sure Charlie has had time to complete her tour of duty, I'm on the phone.

"Hello." I hear excited expectation in her voice." Charlie…" she cuts me off before I finish my sentence.

"Can you come over — right now?"

"Damn straight. Is something wrong?" I ask worried.

"No. I just want to see you."

"I'm out the door."

When Charlie opens her door, I'm engulfed in the fragrance of gardenias and something delicious cooking. My mouth begins to water in anticipation of both. Charlie takes my hand and pulls me forward into the foyer, and kicks the door closed as she envelops me in a tight hug — I hug back. The hug morphs into a passionate kiss, and that sets the tone for the rest of the evening. I never found out what was cooking; it was forgotten soon after that first kiss.

It's dawn when I awake. I open my eyes and stretch. That's when I discover I'm naked. Charlie is still snoozing, so I slip out of bed, grab my clothes and head for the head. I try to be quiet as I get dressed. However, when I look into the mirror, I groan at what stares back at me. "Oh, my God!" I say at my reflection. *The trial has taken its toll on my appearance. I look my father's age and more.* She must have heard me because she calls my name.

"Tony?"

"Yes, love," I answer.

"Come back to bed."

"As much as I'd like to, I can't. I've got to get home and change. We reconvene at nine." I fold my suit jacket over my arm and drape my tie around my neck as I exit the bathroom. When I see Charlie bunched up in the sheet with her raven hair tasseled and sleep still lingering in her eyes, I regret having to leave. I get that funny feeling again and have to fight myself like hell to make it out the bedroom door without succumbing to further temptation.

"What, no kiss goodbye?" she teases.

"Not unless you're prepared to extinguish the four alarm that's still smoldering beneath this calm and collected exterior."

She looks at the clock, "Guess we don't have time...do we?"

"Ah, shucks," I murmer as I jerk off the tie and begin to toss my clothes on a small decorative trunk positioned under the window.

The next rational thing that enters my brain is that its seven thirty and here I am languishing in the euphoria of the most incredible morning of my life.

"Do you always wake up like this?" I ask.

"Like what?" she teases.

"Never mind. There's no way you're going to lure me there again — at least not until tonight. I seriously do have to get going."

Wrapped in a sheet, Charlie walks me to the door. One quick benign kiss and I'm out in the corridor. I break several traffic laws in my manic rush home to prepare for the day. Showered, shaved, and oh yes, dressed, I enter the courtroom just as Ducky takes the bench.

◆◆◆◆◆

"THOUGHT WE'D LOST you," Theo jests. "From the looks of you, I think maybe we did — at least for a few hours."

I shoot him a wry smile. He nods. Our attention is drawn to the bench. Court is called to order. Besides Ducky and his clerk, only Farnsworth, Theo and I are present. Hammond apparently didn't think it important enough to appear. Ducky begins by saying, "Today is Judge Facinni's bond return date and the record will reflect his appearance. Needless to say, the jury has not reached verdicts in the short time it has had to deliberate. Because of the nature of the case and the massive and pervasive publicity it has received, the jury was sequestered for the night and lodged at a local hotel. They were bussed back here at 8:00 a.m. and have been deliberating ever since. Please leave telephone numbers with Thelma so that she can notify you when verdicts have been returned. Then, of course, all of you will need to be present in court. Judge Facinni, your bond will be continued to that time. Unless there are questions, the court will be adjourned."

Both sides say they have none.

Since the courtroom is virtually empty, Ducky abandons banging his gavel and just heads for his chambers.

Once we're outside, Theo says, "Let's go grab breakfast; I'll buy."

I suddenly realize that I'm ravenous. "Where do you want to go?"

"Let's go to Bratton's," Theo responds. "It's just a couple blocks up the up the street."

Bratton's is an upscale restaurant whose patrons are automatically up-sized. As I polish off a supersize Bratton's omelet supreme with potato pancakes, I find Theo staring at me.

Suddenly, I'm embarrassed and pause in the midst of transporting a forkful of potato pancake to my mouth. "Missed dinner and breakfast," I mutter.

"Oh, I see," he says as he shakes his head and raises his eyebrows.

The way he said that made me realize he probably *did* see. Theo knows that my relationship with Charlie is more than casual, though I've never told him and he's never asked. He knows that gentlemen do not talk about such things. I blush and watch Theo pretend not to notice my embarrassment as he pulls his cell phone from his pocket, flips the cover open and examines his messages.

"Anything?" I ask.

"Not yet, but the jury has only been out for a total of about six hours counting yesterday's deliberations."

I cram the remnants of my breakfast into my mouth and wash them down with coffee. I stifle a belch and dab at the corners of my mouth with a cloth napkin which I carefully refold and set next to my plate.

"H-m-m-m, didn't know potato pancakes were such good therapy," I say as we rise to leave. "What now?" I ask. Since I've never been on this side of the coin, I'm at a loss as to what I should be doing and find myself obsessing about the verdicts.

"Don't know about you, but I have a mountain of work waiting for me back at the office. Keep your cell phone handy and I'll call you as soon as I get word. The court has to wait for all parties to be present, so it could take at least a half hour or more for everyone to assemble after we're notified," Theo then adds, "Try not to drift too far away."

We walk back to the courthouse and Theo leaves. I stand in the parking lot looking at the overcast sky and try to think of what I would be doing if all of this hadn't happened. Even though the nightmare has lasted less than a half year, it feels as though I've been in limbo forever. I feel much like I did the day my divorce became final; like a ship adrift without a rudder. I try hard not to allow the circumstances sink me.

My apartment now seems foreign and empty. I constantly miss Karma greeting me at the door and rubbing her agile body up against my legs all the while purring contentment. I realize I was the Kitty Kuisine connection and she was just buttering me up but I like to think she loved me too. I hang my overcoat in the foyer closet and go into my office. My cluttered desk further depresses me. I haven't taken the time to sort through the accumulation of mail and when I see the mess, I cringe as I sit down and begin. I have three categories that I sort my mail into: respond, pay or trash. Most of it goes in trash. I congratulate myself when I get to the bottom of the pile. I thought it would take much longer. Since I'm on a roll, I figure I'll go ahead and pay my bills. Writing checks is a no-brainer. Dealing with responses takes too much concentration and I'm just not up to it at the present time. An hour later, I'm feeling much better about my progress. It's almost four so I call Charlie — my favorite part of the day — any day.

"Hey, Beautiful, what are you doing?"

"Hey, yourself. I've been waiting to hear from you," she responds.

"Oh, sorry. I thought you were on duty today."

"I was. My shift ended at three."

I rear back in my leather chair and prop my feet on my desk. I love talking to this angel. "How 'bout we go to the Horizon Room for dinner. This may be my last night as a free man." I've been avoiding facing it but now that I've said it, I begin to feel melancholy. Charlie picks up on the sadness in my voice.

"Buck up, Slugger! It's not over 'til it's over."

"Sure, easy for you to say." I pause, "How 'bout dinner?" I ask again.

"You're on. I'll pick you up at six. Does that give you enough time to get ready?"

"Yep. I can be ready right now! I still have on my Sunday-go-to-meetin' garb."

"That's great. However, I need the time, unless you want your date decked out in NYPD blues."

"Honey, I don't care what you wear. My preference is nothing."

"So I've noticed. See you at six. And…hold that thought!"

✦✦✦✦✦

I STAND UNDER the green canvas awning outside the Blackstone exchanging war stories with Sammy, the doorman, as I wait for Charlie. When I see her SUV turn the corner, I say, "There's my ride," and slap Sammy on the back before I step to the curb.

"See ya, Judge, and good luck!"

"Thanks, Sammy."

I open the passenger door and greet Charlie. "Well, just look at you!" Dad's eye-candy analogy pops into my weary brain. The marine-blue silk dress clings to her figure like saran wrap and shows just enough cleavage to excite the imagination.

"You like?"

"Very much so. Funny, I've never noticed it before, but your eyes are the color of that dress."

Charlie laughs. "It's an optical illusion. Since birth, my chameleon eyes pick up the color of any blue I wear: light, dark, navy, aqua, you name it. A gift from my mother's side of the family."

"Un-huh, And your five sisters?"

"Nope, just me. Maybe because, after five births, I was relegated to be content with Mom's leftover genes." Charlie glances over her shoulder and eases the SUV back into traffic gracefully maneuvering her vehicle into the constant flow. Just as we enter The Horizon's parking garage my cell phone rings.

The waiting has put me on edge and I fumble, dropping the phone. When I finally have it under control, I flip the cover and almost shout. "Hello!"

"Tony, its Theo. Take it easy; no verdict yet. The judge sent the jury to the hotel for the night. They're to report tomorrow at nine."

My hands are still shaking as I reply. "Okay." I pause a moment trying to think. I seem to have forgotten all the telltale signs regarding which way a jury is leaning. "Theo, is that a good or bad sign? After all, a day and a half is more than ample time to reach a verdict."

"Relax, Tony. It isn't a sign, good or bad. The jurors just need time to examine the evidence and engage in deliberation. After all, there are four counts to consider and a day and a half is nothing to be concerned about. Sorting through all the evidence relative to each count and applying the law is not an easy matter."

"Yeah, of course…You'd think this was my first rodeo."

"Well, in essence it is. That is unless you've been tried for murder before and failed to disclose that insignificant little detail to me."

We share a laugh and say our goodbyes.

"Nothing yet," I say to Charlie as I close the cover on my phone and pocket it. "Ducky sent the jury to bed for the night. Reconvening at nine tomorrow."

"I gathered that from your end of the conversation. Are you going to be morose all evening?" she asks.

"Sorry, can't help it. It's not only my life but Dad's as well. I know he's on pins and needles waiting. A conviction would kill him, and then he'd be victim number five."

"Don't do that, Tony. You know that's not true!"

Seems as though I set the mood and dinner was a bust. I just couldn't relax and enjoy the meal or the company.

As we leave the restaurant, Charlie says, "I'll take you home. You could use a good night's sleep."

"Sorry to have ruined our evening. Guess I'm too distracted to appreciate the here and now."

"Nonsense; no need to be sorry. I think you're holding up extremely well. Just hang in there. I'm a phone call away."

I enter my home. It feels cold and empty. Charlie has enriched my life beyond words, and if I lose her, I'd be a lost soul. I know I should call Dad but I'm too tired to sound confident. I don't want to worry him anymore than necessary so I pass. *I'll call him tomorrow.* More exhausted than I remember ever having been in my life, I skip my nightly routine, throw my clothes on the ottoman and fall into bed clad only in my T-shirt and boxers. My last thought before I drift off is *Perhaps my teeth won't rot out if I skip one brushing...*

Suddenly it's morning. I didn't pull the drape last night and my bedroom is drenched in sunlight. I rub my sandpaper eyes and look at the clock: 7:30. *I must've died when I hit the sack.* I throw Grandma's flower-garden coverlet back and get up. I'm stiff and realize I probably didn't move the whole night, judging from the way my legs are cramped. After a few moments, I and my body compromise, and we awkwardly make it to the bathroom. Hoping the warmth will loosen my joints, I turn the shower on pretty hot and stand under the stream until I run out of hot water. After toweling off and shaving, I feel refreshed. I amble to the kitchen where I start a pot of coffee before I dress.

There is no need for me to go to court until I'm called so I take my coffee and go to the door to retrieve the morning paper. After all the adverse publicity, I'm now gun shy and hesitate before opening it. It seems like every day I'm either headlines or at least a front page article. I take a deep breath and bravely unfold the paper. The only mention of my name is that the case has gone to the jury. I breathe a sigh of relief.

◆◆◆◆◆

WILLY SITS IN his grubby room in the sleazy hotel also reading the morning paper. He had changed his disguise to attend closing arguments. He is determined to be present when the jury comes back with guilty verdicts. *Can't wait to see the look on the judge's face when he has a life sentence imposed upon him.* Willy had heard through the grapevine that a warrant had been issued for his arrest so he was laying low. It was now just a matter of time before he would move to another zip code, preferably a warmer one. *I should even the score with that bitch, Rothburg, and her nosey brat before I boogie, but can't afford to take unnecessary chances now. Maybe someday...*

Willy had procured his new disguise by rummaging through dumpsters. He now presented himself as an old crippled man who carried a cane and walked with a limp. In order not to miss the exciting climax of his handy work, Willy, donned in his *new* outfit, rode the bus to the courthouse. He took up a position on a bench situated on the walkway in front of the courthouse. From this vantage point, he would be able to observe the courthouse comings and goings and would instinctively recognize when the jury was back by the flurry of activity that would ensue. He was well-versed with the criminal justice system. The media would converge on the scene along with the attorneys, and best of all, Facinni.

Facinni would have to be present to receive his just reward. Willy didn't care how long he would have to wait in the bitter cold. Sometimes juries took days to come to an agreement and he was steadfastly determined to be present when they did.

CHAPTER

12

The twelve jurors sit around the large walnut conference table in the jury deliberation room. The bailiff had brought in a generous supply of sweet rolls, coffee, milk and juice. Webster Singleton, a wealthy middle-aged man that operated several Buddy Burger franchises throughout the city, had been elected foreman of the jury. As soon as everyone had settled down, after helping themselves to the continental breakfast, Singleton began:

"Good morning," he turns and cuffs a cough before continuing. "I'm not sure how we go about doing this since we wouldn't reach even a consensus after four full hours of deliberation. The only exposure I've had in this area is from watching the old black and white movie, *Twelve Angry Men*."

All but one of the jurors laugh.

"If anyone has any ideas as to how we proceed, please don't be shy about sharing them. My first thought is that we should take another straw vote to see if our lone dissenter has changed his or her mind. Then, of course, if we have unanimous verdicts, we need deliberate no longer and can be released within the hour."

More laughter.

"That's what I thought as well. Okay, I see you each have a pen and pad. Since we have four forms of verdict to consider, one for each murder and one for the animal cruelty charge, please place the numbers one through four along the left hand margin of your paper. After each number, write the names of the victims in the following order. Number one — Karma; number two — Len Wycowski; number three — Doreen Lancaster and, number four — Jeffery Wilkinson. We'll use this format throughout our deliberations" Singleton stops long enough to create a verdict form for himself.

"Since you have three choices for each count, except, of course, for the animal cruelty charge, you will use one of the following phrases to indicate your verdict: guilty of first degree murder, guilty of second degree murder or not guilty, except the cruelty charge. That one is either guilty or not guilty. Now, go ahead and fill in your choice adjacent to each victim's name."

The room became quiet as the panel poured over their makeshift forms. After a few minutes, everyone put their pen down.

"Okay, looks like we're all finished. Now, take your form, fold it in half, put it in this box, and pass it back to me."

When the box made its way back to Singleton, he took it and began one-by-one to extract the forms. He designated another juror, Kay Lambert, a nurse by profession, to keep track of the verdicts as he read them aloud. At the end of the tally the jury was split. Eleven voted not guilty on all charges. One juror voted guilty of first degree murder on the first three charges as well as the animal cruelty charge.

"Looks like we're deadlocked," Singleton said. "Eleven for acquittal, one for conviction. Mrs. Jump, I assume from the position you have taken throughout the duration of the deliberations that you are the lone holdout. Is that correct?

"Correct," Mrs. Jump responds. "And I'm not inclined at this point to change my mind, unless I can be convinced otherwise."

Mrs. Jump remained unflappable, and by the end of the first full day, the jury was still deadlocked. When they assembled the next morning, Singleton asked in a conciliatory tone of voice, "Would you mind stating your position one more time?"

"Well, I believe it's much too obvious that Judge Facinni was trying to create the crime scenes to make it look as though he was framed." Margaret Jump paused for a moment before continuing, "Lord knows how much publicity this whole thing has generated for him."

"YOU'RE KIDDING!" Lawrence Collier, another juror shouts. "You're willing to send an innocent man to prison, or worse, on that idiotic reasoning? You were present during final arguments and heard the evidence that contradicted that theory. I'm...I'm speechless."

Chi Li Yen chimed in at that moment. "I totally agree with Mr. Collier. The whole idea that an intelligent, accomplished man would put his life on the line for a newspaper headline is inconceivable. My ancestors believed in death before dishonor, but your understanding of the proceedings goes way beyond that concept. You act like someone that has an axe to grind..."

Tears began to form, and Mrs. Jump reaches for a tissue and dabs at her eyes. Amidst the tears, she relates: "When I grew up, we were very poor. My father was unable to keep a job for very long, so my mother worked. I grew up resenting those with wealth because my two brothers and I had to scrape for everything we had, often being teased by our classmates for the tattered clothes we wore. Our pride would not allow us to accept handouts or public assistance."

As Mrs. Jump reaches for more tissues, Singleton passes her the box. Attempting to stiffle her emotions, she continues. "Those with means seem to buy their way in life. That appeared to me to be unfair. I guess I've allowed the resentment that has festered within me to take over my better judgment. Seeing Judge Facinni sitting there, in a starched, white, cuff-linked shirt, silk tie and expensive pin striped suit, being represented by a high-powered attorney, fueled my resentment. It conjured up something my grandfather used to say when mafia figures, who were guilty as sin, were acquitted: 'It's money, not justice, that drives acquittals.'"

Looking at her fellow jurors, Mrs. Jump confides: "I'm ashamed to say that I wanted to prove privilege cannot buy an acquittal. I wanted to make Judge Facinni 'the poster child' or better yet, 'the whipping boy.' It has taken this experience to make me aware, that whether rich or poor, the unjustly accused should, under no circumstances, be convicted. I, therefore, change my vote and vote for acquittal on all counts. Not because the majority has voted for an acquittal, but because it's warranted."

Singleton stands and announces, "We have our verdicts," and looks at Mrs. Jump who nods her head. The rest of the jurors look relieved. Chi Li Yen reaches over and squeezes Mrs. Jump's hand.

◆◆◆◆◆

I STAY CLOSE to home. I've been too anxious to concentrate on doing much else. I call Dad to reassure him I'm doing okay, but I feel he senses the anxiety in my voice. He ends up reassuring me that everything is going to be "okay." After concluding the call, I turn the television on and flip through the channels. Nothing. I wander from room-to-room waiting for word as to whether the jury has reached their verdicts, as they are into their third day of deliberations. Theo again advises me not to worry. "Complex cases require intricate analysis," Theo reminds me. Unfortunately, patience is not one of my virtues.

Charlie has been investigating a drive-by shooting and has been pretty absorbed the last couple of days, so I haven't seen her either. I'm experiencing cabin fever or something similar. If this is a taste of what incarceration is like, I think I'd rather be executed.

◆◆◆◆◆

WE'RE MORE THAN halfway through the forenoon of the fourth day of deliberations when the phone rings. I grab it up and bark, "Yes!"

"Tony, the jury has reached its verdicts. We're reconvening at 2:30."

I look at the clock. It's 11:20. "Okay," I say and swallow hard. "Guess I'll see you there."

"Yes, you will." Theo replies. "Yes, you certainly will. By the way, Esther has iced some champagne so after the proceedings, we'll come back here for the victory celebration."

"I wish to hell I had your confidence," I say, then reflect out loud, "Well, whatever. At least my fate will be determined — good or bad!"

"Hey! None of that. Esther is an excellent judge of outcomes and she doesn't ice champagne lightly. Her reputation is at stake. As we discussed before, you cannot predict what a jury is going to do, so I go with Esther's gut every time. She's as accurate as a crystal ball."

"Theo, if that was meant to be reassuring, it fell short."

Theo laughs and we end the call.

◆◆◆◆◆

WHEN WILLY OBSERVES the media setting up on the courthouse lawn, he rises and tosses the newspaper he has been reading into the trash receptacle. He then walks up the marble steps to the courthouse entrance. Willy pauses before entering through the double brass doors. He turns and observes the TV crews and photo journalists volleying for position on the snow-covered lawn. *What a circus! At least there'll be some good photos in the newspaper for my scrapbook.*

◆◆◆◆◆

"AFTERNOON, JUDGE," A security guard says as I approach the courtroom. He opens the doors for me and I thank him. The courtroom is filled. My knees turn to jelly and I worry my legs will fail me at the most inopportune time. I notice Theo and Ray are already positioned at the defense table. There is an undertow of noise as those present converse in whispers. We wait for the judge and jury to make their entrance. My hands are sweating and I hope my anxiety isn't all that apparent.

I can't help it and I jump when the door leading from the judge's chambers opens and Ducky makes his grand entrance. Everyone rises.

"Please be seated," the judge says. He scans the standing-room-only courtroom before he says, "Bailiff, please bring in the jury."

As I sit waiting, I'm surprised my suit jacket isn't pulsating in rhythm with my pounding heart. Theo scribbles "Easy does it" on the legal pad he has placed between us on the table. I manage a smile and hope it looks sincere. The jury is now seated and the judge says, "Ladies and gentlemen of the jury, have you reached your verdicts?"

The foreperson, Webster Singleton, stands. "We have, Your Honor."

"Bailiff, please bring me the forms," Ducky says.

There are four separate verdict forms, one for each count. Singleton hands the paperwork to the bailiff and takes his seat. I watch Singleton look at me. *What's he thinking?* I study the jurors and note nothing exceptional from their expressions. There is no dead giveaway. Ducky takes his time studying the verdict forms. What seems like light years later, he clears his throat and adjusts his glasses. Theo and I stand and wait. Finally Ducky speaks.

"Count One, the charge of Animal Cruelty...*not guilty.*"

I am relieved but that charge is the least of the four.

"Count Two, the charge of First Degree Murder — Victim Leonard Wycowski...*not guilty.*"

I almost faint. Theo steadies me.

"Count Three, the charge of First Degree Murder — Victim Doreen Lancaster...*not guilty.*"

I wait for the last shoe to fall.

"Count Four, the charge of First Degree Murder — Jeffery Wilkinson...*not guilty.*"

Relief swarms over me and I sag. Theo again has to steady me.

I'm numb and do not believe my ears. Now Theo has me in a bear hug which reassures me that I have heard the verdicts correctly. If it weren't for Theo's hanging on to me, I would have collapsed.

◆◆◆◆◆

ALMOST AS SOON as the judge concludes the reading of the verdicts, there is commotion emanating from the balcony. I look up and see a ragged old man waving a cane around and shouting, "NO! NO! NO! THAT'S NOT THE WAY IT'S SUPPOSED TO END!"

Women scream and the spectators in the balcony scatter. People run down the stairs hampering the guards in their quest to get up the stairs. Despite the chaos, three security guards manage to plow through the throng and reach the balcony. I hear one guard shout, "HEY BUDDY, STOP THAT. PUT THE CANE DOWN RIGHT NOW." I observe the crazed man continue his tirade as the three guards attempt to subdue him.

"LET ME GO! I'LL TAKE CARE OF THAT ROTTEN SON-OF-A-BITCH MYSELF FOR WHAT HE DID TO ME. I'LL KILL THE BASTARD. DAMN YOU! YOU'RE ALL COWARDS! LET GO OF ME!"

The guards can't get a good grip on the old man because of the close quarters in the balcony. He expertly ducks and dodges their attempts and appears to have superhuman strength. As the man struggles with the security guards, he finally breaks free of the confined space and makes a wild dash for the railing. I watch him peer over the edge. That's when I recognize him, it's Willy McCrombie.

"Theo, that's him. That's Willy."

Theo and I stand there, paralyzed, and watch the saga unfold before our eyes. Willy continues to struggle with the guards. Now they're all perilously close to the edge and strain against the railing. Willy fights like a mad dog, swinging his cane and ranting. He grabs at the guards with one hand while swinging his cane with the other, landing a couple of hefty blows in the process. One of the guards has his Taser out and points it at Willy.

"STOP! STAND DOWN OR YOU'LL BE TASED."

This just adds fuel to Willy's fire and he fights all the harder.

"YOU YELLOW BASTARDS. AFRAID TO FIGHT LIKE MEN! COME ON, JUST TRY IT!" Willy shouts, all the while swinging his cane wildly in the air.

The guard has no recourse but to tase him. When Willy is hit by the electric jolt, he staggers back against the railing, loses his balance and topples over the edge before the other two guards can grab him. Willy falls backwards over the railing and lands with a thud, face up, on the prosecution table. Although they had been watching the scenario unfold, Willy's fall was a sudden surprise which caused Hammond and Farnsworth to jump up slamming their chairs against the lower railing that separates the spectators from the participants. Farnsworth screams "WHAT THE HELL..." as he and Hammond scurry to the other side of the courtroom. Theo, Ray and I just stand there and stare in disbelief at the body sprawled on the table next to us. From the angle of Willy's neck, it appears to be broken. He lays there lifeless with his eyes open—those evil eyes staring into eternity.

Ducky shouts, "SOMEONE, CALL AN AMBULANCE!" The courthouse security guards scramble and I notice a couple of them are speaking into their shoulder mics.

Ducky stands and bangs his gavel, over and over, until the courtroom settles down. After Ducky has restored a semblance of order, he asks, "Does anyone know this man?"

Theo stands. "Yes, Your Honor, we do. His name is Wilber McCrombie, our alternate suspect: the man we have insisted all along is the actual murderer. This is the individual Judge

Facinni sentenced over twenty years ago — the one who threatened to get even with him."

"Oh, my God!" Ducky asks again, as he rubs his brow, "Has someone called for an ambulance?"

"Yes, we have, Your Honor," one of the guards answers.

"Thank you." Ducky looks down and shuffles papers around on his desk before saying, "The jury verdicts must have set him off." Quite obviously, Ducky is unsure as to what to do next. He finally mutters, "Well, anyway, it appears justice has been done, or perhaps overdone." Ducky looks at Willy who is still sprawled on the prosecution table. Within minutes, medics arrive with a gurney and remove the body. As soon as they have departed, Ducky continues.

"We must conclude this trial before we do anything else." He raises his eyes to meet mine. "Judge Facinni, you have been found *not guilty* on all charges, and you are now free to leave. Your bond is hereby exonerated." Ducky then looks at the jury. I notice most of the jurors are in a flux and appear tentative. "Ladies and gentlemen of the jury, you are also released from your duty to the state and free to leave. Thank you for your service. Bailiff, please escort the jury out."

As soon as the jurors clear the courtroom, Ducky announces, "Court is adjourned!" He then whacks his gavel against the wooden plaque on his desk. It sounds like a gun shot, and those that are still present, including myself, jump. At that point, the courtroom is almost empty and the stragglers scurry toward the door. I look around and see Charlie standing against the back wall of the courtroom. I motion for her to come forward and she does.

"Hey, Beautiful," I say as I take her hand. "How's that for a finale'?"

After giving me a congratulatory hug, Charlie looks at Theo. "This even trumps your hero, Perry Mason."

Theo smooths his mustache with his thumb and forefinger and says with a wry smile, "Yes, that was pretty dramatic, wasn't it. However, I can't take credit for the finale."

Then he stands and says, "Come along, Esther has uncorked the champagne and she will have it consumed if we tarry too much longer."

When we exit the courthouse, we are mobbed by the media who have returned from their pursuit of Willy as he was being transported on a gurney and loaded into an ambulance. They are now swarming around us snapping photographs and bombarding us with questions. Theo gestures to some of the courthouse guards and solicits their aid in escorting us to his vehicle. I'm still rattled from the chain of events that just unfolded but find solace once we're safely inside Theo's Rolls, away from the television crews and pesky press. Charlie squeezes in and positions herself beside me in the backseat. She lovingly loops her arm through mine and whispers, "Tony, Darling, it's over! It's finally over." Suddenly, I feel lightheaded, as though I'm suspended between reality and fantasy. *Can it really be over — just like that! Can it be?* I'm too emotional to speak, so I slip my arm around Charlie's shoulders and pull her closer to me.

◆◆◆◆◆

ONCE WE ARRIVE at Theo's office, I find my victory celebration is bittersweet. In retrospect, I'm ashamed to admit that I feel no remorse for Willy. He killed four of my close friends and almost destroyed my life. I don't morn Willy's demise; however, I can't help but think of the victims, including Karma, who fell prey to Willy's evil quest for retaliation.

Esther has laid out a delectable assortment of *hors d'oeuvres* and proceeds to pour each of us a glass of champagne. When everyone has glass in hand, I clear my throat and I raise my glass.

"Here's to Len, Doreen, Jeff, Emory and Karma. *Requiem in pace.*" Looking heavenward, I say, "May you now rest in the eternal peace meant for us all."

The others raise their glasses in salute and we all take a sip. Then I turn to face Theo. "Theo, I'll never be able to thank you enough…" I'm overcome with emotion and unable to finish. Theo comes to my rescue.

"Well, thank you Tony. However, you may change your mind when you get my final bill—but there's no extra charge for hazard pay or babysitting."

Theo and I laugh as we share our private joke. Charlie, Esther and Ray look at us like we've lost it.

Esther breaks the spell and announces, "I've made reservations at the Horizon Room for dinner. I hope I wasn't presumptuous. Theo and I would like for all of you to be our guests."

"We would?" Theo asks. I watch as Theo notices the look of distain on Esther's face. He then immediately does an about-face. "Why yes, we would!"

I glance at Charlie. She nods. "Our favorite place…"

"Wait," I say, "before we do anything else, I have to call Dad."

"Of course. Use my office, Tony. We'll wait out here," Theo says.

My hands are still shaking as I dial Dad's number. I know he's waiting for the call and he answers on the first ring.

"Hello! Tony, is that you?"

"Yes, it's me."

"Don't tell me," he says, "I already know. You've been found *innocent.*

"Found *not guilty,*" I correct. But same result…how did you know?"

"Just do," he says.

We share a moment of silence. Then Dad says, "All things are possible with God. He didn't create us to make us suffer. Suffering is 'man's doing' not God's. Trust in a higher power. Justice may not always prevail, but it is always within reach."

"If I live to be 1,000, I'll never have the wisdom you do," I say considering it a truism.

"You've learned more in 58 years than I have in 88. Build on it, and by the time you reach my age you'll make me look like a neophyte."

"Ha!" I say.

"One more thing," he says and adds emphatically, "I love you, Sonny!"

"Love you more!" I say just as emphatically.

"See!" he says. "You're already attempting to exceed me!" He then abruptly hangs up the phone.

EPILOGUE

I toss the morning paper aside just as my doorbell rings. I instinctively know its Charlie. I open the door, sweep her into my arms and swing her around.

"Hey, Slugger, easy! I'm carrying fragile cargo."

Oh, my God! Charlie must have noticed my horrified expression and squeals, "Tony, you should see the look on your face! You didn't think I meant..." and she doubles over with laughter. Unnerved and somewhat embarrassed, I stand waiting. When she's back in control, she holds up a pink gift bag secured with a large pink bow.

Still pretty shaken from what I thought she was referring to, I ask, "What is this?"

"Only one way to find out," she giggles, handing me the bag.

When I take it from her, it wiggles slightly. I jump at the unexpected movement and almost drop the bag. Now my curiosity is on overload. I take a quick look at Charlie; she is grinning like the Cheshire Cat. *What in the hell...*My attention is drawn back to the gift bag. I slowly extract the top layer of pink tissue and carefully peer inside. Two large green eyes peer back at me. Surprised, I jerk back, and as I do, I hear: "Meow!"

Placing the bag on the floor, I carefully reach inside and gently lift the sleek black creature up and out. "Are you kidding me? What…when…how in the world did you find Karma's twin?"

"Thought you knew, Slugger. I have friends in high places." Charlie replies still grinning.

"So you say."

Once the creature is set free, it slowly starts to explore its new surroundings. It's a feisty little beast, and when I reach for it again, it tries to claw me. *Yep, I can tell it must be a close relative of the late great Karma.*

Charlie comes close to me, still smiling, "What number Karma is this one?" she asks.

"Don't know, I've lost count. We'll just call her Karma, in honor of all her predecessors." Then it occurs to me I hadn't yet actually determined the sex of my new family member, so I ask, "It is a her, isn't it?"

"Did the pink bag and bow give it away, Sherlock?"

I can never get ahead of this woman — she's too fast for me. "No, not exactly. I know how crafty you are and assumed the trappings were a ploy to throw me off track."

"Sure you did!" Charlie moves closer and hooks her arm through mine. "Anyway, I *know* how partial you are to females…"

I slip my arm around her waist and pull her to me. "Damn straight, woman! Damn straight!"

THE END

One night...one moment...
changed her life forever

THE
LEGACY

A NOVEL BY
JUDITH BLEVINS

AVAILABLE IN PRINT & EBOOK
12/8/15

Read on for a special preview

CHAPTER 1

KABOOM! Thunder roared as a bolt of lightning streaked across the black sky, and the rain began in earnest. It was early spring in southern Louisiana, and torrential downpours were expected. The thunder competed with Grant Alexander's singing, and lightning illuminated the Lincoln's interior. Caroline leaned closer to Grant, her husband of two years, and slid her hand along his thigh. Grant squeezed her hand in reply, transmitting an unspoken promise. He continued to sing *O Sole Mio*, as he steered the car with his left hand and imitated conducting an orchestra with his right. He was on a personal high having received a standing ovation after performing his piano concerto with the Westchester Philharmonic Symphony Orchestra of New Orleans, earlier that evening.

New Orleans was a playground for the rich and famous, and Thompson Sinclair, CEO of *Spinners, Inc.*, a recording conglomerate based in San Diego, had been in the audience. Grant hoped his piano solo might launch him into a recording career if Sinclair liked his music. Grant recognized his talent was exceptional, and the audience confirmed that with the standing ovation. Even Edwardo Ponzetti, the conductor, bowed to

Grant at the conclusion of his solo—a gesture the orchestra seldom witnessed.

"Be careful, Grant. The rain is coming down so hard; perhaps we should pull over and wait it out. We could stay in a hotel and spend a romantic night together." Caroline said.

"I have it all under control, my dear wife. I don't want to stay in a hotel; however, I'll take you up on that romantic night suggestion when we get home," Grant answered. "Damn weather! You would think it would cooperate and be as spectacular as my performance was tonight."

Caroline noticed Grant was gripping the steering wheel very tightly. "Yes, Grant," she said, as she peered through the windshield.

"As it is, I can barely see the road," Grant said, squinting. He leaned forward and searched for the center stripe. "The rain is so heavy the windshield wipers can hardly handle the downpour."

"Are you sure it's wise to continue?" Caroline asked, in a shaky voice.

Grant had quit singing and was studying the road, carefully. "Quiet! I have to concentrate."

Suddenly, the vehicle fishtailed on the wet pavement and careened toward the shoulder.

"Son-of-a-bitch!" Grant cried, fighting the steering wheel trying to stabilize the car.

"Grant!" Caroline screamed. Her husband whipped the wheel first one way and then the other, but his efforts to regain control were in vain. The Lincoln tore through the guard rail and shimmied onto the muddy shoulder.

Caroline screamed, again. She hadn't fastened her seatbelt and was being tossed about like a rag doll. Grant continued to turn the steering wheel trying to gain leverage, as they careened off the shoulder of the road.

"Oh, God," Grant cried, seeing a giant oak tree looming before them. He instinctively reached over and pulled Caroline into him an instant before impact. The vehicle slammed into the tree, twisting metal and shattering glass. It rebounded from the injured bark and then jolted its unconscious cargo to a rest.

◆◆◆◆◆

THE OCCUPANTS IN the car travelling behind the Alexander vehicle witnessed the accident. The driver pulled over and turned on the emergency flashers.

"Looks like a bad one," he shouted over the rain pelting the roof of their Subaru. Drs. Stephen and Eleanor Monroe grabbed their medical bags from the rear seat and hastened to render aid. Stephen, upon reaching the driver's side, shouted to Eleanor, "Oh, my God. It's Grant and Caroline Alexander. I think Grant may be dead." Stephen was Grant's longtime physician and recognized him instantly, although Grant's face was bloody from a gash in his forehead.

Eleanor, in the meantime, had gone around to the passenger side of the wrecked Lincoln. Caroline lay motionless in a twisted position, covered with blood. Eleanor took a deep breath and carefully put her arm through the broken glass of the passenger window. She found Caroline's wrist and searched for a pulse.

"Caroline is alive, but badly injured!" Eleanor shouted. "She's losing a lot of blood. It's coming from a nasty gash on her neck but, thank God, it isn't the jugular. An ambulance isn't going to cut it. I'll call for Life Flight helicopter."

Eleanor stepped away from the car, pulled her cell phone from her jacket pocket, and hastily dialed 911.

"This is 911. What's the nature of your emergency?"

"Operator, my name is Dr. Eleanor Monroe. There's been an accident on Highway Six, at mile marker sixteen, a few miles from the French Quarter. We have critical injuries and are requesting a life flight, as soon as possible."

"I'm calling it in, now. Stay on the line."

"Thank you."

"I got a confirmation. They're ten to fifteen minutes out."

"We may not have that much time."

"I'll relay that to the medical team. God be with you."

"Thanks for your help...and your prayers."

Eleanor tapped her cell phone and jammed it back into her pocket. Since the passenger door was partially opened from the force of the impact, she squeezed through and set about doing a more thorough examination of the injured woman.

"I'll try to slow the bleeding," she shouted, "but, at this rate, she won't last long. I don't think the chopper will get here soon enough to save her." She looked across at Stephen, whose grim features matched her own. He looked down at his patient and shook his head.

The Lincoln's driver side door was gaping, hanging from a hinge. Grant's body had slammed into the steering wheel and was draped over it. Stephen had eased him back against the seat and brushed glass off his tuxedo. Pulling his handkerchief out of his pants pocket, he gently dabbed at the blood on Grant's face. His face was white underneath. Stephen retrieved his stethoscope from his medical bag and, after doing a cursory examination, looked at his wife.

"He's beyond our help. I'd guess he has massive internal injuries after slamming into the steering wheel." Leaning into the car, he scrounged around in the backseat. "Do we have anything in our car that we can use as a canopy?"

"I'll look, but I doubt it," Eleanor said. She backed out into the rain and headed for their Subaru. She slipped in the mud and landed on her knee. "Damn!"

Stephen shouted after her, "While you're at it, pull the car up closer. We need more light."

Eleanor swiped at her muddy Italian wool slacks, without much success. "Good idea. Let me find a cover, first."

Minutes later, Eleanor pulled the brake on their car, its headlights cutting a swath through the near horizontal streaks of rain. She stepped out, opening a large blue and white striped umbrella Stephen used when playing golf.

"I found this in the back," Eleanor said. "Will it do?"

"Yes, it'll do nicely. Can you hold it while I extricate Grant?"

Eleanor propped the umbrella against the open driver's door, positioning it in such a way as to shield Grant's limp body from the downpour. Stephen pulled Grant from the wreckage and laid him on the wet grass beside the Lincoln.

"I don't believe it. I just saw him, yesterday. He gave me our tickets to the symphony." Stephen placed his fingers on Grant's neck, once again. "Hey!" He shifted his position so he was closer. "There's a heartbeat!" He looked up at his wife. "But, it's really faint."

Eleanor massaged her brow with her thumb and forefinger, wondering whether to share a thought that had occurred to her. Kneeling beside her husband, she asked, "Stephen, if...if Grant doesn't make it...you know, if there's nothing we can do for him...we may be able to save Caroline. If we act, quickly. I slowed her bleeding down, but she desperately needs a transfusion."

Stephen put his hand on her shoulder. "Eleanor, what are you suggesting?"

She rose and hurried back to the passenger side of the Lincoln. She found Caroline's black evening bag and dumped the contents out, searching for a driver's license.

"Stephen, she's AB positive," Eleanor exclaimed, holding the license up. "You and I are both A. Do you remember Grant's blood type?"

"Yes. He's type O positive, universal." He placed his own jacket under the bleeding man's head. "Easy to remember. Why?"

Eleanor returned to her husband's side. She observed her husband gently wiping blood from Grant's face with those miraculous hands of his. She had assisted Stephen with numerous surgeries during her internship at Immaculate Heart of Mary Hospital, in New Orleans, and was in awe of his surgical skill. As they worked side-by-side, their professional relationship had grown into romance, and they'd fallen in love. They were married soon after Eleanor completed her internship. Eleanor believed in predestination; they were meant to be together.

Pushing her musings to the back of her mind, Eleanor sighed. "If we could jerry-rig a transfusion line between the two of them, while Grant's heart is still beating, we may be able get enough of his blood into her to save her life." She scrutinized the expression on Stephen's face and pushed forward. "What do you think?"

Stephen swiped rain from his eyes. He regarded his dying friend and then his wife, his brilliant, amazing wife. "By God, it's worth a try. What have we got to lose?"

Eleanor nodded briskly. "Our license to practice comes to mind..." She suddenly started shivering, whether from the rain or from stress she couldn't decide. She tightened the belt on her coat and helped her husband up.

Stephen said, emphatically, "We very well could, but can we live with letting someone die because we're afraid of the consequences? We took take the Hippocratic Oath. Saving lives is our job, so...let's get on with it."

Trying to hide a smile, Eleanor said, "Yes, let's." Rain-soaked and still shivering, she took the medical bags to the rear of the wreck, where she could see better in the beam of the Subaru's headlights. She searched for anything they could use to establish a transfusion line.

In the interim, Stephen returned to the passenger side of the Lincoln and squeezed in. Leaning into the back seat, he found a Saints stadium blanket and, wrapping it around Caroline, he gently picked her up and carried her to the driver's side of the car. He laid her next to her husband.

Eleanor, who had completed her search of the medical bags, approached and said, "Look, I found these. Do you think they'll work?" She showed him three packages of sterile catheters, surgical clamps, hypodermic syringes, and alcohol wipes. "Not too fancy, but…"

Stephen peered at the items and shook his head. "Do you have a miracle tucked away in that collection?"

"Dearest, I've seen you perform miracles. It's in your DNA. You *can* do this; I know you can, even if the odds are stacked against us."

Stephen peeled off Grant's jacket and ripped open his shirt. "With that kind of faith, how can I miss?" Fumbling in the dying man's pants pocket, Stephen found a clean handkerchief which he applied as a tourniquet.

Eleanor set about sterilizing the man's arm with alcohol swabs, as Stephen began to prepare Caroline. The doctors worked feverishly for several minutes and finally had a make-shift transfusion line hooked between the arms of Caroline and Grant.

"Okay, partner, say a prayer and, just to be on the safe side, cross your fingers. I'm concerned that we don't have a sterile enough environment to work in, but, what the hell! If we don't do something, they're both dead, anyway." With that, Stephen removed the tourniquet from Grant's arm and the blood began flowing, slowly at first, but when Stephen started a gentle CPR, the flow increased.

After a few minutes, while monitoring a blood pressure cuff, Eleanor said, "You are a genius! Her blood pressure is rising!"

"That's good to hear." The relief in Stephen's voice was evident. "I had my doubts," he muttered, as he continued the CPR. "And, my love, you're the genius. This was your idea. You're the brains, I'm just the brawn."

"This may have been a long shot, Stephen but never underestimate your skill. Not many MDs would have even attempted such a feat, much less successfully."

Before Stephen could answer, they heard the flap, flap, flap of the blades, as the rescue chopper approached.

Eleanor stood up and began waving her arms at the chopper. Stephen sat back on his heels, rubbing his aching arms. He was cold and wet. He put his fingers on Grant's neck looking for that faint pulse, but found none.

"He's dead," he shouted to Eleanor. Then he leaned closer to Caroline looking for signs of life. He heard her groan, as he touched her wrist. Jerking his head up, he looked at Eleanor who was still waving at the chopper.

I think she's going to be all right, dear! She's weak and a little hoarse, but she just whispered that she was going to live. Her exact words were, 'I will live on.'"

"Now that's what I call determination," Eleanor replied, as she joined her husband at Caroline's side, and the doctors grasped hands. Eleanor made the sign of the cross and looking heavenward, said, "Dear God, bless Grant and take his soul to heaven and into your loving arms. Thank you for the miracle we prayed for. Now, at least, Caroline has a fighting chance."

The chopper was on the ground and the flight crew was running towards them. Stephen removed the makeshift transfusion line and took Grant's arms, carefully folding them across his chest. Placing his hands over Grant's, he looked up at his wife. "What a shame. These hands will never play the piano, again."

Eleanor nodded. "An amazing talent lost forever."

ACKNOWLEDGMENTS

Special thanks to fellow mystery writer, retired prosecutor, defense attorney and judge, Carroll Multz, for his encouragement, editing skills, inspiration, and most especially, his expertise in assisting in the creation of the jury trial sequence portrayed in this novel.

My gratitude also to Tammy Ballagh for her excellent editing skills and to dear friends, Gary and Shirley Carr, for their technical assistance.

Last but not least, to my publishing partner, Blue Harvest Creative, I am eternally grateful.

ABOUT THE AUTHOR

Judith Blevins has spent her entire professional life experiencing the mystery, intrigue and courtroom drama that unfolds daily within the criminal justice system. Her previous experience as a court clerk, then serving five consecutive district attorneys in Grand Junction, Colorado, has provided the inspiration for her stories.